ROYAL CHASE

ALSO BY SARIAH WILSON

The Ugly Stepsister Strikes Back

The Royals of Monterra Series

Royal Date

ROYAL CHASE

SARIAH WILSON

Montlake Romance

This is a work of fiction. Names, characters, organizations, places, events, and incidents are either products of the author's imagination or are used fictitiously.

Published by Montlake Romance, Seattle

www.apub.com

ISBN-13: 9781503952041
ISBN-10: 1503952045

Cover design by Kerrie Robertson

Printed in the United States of America

For Caroline Carr and the Kindle Scout team—
I don't know why you worked so hard
to make my dreams come true,
but I'll be forever grateful that you did.

Prologue

HRH Dante:

I'm in the middle of finals, so I decided to ask you this in a way more familiar to me.
Do you:
A. Miss me.
B. Really miss me.
C. Really, really miss me.
D. All of the above.
(P.S. My answer is D. Can't wait to see you again.)

"Lemon, there's something I want to ask you."

I put down my fork, folding my hands on my lap. I ran my tongue across the top of my teeth, making sure there was no food stuck there. I squared my shoulders and tilted my head slightly to the right as if listening intently, hoping I wasn't giving anything away with my expression. So that he would think I was surprised.

The restaurant was dark and romantic, the music soft, the food exquisite. It was the perfect setting for a proposal.

And I knew he was fixing to propose. He'd asked for my daddy's blessing, and my father couldn't keep a secret from me if his life depended on it. I was just a teeny bit shocked when Daddy called to give me a heads-up. I couldn't remember even saying anything in response. I sat on the edge of my bed, phone cradled in my hand, stunned. It had been the last thing I expected.

I'd been there when my best friend, Kat, got engaged, and I'd never seen her happier. I should feel excited like that. Happy. Giddy. I didn't. I decided the shock was blocking my ability to react appropriately.

"I know this seems fast . . ." he said. No kidding. It was fast. Maybe that would explain why I wasn't quite as enthusiastic as I'd hoped to be. To be honest, we'd really only dated for a couple of weeks over spring break.

"But we've known each other for so long." That was true. I'd known him for forever.

Maybe the reaction I expected would come when he actually proposed. He'd flash a diamond, ask me to marry him, and then it would happen. Then I would feel the way I was supposed to feel.

He hesitated, just looking at me.

"Yes?" I prompted. Still waiting. Still nothing.

"I think this is right. I think we're right."

He gestured to our waitress, who brought over two flutes of champagne on a tray. She set them down on the table, and my heart sank a little. This seemed so clichéd, so done-a-million-times. I'd wanted something special, and this was about as stereotypical as you could get.

But as I looked inside the glass, I didn't see a ring.

Maybe I was wrong. Maybe Daddy had misunderstood. Maybe it was all just . . .

Then he was down on one knee, looking at me. The restaurant went quiet, and I heard the other patrons whispering. Everyone stared at us.

No excitement. No happiness. Just . . . nothing.

"Lemon Isabel Beauchamp, would you do me the great honor of becoming my wife?"

I looked at this handsome man whom I had known my entire life. He had been my first love. The first boy I ever kissed. My parents adored him. He was ambitious and worked harder than any man I'd ever met. He would be a partner in his father's law firm by the time he was thirty. He enjoyed all the things my grandmother despaired of me ever liking—opera, art museums, country clubs—and by marrying him I would finally be the woman my family had always wanted me to be.

He was stable. Safe. Comfortable. Familiar. And part of me had always loved him. We could have a good life together. Tomorrow I would graduate with my master's degree in marketing and branding, I would find a job in Atlanta, and then we would settle down and everything would be just as I'd always pictured.

The only problem was that I had imagined I'd feel happier than a tick on a fat dog when I got engaged.

Instead I only felt empty.

To make things worse, thoughts of Dante crept in. The last time we were together, what had happened between us, and how embarrassed I'd been. I thought of how much I wanted to change, to not be the person I was. The woman who always made the wrong choice.

This man was the right choice. He would give me the future I wanted. I knew he would never hurt me.

"Yes, Sterling," I said. "I will marry you."

Chapter 1

HRH Dante:

I've wanted to tell you this for a long time, but I wasn't sure how to say it. It will change everything between us. But I can't keep this secret from you any longer. I'm . . . Batman.

Loud sobs erupted from the stall behind me. I dropped my Great Lash mascara and turned. "Hey, are you okay?"

Whoever was in there tried to stop crying and catch her breath. There was another blubbering whimper, and then the sound of a nose being blown. The toilet flushed and a girl walked out in an evening gown, eyes red, looking embarrassed.

"Sorry," she said, her breath still ragged. "This is all stressing me out."

"Is there anything I can do to help?"

She shook her head. "I'm fine. Just needed to blow off some steam before tonight. I'm sure you know how it is."

She wasn't the first girl to cry in a bathroom stall on this show, and I was sure she wouldn't be the last. I fluffed my short, blonde bob with my fingers, and then finished putting on my mascara, keeping an eye on her while she smoothed out invisible wrinkles in her dress. I had only been here for a couple of days, but I was ready to lose my mind with all the drama from the sequestered contestants. I didn't know how the producers put up with it. I didn't know how Dante was going to deal with all the madness.

Not that I minded Dante suffering just a little. It was his fault I was here.

"I have to tell someone. I feel like I'm going to burst. I saw the guy. You know, the guy we're all here for?"

The girl thought that I was one of her competitors. It was too complicated to explain who I was, and telling her might give away Dante's secret. The secret the producers were trying very, very hard to keep under wraps from the contestants on the show.

"You saw him?" I asked, trying to assess the damage. The show was deliberately keeping Dante away from all the wannabe wives. How had she managed to catch a glimpse?

"Across the courtyard. He was being led into some room with this big entourage. Anyway, I think I recognized him."

I had been putting on my favorite Tom Ford red lipstick, but her words settled into the pit of my stomach. She washed her hands in the sink next to me. Her reddened eyes looked at my reflection in the giant mirror. Some detached, unfrantic part of my brain noted that our eyes were the same shade of dark brown.

I finished applying my lipstick and tried to sound casual. "Really? From where?"

"I think I saw something online. I don't remember. Anyway, I'm pretty sure he's a prince."

My mouth went dry, and my heart beat quickly. "What makes you say that?"

"I can't be sure, but I think he's the brother of that European prince who's marrying that American girl."

That American girl was my best friend and former roommate, Kat. And that European prince was Kat's fiancé, and my current client, Nico. The brother was His Royal Highness, Prince Dante of Monterra.

But no one here was supposed to know that. I didn't respond, which didn't seem to matter as she just kept talking.

"I can't wait to tell everyone else," she said as she shook her hands and turned off the water. "They are going to *die*."

They would die and this whole thing would be over before it ever even started. We were in Southern California filming *Marry Me*, a reality show where dozens of women vied for the true love of one eligible bachelor—a love that would last forever and ever, or until the show ended and the publicity tour was finished.

And sometimes the pseudo-couple wouldn't even make it that long.

It was my marketing plan that had started this. I had decided that putting one of the royal brothers on the show would bring tons of attention to Monterra and boost their tourism numbers. Nico had backed out because he had fallen in love with Kat, and Dante had agreed with one very big condition—that I would be his liaison on the show for the entire six weeks of filming. I'd had to postpone all my other plans to focus solely on him. I'd given up a lot to be here, including seeing my fiancé and planning my wedding. I couldn't let this woman ruin everything I had worked so hard for. Especially since the royal family of Monterra was my only client. I wouldn't let it all fall apart. I needed to stop her.

"Have you told anyone besides me?"

"A couple of girls. The producers are doing a really good job of keeping us apart."

My throat felt too tight. A couple of girls? This was worse than I thought. I had to act now. Fortunately, I'd always been quick on my feet. Lipstick in hand, I brushed past her as she dried her hands with a paper towel and managed to get a good streak on her light turquoise evening gown.

"Good heavens, I am so, so sorry," I said. She stared at me, confused. I tried to look apologetic. "I got lipstick on your dress."

"What? No, no, no." She rushed back to the mirror to look at her hip. "Do you know how much this cost?"

"Here, give it to me. I get lipstick on my clothes all the time. I can get it off."

"You want me to take off my dress?"

I took off my blazer and held it out. "You can put this on. I'll go get this stain out and bring it right back. No one will ever know." I turned her around and pulled down her zipper, hoping she wouldn't stop me. I needed to keep her in this room and away from all the other hopefuls.

She stepped out of her dress and put on the blazer. She crossed her arms and glared at me. "You'd better bring that thing back to me in perfect condition. It's worth more than your life."

I nodded as I arranged the dress over my arm. I had the momentary urge to play the "my daddy owns an oil company" card but refrained. I tried to stay calm.

"Bless your heart," I said. That got out some of my frustration, as people who weren't from the South never quite understood the true implication of that phrase and took it at face value. "I will take care of everything. I'll be back right quick. Stay here."

She wasn't going anywhere. She let out a loud sound of disgust and sat on the small couch, still glaring at me.

I pushed the bathroom door closed behind me, wondering if I could lock it. There were production assistants and grips and lighting guys all over the place, and I pushed my way through them to get to the production hub. I had to find Taylor. She would know what to do.

As I turned down an empty hallway, I felt him before I saw him. The air around me became charged, and every single one of my nerve endings snapped to attention. I knew he was behind me. Then he put his hand on the small of my back and walked around me when I stopped short. I cursed my wobbly knees. Someday, somehow, I would learn to control my attraction to him. Keep him from physically affecting me. It was beyond ridiculous that I still acted like a debutante at her first ball whenever he was near me.

It didn't help that he happened to be ridiculously gorgeous. His Italian ancestry was obvious—black hair, olive skin, and light brown eyes that literally sparkled. I'd never seen anything like his eyes before, and they had a sort of mesmerizing effect whenever he looked at me. And he seemed to look at me a lot. He was tall and built and always had a clean, crisp scent from an obviously expensive cologne that I could never quite identify and refused to ask about.

Dante stood too close to me. I resisted the urge to shut my eyes as I ordered my nerve endings to behave.

"There you are, *Limone*." His voice was silky and laced with humor and an undeniable charm. He only called me *limone*, Italian for lemon, when we were alone, which made it unbearably intimate and personal. So whenever he said "*Limone*," it weakened all my defenses and gave me the shivers.

And I was pretty sure he knew exactly the effect it had on me.

"No kiss hello for your dear friend?" he teased.

"You wish," I retorted.

"You're right, I do wish," he practically purred, like some giant predatory cat, and my heart thumped painfully in response. Goose bumps broke out on my arms, and I accidentally swayed toward him.

Desperate to retain control, I ran through my list of reasons I could never be with him. That usually helped to calm my racing pulse. He was unserious, lazy, unambitious, flaky, a womanizing flirt, and would, without a doubt, cheat on me if I was ever stupid enough to hook up with him.

Unfortunately, every time I reminded myself why Dante and I could never work out, another annoying voice popped up to point out everything I liked about him. His sense of humor. His intelligence and wit. His loyalty and affection for his family. How he would sacrifice for the people he loved—he was only on this show for Nico's sake. Then my brain happily skipped to the things we had in common, like how we both loved to ski. How he had always been a good friend to me; how even after the incident at the New Year's Eve costume ball in Monterra he continued to text me funny and sweet things on a daily basis.

I told the voice to shut up. None of that mattered. Kat had told me once that she wouldn't research Nico online because she didn't want someone else's opinion to change how she saw him.

Not me. After Kat's accident, as I sat next to her hospital bed, I looked up every single thing I could about the royals. Especially Nico and Dante. I devoured every story, every article, looked at hundreds of pictures. I wanted to be informed. And it was then and there that I knew nothing could ever happen between Dante and me, given his propensity to flit from one supermodel to the next.

I knew what life would be like with him. So many of my mother's friends looked the other way while their husbands ran around with women half their age. Everyone felt sorry for the wives, but they wouldn't leave—either because of the money or the children or the public embarrassment. If I was with Dante, my humiliation would be on an international scale. I'd be a worldwide laughingstock. I couldn't deal.

He'd already proven himself to be a player the night after the accident. I saw him in the hallway flirting with one of Kat's nurses. I was worried about my best friend staying alive, and he was trying to get some. I was wildly attracted to him, but I was always wildly attracted to men who seemed intent on ruining my life, and did. Every man I had ever dated had cheated on me. As part of my resolution to treat myself better, I decided to keep him at arm's length.

And I had to remember that flirting was as natural to him as breathing. He couldn't help himself. But he was so well practiced that he often seemed sincere, and I had to constantly remind myself that it was all an act.

An act that would be easier to ignore if he didn't look like a movie star.

When I had showed my sorority sisters pictures from my Christmas vacation in Monterra, most of them had begged for the cell numbers of Dante and his identical twin, Rafe. One of my sisters had dubbed the twins "the faces that launched a thousand sighs." I couldn't argue with her over that one. They probably would have begged for Nico's number too, but I told them all that he was with Kat and I was determined that nothing would change that.

Someone had asked how I could tell the twins apart, to which my friend Jenna had said, "Why would you need to? Who cares? Date both!" After I had glared at Jenna, I explained that beyond the obvious—Rafe wore glasses and Dante didn't—their personalities were total opposites. Dante was fun and flirtatious, Rafe more serious and reserved. There was a deep sadness behind Rafe's eyes, even when he laughed and teased. I asked Kat once if she'd ever noticed it and she'd said no—which was probably due to the fact that she spent all her time looking at Nico. Not that I could blame her.

My pulse raced and my heart throbbed from Dante's nearness, so I reminded myself of the one thing that should make every inner voice go silent and my knees hold still.

I was engaged.

Engaged and getting married in only six short weeks. Sterling and I had agreed to get married the weekend after the show had finished filming.

"What is it? What's wrong?" Dante asked. "And why are you carrying a dress?"

I hated that he could tell right away that something was going on. I didn't like feeling like he knew me. "There's a girl in the bathroom who knows you're a prince, and I had to do something to keep her there until I could tell someone on the production team."

"So you disrobed her?" This amused him way too much.

"I couldn't think of another way to keep her away from the other girls," I said, walking away, determined to find Taylor and leave Dante with whoever was supposed to be babysitting him.

"Don't be defensive. It was very clever of you." He paused. Though I was practically running, he had no problem keeping stride with me. "Is this a new rule?"

"Is what a new rule?" I asked over my shoulder. It was easier to control my attraction when I didn't look directly at him. It didn't eliminate my symptoms entirely, but it did help.

"Does this mean that anytime you do something I don't want you to do, I can take your clothes?" I stopped. He'd asked the question so innocently, but my skin immediately flushed in response and I couldn't look him in the eye.

"Ha-ha," I replied, forcing myself to walk on now unsteady ankles. "Now, if you'll excuse me."

He gave me a half bow. "By all means, go save the day."

I thought I had escaped, right up until he reached out and gently grabbed my hand, forcing me to turn and look at him. Which promptly made me hold my breath and my heart stopped. "Dante, I talked to you about this . . ."

As if realizing what he had done, he held both of his hands in the air. Like he was surrendering. "I know, I know. I'm not supposed to touch you. I try and remember that I'm not allowed, but my heart forgets." He said it with a wink and a playful grin that made me remember the first time he ever kissed me.

Last Christmas I had made my best friend come with me to Monterra, a small European nation between Italy and Switzerland that most people had never heard of. Some friends in my ski club mentioned that Monterra had some of the best powder and some of the cutest guys. My parents had plans to go on a cruise to celebrate their thirtieth wedding anniversary, and I asked if I could take Kat to Monterra to go skiing for Christmas.

The first day we were there, on the one day that Kat had promised to ski with me, she had a terrible accident. She had planned to meet me on the bunny slope. I had been skiing around waiting for her when I heard yelling and whistles farther down the mountain. Curious, I went off to see what was going on. There was Kat, strapped to a board and being pulled toward a waiting helicopter. I couldn't recall another time when I'd ever felt so panicked or worried. I had tried frantically to get to her, to make sure she was okay, and someone grabbed me to keep me back. To hold me. To comfort me.

It was Dante.

He held me tight as I cried, causing my fear to dissipate while she was loaded in. Another man (Nico, I learned later) climbed in behind Kat, and Dante yelled something to him in Italian. He waved for us to join them. I sat right next to Kat, holding her hand, praying for her to be all right. She was awake, which was good. But I couldn't seem to stop crying. I told her she was going to be okay, which I desperately hoped was true. I could feel Dante behind me, and even though I didn't know his name then, I was so glad that he was there. He was so calm and sure while I fell apart. Kat threw up and passed out, and Dante held me again while I cried and the paramedics took care of her.

It had been all my fault that she was in that situation. She'd only skied once before, and she'd somehow gotten onto one of the harder runs and had almost died. I shouldn't have made her come with me. If she had died, I never would have forgiven myself.

I was confused when we arrived at the hospital and all of the staff were bowing and scraping to the two men as Kat was rushed into an examination room. I heard someone call them "Your Highness," which shocked me. I was told to sit in the waiting room by a nurse in broken English, while Dante and Nico spoke to some of the doctors. I pulled out my phone and did a search for "royal family" and "Monterra."

And found pictures of Nico and Dante. Princes.

Charming, playboy princes from the look of things. Dante seemed to have a different girl for every occasion. I knew his type. I constantly dated and got cheated on by his type. I was well aware of how our story would end. Regardless of how considerate and nice he'd been, I wasn't about to play his game. I planned to keep my distance. Maybe even find a different guy to lust after while I was there.

Once Kat had recovered and had started responding awkwardly to Nico's sweet advances, I decided I needed to let off a little steam.

When I said as much to Dante, he told me he sometimes ran a pseudo-nightclub out of the castle's dungeon. Which was weird, and I told him as much. He laughed, up until I asked him to invite some other friends along. Some male friends. His face fell, and he looked so sad it was all I could do to stick to my guns. I wasn't going to let him sway me.

Which turned out to be famous last words.

Chapter 2

HRH Dante:

How much does a polar bear weigh? Usually enough to break the ice.

At the hospital Dante had introduced me to some of his friends, including his twin brother, Rafe, and several other young nobles. One in particular stood out—a man named Salvatore, who was some kind of duke. He was handsome, but nothing compared to the men of the royal family. It was a bit like a star standing next to a group of suns.

But he was cute and had flirted with me, so I decided to focus my energy on him. Our flirtation fizzled out, but I was determined to regain his attention. If I didn't have someone else, I knew I wouldn't be able to resist Dante.

And Dante turned out to be pretty irresistible.

We were in his nightclub, dancing to a playlist that Dante had arranged himself. Someone had sprayed neon glow paint all over the stone walls, and there were comfortable benches set up with tables. The club even had a bar in one corner where everyone just helped themselves.

I stayed away from the alcohol, because Dante had a predatory look in his eyes and I needed to keep my wits about me.

I sat down on a bench, pretending to ignore Salvatore the way he was ignoring me. He was talking to two women who appeared to be models, and they chain-smoked in a corner while looking bored by everything.

He was shunning me because of what I'd told him. Kat planned on staying a virgin until she got married, and for some reason I'd made the Lord a promise while she was in the hospital that if He would make her better, I'd do the same thing. I would give up my one-night stands and cheating boyfriends and become celibate. In that moment I would have promised anything if it had meant she would recover. In hindsight it might have been a bit rash, but it was a promise I planned on keeping. Or, at least, trying to keep. We were leaving Monterra in a little less than two weeks, and I didn't want to sleep with a man I'd never see again. I was tired of random hookups. Tired of how gross and used they made me feel.

And his rejection bruised my pride. I wasn't used to men not paying me any attention. I sat there, feeling sorry for myself, but not willing to change my mind to make some boy like me. If all he wanted was someone to sleep with, he could get one of those underfed bimbos instead. I'd move on. As if he could read my mind, Dante came and sat next to me. Like he had somehow sensed my vulnerability from across the room.

"Interesting nightclub," I told him as he completely invaded my personal space. "I've never seen anything like it."

"You don't have one in your dungeon?"

I raised an eyebrow at him. "I don't have a dungeon."

"Really? How strange," he teased as he lifted his cup to his lips. His very kissable lips, by the way. I made myself look away. I could feel him, almost touching me but not quite, a delicious heat emanating from his body.

I should have made him go away. Instead, I asked, "Why did you create all this?"

He shrugged. "If we go out, our security details have to go out with us. If we do it here, then we don't take anyone away from their families."

My heart did a funny little flip. That was extraordinarily thoughtful and sweet. I was about to tell him so, when I stopped myself. I was supposed to be keeping my distance and not encouraging him.

So I stayed quiet, listening to the music, watching but not watching Salvatore.

"I don't know why you're making this effort. He's not worth it. And this will never work with him." He put one of his arms along the back of the bench, right behind me. His very strong, masculine arm. The one that had felt so nice wrapped around me earlier at the ski slope.

"Work with who?" I forced myself to ask.

"Salvatore. You're pretending to ignore him. He only wants what he can't have."

"That's true of most men." Had everyone in the room guessed what I was up to? That I was trying to get Salvatore's attention?

"He's worse than most. I don't know why you want to be with someone like him, but since you do, I have an idea."

Somehow he managed to get even closer to me. "You should kiss me, and that will make him crazy. He's always been jealous of me and my brothers. He's the two hundred seventy-sixth person in line for the throne, and I think he's been trying to figure out how to kill two hundred seventy-five people without getting caught."

My body thought this was a fantastic idea, as I was already leaning toward him, face tilted up. My brain tried to run interference, but I made it be quiet. I refused to poll my heart on the matter.

He leaned in, smelling my neck, which made me feel a bit woozy.

"What is that scent?" he asked.

"Lemon sugar," I said, my heart beating too quickly.

"Sweet and tart, like you," he said before he planted a soft kiss at the amazing spot where my neck met my shoulder, and the earth shifted on its axis.

I decided it had been far too long since I'd last kissed somebody if this was how I was going to react. I also thought for a moment that I should stop him, but the only thing I said was, "My lip gloss is lemon-flavored, too."

Which was such a blatant invitation, and from the fire in his eyes and the seductive smile on his face, he knew it.

"I do appreciate the commitment to your name." He set down his drink and used his free hand to run his fingers up and down my arm, which gave me chills and hot flashes at the same time.

"Well, not everyone gets to be named after a fruit. You have to have fun with it."

He pressed another kiss to my throat, and I closed my eyes as a tingling warmth spread slowly through my body. Nothing had ever felt this good, ever. I wanted an excuse for behaving like a love-starved teenager. Alcohol. Loneliness. Wanting to make what's-his-face jealous. Something to explain why I was reacting like this to Dante.

I had nothing.

He took my head in his hands, his fingers softly massaging my scalp, rendering me boneless. I heard something somewhere off to my right and was starting to turn when he stopped me, holding me still.

"Don't look at him. This will never work if you do."

"What won't work?" My brain was a fuzzy haze of buzzing sparks. I felt like someone had dipped me in warm molasses and now I couldn't move or think.

Another smile. "Making Salvatore jealous."

Right. Salvatore. That was his name. We were making him jealous.

Only I didn't much care about making him jealous anymore.

But I couldn't let Dante know it.

"That is such a total line," I breathed. For all I knew this was his MO—telling girls he could make their potential boyfriends jealous if they would just kiss him.

And if they were smart, they'd let him do it.

"Could be," he agreed. "Only one way to find out."

I waited for him to kiss me. Wanted it more than I'd ever wanted anything. Instead he caressed my face and looked at me. I scooted closer. I was tempted to kiss him, but I'd never kissed a man first. It was kind of a rule.

A rule I was seriously considering breaking.

His breath washed over me. He had been drinking, but his breath smelled like mint. Like he knew he was going to kiss me or somebody else. Maybe I should have been outraged, but he was way too good at what he was doing.

He had turned me into putty in his hands.

"Are you ready?"

I practically jumped out of my skin at the sound of his voice. I wanted to speak, but my mouth had gone so dry I couldn't. Every other sight and sound had faded, and I could see and feel only him.

He leaned forward and nibbled gently at my lower lip. His prelude to his kiss was making me go just a tad insane.

Then his warm and surprisingly soft lips were fully on mine, and I half expected to hear the "Hallelujah" chorus as a jolt of excitement and heat slammed into me. I wrapped my arms around his neck, pulling him close.

I had planned on keeping my eyes slightly open to see if Salvatore was watching. But they fluttered shut of their own volition the second Dante's lips touched mine. Like his lips were drugging me and it was all I could do to stay coherent.

His hands weren't just holding me where he wanted me—they were caressing my face, my neck, leaving fiery trails of yummy goodness everywhere he touched. Somehow I had gone from sitting next to him to pressing close against him, my hands moving from his neck to his hard warm chest, where I could feel his rapid heartbeat against my palms.

All of my nerve endings were wriggling in delight as his mouth slowly and sensuously moved against mine. I was giddy and light-headed.

And then it was over. When he stopped kissing me, it felt like a physical pain and all I wanted to do was grab him and kiss him again and again and again.

My cheeks were flushed, and I put a hand against one, just to cool it down. Dante smiled at me.

"Don't look now, but somebody's coming over here." He whispered the words into my ear and an actual shiver ran down my spine, making me want to turn my head and finish our too-short kiss.

"Do you think he's jealous?" I asked, not really caring right then, but liking the opportunity to whisper back, to be close again.

"Definitely. But be careful—there's jealous and then there's Othello."

I wanted to laugh, but I was still so caught up in all the sensations he had caused that I only looked at him. There was something in his eyes, something I couldn't explain, but it made my heartbeat do triple time.

Then Salvatore was there, and in his heavily accented English he asked, "Do you want to dance?"

Part of me wanted to tell him to forget about it, that I was just fine where I was, but some random model-esque woman sat next to Dante, kissing him on the cheek. She threw one of her legs on top of his and leaned in to whisper something in his ear. He laughed.

This. This was why I wanted to stay away from Dante and focus my attention on Salvatore. He had just given me one of the most amazing kisses of my life and ten seconds later he had another girl draped all over him. It made my stomach turn. I didn't need this.

I didn't need him.

Dante flashed me a satisfied grin as if to say, "See? I told you it would work."

I'd never wanted to punch somebody so badly in my life. But I didn't know whether I wanted to hit him or her. Both, probably.

I refused to look at or talk to Dante for the rest of the night. And just as he had predicted, Salvatore didn't leave my side. Before I hadn't even existed, but now I was the center of his universe. He was funny and charming, but not as funny and charming as Dante. But it didn't matter. I refused to go down that road. Tonight was a spectacular example of why.

That soft, sweet kiss had very nearly made me spontaneously combust. I wondered what would happen if he ever kissed me and meant it.

I wouldn't have to wonder for long.

I explained the situation with the girl in the bathroom to Taylor Hodges, my former sorority sister and recently promoted field producer of *Marry Me*. She was on a headset faster than a hare with a hot foot, talking to whoever was in charge, and the decision was quickly made that the girl in the bathroom would have to be let go. They ascertained that her name was Brittney, and they located her luggage, returned her stained dress even though I didn't get the chance to clean it, and had her in a taxi and on her way to the airport before I even knew what was happening.

And she took my blazer.

An order went out to sequester all of the girls in their hotel rooms so the production team could find out who knew what. As far as the team was concerned, the show would be ruined if even one girl suspected Dante had a title.

An emergency meeting was called in the conference room, and Dante was invited. He nodded his head toward the door, letting me know that he wanted me to come too. The room was crowded with executives and crew members, all talking at the same time on their phones and to each other.

Assistants ran in with reports from each of the girls. Brittney had told two other girls about Dante, and they were sent home just as quickly. The other women still appeared to be in the dark.

Unfortunately, the show only had two alternates, which left them with one slot open.

"We could just do it with twenty-four women," said one of the executives.

Another executive, a woman with a severe silver bob, shook her head. "But we always have twenty-five! Always! Not only will it upset the viewing audience, but the other girls will wonder why we're one short. It will tip them off that something's going on. We can't risk it."

"We're filming the first episode tonight," said a heavyset man with a baseball cap. "Everything's been set up and ready to go, the permits have been pulled, and if we delay things even a day, it will mess up the entire schedule."

"We can't afford that," someone else said, and several people nodded their heads.

"Matthew is going to kill us if we mess this up," said a small, accountant-looking man in a three-piece suit.

Matthew Burdette was an executive producer. He owned a massive conglomerate with a very famous production company, and he had his fingers in television and movies and owned a crapload of radio stations. His wife, Stephanie, was a former A-list movie star turned talk show host. Together they ruled Hollywood. He was not a man you would ever dare cross, especially in my line of work. He could effectively keep me from working with any TV or radio show ever again if I made him mad.

And he had a temper.

"Who's going to call him?"

The room fell silent. Nobody was willing to risk professional suicide.

"What about Lemon?" Dante had been standing quietly in the corner, observing the chaos.

"What about Lemon?" I repeated shrilly. He wouldn't, would he?

"Lemon could fill the empty slot," he said. He didn't look at me. Which was smart, because if looks could kill, he'd be lying in a white chalk outline.

Taylor jumped to her feet. "That's perfect. Lemon is the right age, she's gorgeous, and since Dante's her client, she's not going to tell anyone about him being a prince."

Taylor had been promoted to field producer from director's assistant when I reached out to her with an actual prince for the show. She got the credit and the glory, which was fine. I was just happy that part of my plan to promote Monterra via its crazily attractive royal family was coming together. Matthew Burdette was thrilled by the idea of having a member of a reigning royal family on the show. He loved the idea of capturing the contestants' reactions when they eventually found out, and he didn't want anyone to know beforehand. The audience would know in advance, but the show sequestered the women while they were promoting the twist. They wanted that huge shock, that massive surprise that would make all of America tune in to see what would happen when the show stopped being about landing a husband and started being about becoming a real-life princess.

"I don't think that's a good idea. I'm engaged," I reminded her. Sterling would be upset. So would my family.

"So? No one needs to know that. You're not even wearing a ring," she said. That made me think of a not-too-long-ago conversation I'd had with Dante about my missing ring, and my eyes flicked to his. I could see that he remembered it too, and I felt humiliated. Which made me get angry.

A man wearing thick glasses cleared his throat and pointed out, "She hasn't taken any of the tests. Like the psychological ones."

I'd heard about those. They were like eight hundred questions long to weed out the crazies. I didn't know why it mattered. Every year some

Looney Tunes girl always made her way onto the show. The one you worried might start boiling rabbits and stabbing people through shower curtains. It wasn't like they were great at screening.

"Or the STD tests." That felt really invasive. But with some of the activities that had happened on this show in the past, it was probably necessary.

Dante walked over to me and held up a hand, which made the room fall quiet. "Are you crazy?"

"No, but . . ."

"Do you have an STD?"

So inappropriate. "No!"

"There. Her word's good enough for me."

Everyone exploded, and I couldn't make out what anyone was saying.

"I am not going on this show," I hissed at him, poking his chest. "I'm supposed to be here to make sure they're not portraying you or Monterra in a negative light. I can't do my job if I'm on the show."

Taylor made her way over to us. "Lemon, I need you to do this. I will lose my job if you don't."

Guilt trip successful. I knew how hard she had worked to become one of the youngest field producers ever on the show. I also knew how much her job mattered to her. As much as mine meant to me. "You should just find someone else," I protested weakly.

"There is no one else. There's no time. All our eggs are in this basket. You're the only one I can trust, and I know you'll protect Dante and the show. Please. From one Zeta Beta Gamma to another."

She'd played the sorority card. I couldn't say no to a sister.

"Okay, but on one condition. Dante sends me home tonight in the first round."

The room erupted in cheers, and Taylor hugged me tightly. "Yes, he'll send you home first. Thank you, thank you, thank you!" She ran back to the conference table to strategize.

"Dante? Tonight, you'll send me home?"

He smiled at me, which I took as a yes.

I quickly sent texts to Kat, my mother, and Sterling, letting them know what had happened. I didn't want to call because I could predict how each would react. Kat would be thrilled, because she had been pushing me toward Dante since our time in Monterra. My mother and father would be disappointed in me for the millionth time and would probably put Grandma Lemon on the phone, and she would be shocked that I would besmirch the Beauchamp name by appearing on something as lowbrow as reality television, even for one episode. Sterling would again tell me that I didn't need to do any of this, that he could provide for me, and I should just come home.

I was already stressed enough.

And it was just for one night. One episode. I would say what I had to say, do what they wanted me to do, and then I would be done.

So why did I suddenly feel so nervous?

Chapter 3

HRH Dante:

I think I suffer from amnesia. Do I come here often?

I signed what they called a "standard contract" for the contestants on the show. They made me turn over my cell phone and laptop and checked my luggage. I asked the production assistant what they were looking for, thinking I could help speed up the process, and she said any magazines, music devices, books, or tablets.

"I seriously can't take any of that with me to the house?"

"You seriously can't," she replied, once she'd done a thorough inspection. I already knew the mansion we were staying in didn't have any televisions or computers available, but I thought at least I'd be able to keep my personal devices. Losing my phone was sort of like losing a hand.

"What do you expect everyone here to do?"

"Drink heavily and 'interact' with the other competitors. That's all you can do."

She left with my confiscated items. Thank heavens I'd only be here for one night. I already hated everything about it.

I walked over to my window, pressing my forehead against the glass. I could see the ocean from the hotel, and so far it was my favorite thing about California. I had invited Kat to come out and visit me for a little while during the filming, but she'd declined. I had arranged a press tour for her and Nico because they had officially announced their engagement, and she wanted to have some downtime with him before they started flying all over the world.

She also ordered me to not go all California on her. Said that if I started drinking kale smoothies, we could no longer be friends.

There wasn't much danger of that.

I had been instructed, by another assistant, on what I needed to do that night when I "met" Dante. I had to pretend like I didn't know him, and he would do the same. It was expected that I would do something memorable to catch Dante's attention, because that's what all the other competitors would be doing. No one wanted to go home first.

Except for me.

I didn't have anything appropriate to wear for this show. The women tended to dress formally for Heart Celebrations and had cocktail dresses for the parties and other get-togethers. I had packed only business attire as I'd never imagined I might end up a contestant.

What I didn't tell anyone was that I had watched *Marry Me* obsessively for years. The girls in my sorority had been addicted, and they got me hooked too. I watched every incarnation—like when a woman was at the center and the men competed, or when former contestants were sent to an island location to fall in love with each other—and I ate it up. At first I pretended to watch ironically, but I soon fell under the spell. Even though I knew the couple wouldn't actually end up together, I still loved it.

I had just never wanted to be on it.

Not knowing what else to do, I threw on an Atlanta Braves jersey that was worn and comfy and a pair of jeans. That was different and unusual, right? Everybody else would be dressed like they were ready for the Miss America pageant, so I would definitely stand out.

An assistant offered me the use of a stylist and a team of hair and makeup people, but I'd been doing my own hair and makeup since I was knee-high to a grasshopper. And I didn't need a dress.

I ordered room service and flipped through television channels until it turned dark outside. A knock on my door let me know it was time to go, and a different production assistant with a headset on came in to mike me. That consisted of clipping a pack to the back of my bra, although I insisted on attaching the small microphone to the front of my bra by myself. After the assistant confirmed it was working, he directed me to a waiting limousine.

The hotel was minutes from the mansion. There were several cars lined up in front of mine, and at a distance I could just make out Dante, standing in front of the mansion and greeting each girl as she exited her limo.

My driver settled into position, and when I was only one car away, I got my first good look at Dante. In a perfectly tailored tuxedo. I sucked in a deep breath. It had been a while since I'd seen him in formal wear. I forgot how sexy he looked in it.

My view was obscured by a skinny blonde in a long, hot-pink dress. She walked up to Dante and, in his typical Monterran style, he kissed her hello on each cheek.

"I'm Dante. Pleasure to meet you."

"I'm Annie. As in, Annie time you want."

I couldn't see her face, but I could definitely see his. There was a moment of shock, and then he tried desperately not to laugh. I didn't think that line worked the way she wanted it to. Annie walked away, not letting the conversation continue.

Then it was my turn, and I climbed out of the limo. Dante stood there, waiting for me with a giant smile. I had a momentary lapse where I imagined myself in a wedding gown and Dante waiting for me as I walked down the aisle. If there hadn't been three cameras pointed at me, I would have slapped myself. *You are engaged*, I reminded myself for the three thousandth time. I took a deep breath to calm my dancing nerves.

He leaned down to kiss me hello, his eyes lit up with delight. First he kissed my left cheek, and then the right. My skin tingled beneath his lips. I couldn't be sure, but it seemed like Dante lingered in those kisses for a beat longer than he did with anyone else. Maybe I was imagining it.

"Hold on," somebody yelled out from behind a camera. "Technical difficulties. Give us a minute."

A makeup artist walked over to put some powder on Dante's face, which made me giggle. He grimaced. "Please don't tell my siblings. I will never, ever live this down."

"Oh, this is so going in the blackmail folder," I responded, trying to hide my smile.

"You know you don't have to blackmail me. Just ask, and I'll do it."

My heart got a little twinge, because I knew he was telling the truth. That's just how he was. Whatever I'd wanted to do in Monterra, he always found a way to make it happen. If I asked him to get me the moon, I was pretty sure he'd have a plan within the hour for how he would accomplish it.

Which was both super sweet and disconcerting.

"Go ahead and set up; let us make sure we have the lighting and angles right," a director called out. I moved back to my spot. "Pretend like you're meeting for the first time."

"I'm Dante Fiorelli, by the way. In case I hadn't mentioned it." Another woman had come over to fix his hair. This, thankfully, kept him from kissing me hello again.

"Fiorelli? I thought you didn't use a last name."

The stylists finished messing with him and walked back over to the other crew members. "We don't, but it'd be a little suspicious if I showed up with only one name. Like Cher or Madonna."

"We need to have a serious conversation about your taste in music if that's your frame of reference for one-name singers."

"I have excellent taste in music, thank you very much. I was only trying to use singers I thought you would be familiar with. We all know your taste in music is a bit questionable."

"You leave Taylor Swift alone."

He gave me a half smile, but before he could respond the director said, "All right, ready to roll. Meet again, please!"

This time I held out my hand so that he couldn't kiss me. "Hi, I'm Lemon, from—"

"Atlanta?" Dante finished as he took my hand. I tried not to gasp when he leaned down and kissed my hand. My pulse exploded as my lungs deflated. The smirk on his face told me he knew exactly the effect he had on me. Sneaky jerk. I yanked my hand free.

"How did you know I'm from Atlanta?" He was supposed to pretend that he'd never met me.

"Your jersey," he said. "It says Atlanta on it."

Oh. "Yep, that's me. From Atlanta. Go Braves!" I should have said something clever or funny, or kicked him in the shin for making me all weak-kneed again. Instead, I sounded like an idiot.

I really wanted to wipe that all-knowing smile off of his face, but I couldn't think clearly. His cologne had invaded my senses, and I wanted to grab the lapels of his jacket and pull him closer.

He spoke and I balled up my hands at my side, ordering them to stay still. "I love your accent. I'm Dante."

"Okay."

And I walked away. I was going to look like a total fool on national television. Maybe they'd edit me out for hitting below the stupidity threshold. Although given the sorts of things that happened on this show, that bar was pretty low.

Nobody stopped me to do it over, and I let out a sigh of relief when I reached the front door. When I stepped inside, I was struck by the overwhelming smell of melted wax. I could only imagine how many candles had given their lives in service of the show. An assistant directed me to the Mixer Room, where all the parties and ceremonies would be held.

The room was full of women who were pretty in a generic way—everyone had long hair (mostly extensions) with beachy waves. They all sported fake eyelashes, too-white teeth, and perfect makeup. They wore tight, formal dresses that fit courtesy of Spanx, and heels so high I worried for their safety. Especially since most of the women in here were already half drunk.

"Wow!" someone said over my shoulder. "I was in the car behind you, and I have to say, you two have the kind of sparks where you need a welder's helmet. Yikes. The rest of us won't stand a chance!"

I turned to see a tall and very pretty redhead with dark green eyes. Her hair was a deep, fiery color. Normally you'd expect to see a lot of freckles on a girl like that, but her porcelain skin was clear and smooth. She had a genuine smile on her face, and I felt drawn to her. It reminded me of the first time I met Kat. Where it had felt like I had known her in another life and that we would be the best of friends in this one.

"Don't worry about me. I'll be surprised if I last beyond tonight." I wanted to reassure her because she seemed wired and nervous.

"I'm Genesis. Which I know is a weird name, but you get used to it after a while."

"Were your parents religious?"

"My mom, fanatically so. Hence the name. And you are?"

"I'm Lemon."

She laughed. "So you get it."

The other women stared at us like old cows looking at a new gate. I could see that they dismissed us immediately as possible competition.

Ordinarily that would have gotten my dander up—but since I wasn't competing for Dante's heart, it didn't matter. I would have to tell him about Genesis, though. She seemed very sweet.

I heard Annie talking to the other girls about her arrival. "He couldn't take his eyes off of me. We had such a connection. I bet I get the 'First Sight Heart.' You should have seen our crazy chemistry."

"I certainly saw the crazy part of it," I whispered to Genesis, and she laughed, which caused the women to turn as one toward us, like a bunch of hormone-addled meerkats. Annie glared at me, and I just smiled at her. Because that's what you did with crazy people. Another limo arrived and everyone turned back to the window.

An angry-sounding dark-haired girl in a purple dress said, "I told him that my last boyfriend wanted me to lose twenty pounds, so I decided to lose two hundred pounds in the form of my loser ex-boyfriend instead. If Dante can't like me how I am, then I don't want him, either."

That must have terrified him. I tried not to laugh.

Everyone started talking at once and trying to one-up each other on who had the best line when they met Dante. Nobody listened to anyone else and nobody stopped talking, either.

"I'm a little afraid," Genesis whispered. "What's going on with all of these women?"

"Dropped on their heads as babies?"

She giggled, and we walked over to a couch to wait for everyone else to arrive and to chat without the harpies at the window judging us.

"You look so comfortable. I'm so jealous."

I had actually been feeling a bit out of place in my jeans and jersey, but Genesis was right. I was comfortable. "But your dress is so pretty."

She was wearing a dark green dress with princess cap sleeves and a poufy skirt. "It isn't mine. The stylist had to sew me into it. I just want to take it off and put on some sweats. Same for these stupid fake eyelashes. I feel like somebody glued spiders to my face."

"You've never worn them before?"

She shook her head. "That's not really me."

Another new arrival walked in the room, and every eye went to her. She had honey-blonde Disney princess hair—the kind that fell in perfect waves down to the middle of her back—and soft brown doe eyes. She wore a skirt so tight and short I could see her religion. I felt like I should scour my eyeballs.

"I know her!" Genesis whispered to me in shock. "She's a British actress on that soap opera, *East and West*, which is one of my favorite shows ever. I used to follow her on Twitter!"

"Used to?" The actress seemed to glide across the room to the bar, pouring herself a drink while looking both refined and flawless. I wondered who did her PR. Since I had a grand total of one client so far, this might be my chance to network with her before I got kicked off at the Heart Celebration.

Genesis's voice broke into my train of thought. "She totally blocked me! She took over this longstanding role and started misspelling her character's nickname on purpose, and I corrected her to help her out because it was making people upset on this message board I belong to, and she publicly called me out and said something about people changing and reinventing themselves as they grew and having the freedom to be whoever they wanted, and then she blocked me. Then a bunch of her other followers started ganging up on me. It was not fun."

She said it in one quick breath, and I narrowed my eyes at the actress. Genesis seemed like such a sweetheart that I couldn't imagine anyone being mean to her for any reason.

Although sometimes I was too quick to judge. Maybe the actress got a lot of flak on Twitter and used her block button liberally. She might be really nice. I should give her the benefit of the doubt. Especially if it would help my little fledgling company to succeed.

She walked over to us, and Genesis fell silent.

"Hello. I'm Abigail Morris-Mansey." She had a smooth, posh, upper-class British accent. She held her hand out limply, and I wasn't sure how I was supposed to grab it. So I shook her fingers.

"I'm Lemon, and this is Genesis. Nice to meet you."

"Beg your pardon? What did you say?"

Confused, I glanced over at Genesis. She looked like she wished she could just shrivel up and disappear. "I said, I'm Lemon, this is Genesis."

"Very sorry, but I simply can't understand a word you're saying. You have an extremely thick accent. Excuse me."

My accent was *not* that thick and I knew she'd understood me just fine. I'd lived with women long enough to know that she was playing a mind game and trying to intimidate me. Too bad for her—I didn't intimidate easily. Abigail walked outside toward the pool, carrying a drink in one hand and smoothing down her hair with the other. A cameraman followed after her while she looked out at the horizon, as if thinking deep thoughts.

So much for her ever becoming a client.

"That's her! That's the girl who told production I had an eating disorder!" I heard a woman screech. I turned back to the window to see somebody in a hideous tangerine getup pointing a finger at the window, and I craned my neck to see who was coming in. The new girl had just stepped into the room when the tangerine woman stalked over to the new girl and slapped her.

I gasped, and then ran over to try and separate them. Tangerine Girl was screaming, "You were trying to get me kicked off the show, weren't you?"

At the same time, the other woman was yelling, "You're crazy! What is wrong with you! Get off of me!"

None of the crew stepped in to help. They stood there and filmed, saying nothing. So I yanked the tangerine girl off of the other one and pushed her back. She fell onto her butt, still yelling and screaming.

I put my fingers into my mouth and whistled loudly. The screaming finally stopped. I channeled Grandma Lemon the best I could. "Y'all need to calm down. This is not how ladies behave."

Some more choice words were exchanged, but the other girls managed to separate the fighters into opposite corners of the room. I worried that I might have to spend the rest of the night playing referee.

And that things would only get worse once Dante joined us.

Chapter 4

HRH Dante:

I never realized how much I like surprises until I met you.

I already had a pounding headache, and it didn't seem like it was going away anytime soon. I had spent a long time talking with Genesis, the only other halfway normal person here, and we both enjoyed the show put on by the drunken women who had gone into a tizzy when Dante entered the room.

"He sure is handsome," Genesis sighed.

And in other news, water was wet.

I encouraged her to try to meet him, although I didn't like her odds given the man-eating savages currently monopolizing his attention. He looked over their heads at me and gave me a "sorry" expression and I just waved. That's what we were here for. He wasn't there to spend time with me.

"I'm relieved he only has a bit of an accent," Abigail said to some women off to my right. Dante and Rafe had been allowed to attend Columbia and MIT, respectively, unlike their older brother, who had only been allowed to go to university in England since he was the crown prince and all. Even then they'd only let Nico go because England's crown prince was attending the same school, which would double the amount of security. Dante had once joked that as "the spares," no one cared if he and Rafe came to the United States. Which meant that they had only the barest trace of an Italian accent when they spoke English.

"Some of the girls here have such thick accents I can't understand them."

I would not get annoyed or let her provoke me. Hopefully, Dante would see right through Abigail and kick her off the show too.

She noticed me then and said, "Oh, no offense."

"Bless your heart. Lots taken."

She gave me a dirty look, which let me know that she did indeed understand me, but had singled me out as her first victim in what was sure to be a six-week smear campaign against all the competitors.

I sat down on a bar stool and asked the bartender for some Sprite. Dante made his way over to me, with a cloud of desperate women clinging to his heels. They stayed a few steps back as he sat next to me. His leg accidentally brushed mine, and I refused to acknowledge the way it made my stomach go fluttery.

"You're not drinking?"

I probably should drink. It might help dull the boring. But on the other hand, it would definitely make me more susceptible to him. "Nope. Kat's my spirit animal."

He looked confused. "Your what?"

I noticed that there were no cameras nearby, which meant I could explain without getting embarrassed. "My spirit animal. My life choices guide. She has what I want—a degree; plans for her international children's charity; and she landed the man of her dreams, who just happens to be an actual prince. So I've adopted her lifestyle and am giving up certain things. Like alcohol." It was a weird flaw of mine, and was probably because I was both super competitive and mildly superstitious—if somebody went on a three-day cleanse and lost five pounds, I'd do it for a week and lose ten. Kat went without alcohol and sex and had all her dreams come true, and so would I, only better.

He gave me a knowing grin, while I took my soda from the bartender. Dante asked for a scotch.

"What? It totally worked for her."

"You could have landed a prince too, without forgoing anything."

I sighed and shook my head while he laughed. He stopped mid-laugh with a quizzical expression.

"Wait, does this mean you and the fiancé haven't . . ."

I put a hand over his mouth. The cameras were everywhere, and even though they'd left us alone a minute ago, now we had like five of them pointed right at us. My relationship with Sterling was my personal business, and all of America did not need to know about it. His eyes sparkled with mischief, and I pulled my hand away.

"No, we haven't."

That grin got bigger, and I decided to ignore it.

"Challenge accepted," he said.

"What? What challenge?"

"The no alcohol thing." The bartender came back with Dante's drink, but he waved it away. "It will be my first task."

His first task? "What in the world are you talking about?"

But before he could explain, a petite brunette was at his elbow, tugging at him to come and talk. "I'll tell you later," he said as he allowed himself to be led away.

I didn't know how much time had passed, because I had nothing to do but drink my soda and watch the women preen and posture as they tried to get Dante's attention. He seemed to be loving the situation and had nothing but smiles and compliments for everyone. Always so polite, always so charming.

It was early summer in California, and despite the open windows, I was hot. The overhead lights, all the bodies, the weather—everything contributed to making the room stuffy and unbearable. I didn't know how Dante was doing it in that tuxedo. I was pulling my jersey away from my body to try and let some breeze through, while he looked cool and calm.

Genesis had wandered off, and I'd lost track of her hours ago. Taylor had told me that the producers would be pulling the girls aside for interviews and what they called "In The Moments," or ITMs. She told me that some of the crew called them TMIs, because it wasn't uncommon for a contestant to share way too much information.

Somebody kissed Dante on the cheek, leaving pink lipstick. I quite literally had a flash of red before my eyes as she giggled and wiped his cheek clean.

I'd had about all I could stand, so I escaped to the backyard to get away from the heat, the alcohol-induced fights, and the raging hormones.

There was a pool, and then a massive yard behind it with trees, rows of flowers, and open green spaces. It reminded me of our ranch back in Georgia. I found a massive old oak and sat on the side opposite to the house. Taylor could yell at me later.

I looked up at the full moon and realized that I had no idea what time it was. I was totally reliant on my phone for everything, including checking the time, and so I never wore a watch.

Thankfully, by this time tomorrow, I would have my phone back and things would return to normal.

"Hiding out?"

I jumped, putting my hand over my heart. It beat fast and heavy. Whether that was from being surprised or him being close to me, I didn't know. "You almost gave me a heart attack. What are you doing?"

Dante sat down on the grass next to me, looking out of place in his tuxedo. "Running away. You?"

"Same."

"You are going to owe me for this, *Limone,*" he said as he took off his jacket and placed it on the ground.

"Owe you? Pretty sure you owe *me* now."

He flashed that smile that always turned my stomach to jelly, and I forced myself to look back up at the sky, searching for stars that couldn't shine through the layer of pollution.

"I owe you?" He let out a short laugh. "Don't worry. I plan on paying you back." His voice sounded weird. Ominous. Un-Dante-like.

Before I could ask what he meant, he said, "I heard things got crazy in there earlier." He sounded like himself again. So I told him about the catfight that had taken place. He was laughing as I told the story. I, admittedly, played up the comedic aspects. I liked hearing him laugh. It made me feel all warm and fuzzy.

A twig snapped behind us and we both turned. I was worried that we'd been caught and they'd force us to go back inside.

"It's only Marco." I heard the relief in Dante's voice. Marco was his primary bodyguard, and was one of the nicest people I'd ever met. One of the deadliest, too. I saw him practicing hand-to-hand combat in Monterra once, and I pitied the person who ever tried to get at Dante.

"Hey, Marco!" I called out.

"*Buonasera,* Signorina Lemon." He melted back into the shadows, and we sat quietly for a couple of minutes until it was clear that he was giving us some privacy.

"I'm glad I caught you alone. I've been wanting to talk to you about something."

He suddenly sounded serious, which made me wary and a little nervous. Dante was never serious. I wondered if it was about how he planned to pay me back. Or the task thing he'd mentioned earlier.

"You should tell me about this fiancé of yours."

"I don't know if we should talk about this." It seemed strange to talk about Sterling with Dante. I didn't talk about Dante with Sterling, either.

"You don't have to do anything you don't want to do. We're friends, and I would like to know what's happening in your life." He sounded so sweet and sincere. I ran through my list again of why Dante would be a terrible boyfriend.

Maybe talking about Sterling would help keep us in the friend zone. It would be a reminder to both of us that I was an engaged woman and he needed to stop chasing me for fun.

"What's his name?"

"Sterling."

"Sterling? That's not a name. That's a type of silver."

I pushed him on his shoulder and he listed to one side, laughing. "I'm sorry. I won't tease. Sterling what?"

"Sterling Jackson Brown, the fourth."

"He sounds like a law firm." I went to hit him again and he held up his hands, still laughing. "Sorry, sorry. Please tell me you're not marrying a lawyer."

I sat still for a beat. "What's wrong with lawyers?"

"Everything's wrong with lawyers."

"My mother was a lawyer."

"A lawyer created an angelic creature like you? I don't believe it." He reached out when he said this, brushing a strand of hair from my face and tucking it behind my ear. I held my breath until he took his hand away, and I closed my eyes slowly and opened them again. He made me more skittish than a newborn colt.

"True story. It's how my parents met." Even I could hear the wobbliness of my voice. I hoped he didn't notice. "She was an environmental lawyer, and my daddy had started up his oil company, and they met in court when she tried to shut him down. They started dating once the trial was over. Daddy says he won the case and the girl, and then Momma reminds us that she only lost on a technicality, because she was a great lawyer who should have won."

"How do you know she was great?"

"Because a good lawyer knows the law. A great lawyer knows the judge."

He laughed at that, and I joined him. Most of my time spent with Dante alternated between wanting to laugh with him and wanting to punch him for making me feel things I didn't want to feel.

It was exhausting.

"Did your mother keep practicing law?"

"She stopped when they got married. They wanted a family more than anything. My grandfather died when my daddy was young, and my poor grandmother, who had never worked a day in her life, had to work three jobs just to keep them afloat. They nearly lost the ranch. Daddy always says his proudest day was when he gave my grandmother the deed and made sure she never had to have a job again. He didn't want my mother to have to work either. Or me."

Dante raised an eyebrow at me. He knew how important my career was to me. "Your mother doesn't object?"

"My mother says she's found more happiness and satisfaction in volunteering than she ever did working, and so she's on board with Daddy's plan. But it's not like some old-fashioned or sexist 'women belong in the home' sort of thing," I explained. "It's just that given his upbringing, he adores the women in his life and wants to take care of them."

Which meant that I let my father down on a continual basis. He wanted to shelter and protect me, and I wanted to be out in the world, living my own life.

"So he expects your future husband to keep you barefoot and pregnant?"

I only barely refrained from rolling my eyes. "That's not the point."

"I don't know if I can let you get married."

I pressed my lips together, shocked by the turn in our conversation. What was that supposed to mean?

"Because you can't possibly be planning to be named Lemon Brown. So plain and sad. I think 'Her Royal Highness, Princess Lemon' sounds so much better, don't you?"

"You think Rafe would have me?" He laughed again, but the smile didn't quite reach his eyes.

He picked up a blade of grass and twirled it between his fingers. His very clever fingers that always managed to make me melt every time he touched me. "How did the two of you meet?"

I couldn't tell if it was my imagination, or if we were moving closer to each other. This happened a lot when I was with him. Like our bodies were two magnets that wanted to be together, no matter how hard I tried to resist.

"I've known him my whole life," I said. Our mothers met in Lamaze class, which my momma only attended to humor Grandma Lemon. My momma says it's stupid to give birth without drugs when the good Lord gave us medicine. Anyway, we grew up together, and he was the first boy I kissed. We were thirteen and chasing fireflies." I half smiled at the memory.

"And then?"

"Then we were in high school and he wanted to do more than kiss and I wasn't ready. So he ended things with me because there were plenty of other girls who were willing. Like Ellis Wetherly. It broke my heart." I hoped I didn't sound too bitter or sad. When Sterling broke up with me, he destroyed something inside of me. I was at an awkward age, feeling vulnerable, and when he did it, my soul hurt like fissures spreading across a mirror—small cracks that spread and widened until the whole surface was ruined.

A murderous look crossed Dante's face, and I had seen the men in his family angry often enough to know what that meant. If Sterling had been sitting next to me, Dante would have beat his face in.

I hurried on. "I swore off boys for a while. It killed me every time I saw him in the hallway with another girl. And there were lots of other girls. In our senior year I met a foreign exchange student from Spain—Enrique. I was asked to show him around and we started dating, despite some serious communication issues."

I probably should have stopped. But it was always so easy to talk to Dante. "And then one night, having drank more than I should have, and thinking I was in love, I slept with him. It was awkward and fast and I regretted it the second it was over. I really wished I hadn't done it later when I caught him at a bonfire party in the backseat of Ellis Wetherly's car. I smashed out her headlights, but it didn't make me feel better. Unfortunately, it started a pattern that I've never been able to break. Exciting, passionate foreign men who cheat on me and break my heart. Sterling is the only man who never cheated on me."

"He's also the only man who broke up with you so that he could cheat on you." I hadn't been mistaken. Definitely angry.

I put my hand on top of his, wanting to calm him down, but it had the opposite effect on me. There was this electrical current that seemed to always be waiting beneath the surface when we touched. The second we did, it zipped around my body, making me feel anything except calm, but I left my hand where it was. He didn't move. It was like he was afraid that if he did, I would pull away again. He was probably right.

"I still don't understand why you're engaged to him." He sounded a bit better. Calmer.

"I went home for spring break, and the first night he was there with his family. He asked me to go to dinner the next night and I did, and the night after that and the night after that. I extended my break a week to spend more time with him, and we called and texted when I got back to Colorado. Then the night before graduation he proposed and . . ."

I trailed off, and his eyes met mine. There was a fire there that singed my soul, that burned me up and made me want to beg for it to consume me. Like a lit fuse between us that waited and waited, and then caused a mountain-sized explosion whenever we kissed.

And like so many times before, all I wanted was to be close to him. I was dying to kiss him, but knew that I couldn't. Somehow I had angled myself so that our faces were so close that even though we weren't kissing, if somebody saw us they'd probably think that we were.

My breathing became shallow and rapid, and I tried to repress it. It would only encourage him, and I couldn't let that happen. I should move away. Go back inside. Something.

You're engaged.

But then Dante said, "I hate that anyone has ever hurt you, *Limone*," as he caressed the side of my face, and every last bit of resistance inside of me crumbled.

I knew he would never kiss me, because he was too honorable. But despite my rules, I nearly attacked him then and there. I didn't—because a hysterical Taylor found us and ordered us back inside. As soon as she spoke, I pulled away faster than a rattlesnake getting ready to bite. I couldn't look at him. Dante stood up first and offered me his hand, but I ignored it and him and walked back into the house.

I couldn't believe it. I had to be stronger than this. I was marrying someone else.

And, once again, I'd come this close to throwing away my steady, sure relationship and believing Dante could be more than he was.

Chapter 5

HRH Dante:

If it be thus to dream, still let me sleep!

I pulled Taylor aside to see what had made her so upset. She was typically a go-with-the-flow kind of girl, and I'd never seen her so stressed. "Matthew's here," she said, and my heart stopped.

"Matthew Burdette is here?" I responded. I suddenly felt nauseous.

"This Heart Celebration has to go *perfectly*. Matthew said he wants to film it live. No cuts, no reshoots. Something about it seeming more real and test audiences responding better to live tapings." She doubled over, and I looked around for the nearest thing she could throw up in. "These things never go right. I am so going to get fired."

"You will not get fired," I told her, helping her to sit down on a nearby chair. "Everything will be fine. I promise."

It was a promise I shouldn't have made.

I could feel Dante standing behind me, presumably listening in on our conversation. I continued to ignore him. I shouldn't have been upset with him. It wasn't his fault my messed-up psyche found him irresistible.

But it was almost over. Soon I'd be gone and free of this hellmouth.

The perfectly coiffed host of *Marry Me* walked in, his tailored suit and golden tan making me feel pale and unkempt. "Hello, ladies, I'm Harris Phillips." Cue the excited twittering from women who'd been standing in super-tight shoes for way too long and had had way too much to drink. "If you will excuse me, I need to have a conversation with Dante, and we will meet you at the Heart Celebration."

Dante left with a chorus of good-byes echoing behind him, and we were told to go into the room where all the Heart Celebrations would be held. There were candles of every shape and size all over the place. They had put a riser on the floor, and the back windows opened on the lit-up pool. Past the pool I could see the sun just starting to come up over the horizon. This stupid shoot had taken almost all night. No wonder I was so tired. They arranged us by height, and I was stuck up front in the middle. I was shorter than everyone else because I was the only woman not in heels. I felt like I was on *Sesame Street* playing "one of these things is not like the others."

Genesis was led over to the other side, and I waved to her. She smiled back, and I noticed a small red heart pin attached to the bodice of her dress. She must have won the First Sight Heart. Which meant that Dante had liked her so much at first sight that she didn't have to worry about this elimination, because she was safe.

My mind whirled with crazy thoughts that led me down a dark, jealous path. While I logically knew Dante would date other women and possibly fall in love, I still felt more possessive than I should have. It made no sense. How could I be upset? I liked Genesis so much, too. But it still caused a sharp pang in my heart.

I told myself that they might be really good together. She might make him really happy. It should be what I wanted. It might even help my inappropriate attraction to him if he paid all his attention to the women on the show and left me alone.

The lights were okayed, the cameras were positioned, and the director called for Harris and Dante to enter the room. There was a call for "quiet on the set!" and everyone went still. Harris walked out first to greet us.

"Good evening. Welcome to what I hope will be the first of many Heart Celebrations for you. I guess that everyone here has a pretty good idea of how this works." Some nervous laughter. "If you hear your name, please step forward to accept a heart pin. Genesis has her First Sight Heart." There was low murmuring and rumbling from some of the other competitors, who were apparently just as jealous as I was. "Which means she doesn't have to worry tonight. If you don't hear your name, you will be going home immediately."

It would have been more fun if Harris would have just been honest with us. Like if he'd said, "Good evening, ladies. Dante will choose one lucky woman out of twenty-five, whom he will ultimately drop like a hotcake and embarrass in the national press once this is all over. Hope you enjoy your fifteen minutes of fame, because everyone will forget who you are the second you get sent home."

Instead he finished up with a "Good luck to everyone, and here's Dante."

You'd think I'd be used to him, but I was struck all over again when he came out and smiled at us. "First, I would like to thank all of you for being here tonight. I know that many of you have sacrificed to do this, and I am so flattered and grateful. I'm glad to have had the chance to meet all of you, and it has been an amazing night. I'm sad that I have to let any of you go. I wish I could keep you all."

A few anxious laughs, and lots of twitching and fidgeting. An obviously drunk girl behind me kept swaying back and forth, sighing and singing to herself softly. I hoped she could keep it together until the cameras turned off. For Taylor's sake, if nothing else.

"But Harris tells me I can't, and since I am hoping to find my future wife, this is a necessary evil."

He picked up one of the heart pins and held it. A couple of months ago I'd sent him some full seasons of the show because he'd never seen it before. He'd obviously studied them well. He stood there, staring at us, increasing the suspense. Even my heart was pounding in anticipation, and I knew I was going home. I could only imagine how the other women felt.

"Emily."

Emily stepped forward with a smug look on her face, brushing past the front row. She walked up to Dante.

"Emily, will you accept this piece of my heart?"

"I will," she said and hugged him.

One down, only seventeen more to go.

A parade of Ashleys, Lisas, and Tiffanys went up to accept their pins and pieces of Dante's heart. This represented my worst fears—Dante sharing himself with everyone here, unable to commit to just one woman—and it was all I could do to not cackle inappropriately.

Harris reemerged to remind us that Dante held the last pin in his hand, and that six women would be going home. I heard someone on my right start to whisper, "Please, please, please," as we waited.

"Lemon."

Was someone else here named Lemon?

I stayed in my spot. Sometimes they called the wrong names. He could have been looking at me and meant someone else. Total accident. I'd let him recover.

"Lemon?" he said again, looking right at me.

My mouth dropped open. We had a deal. I was supposed to be getting out of this madness.

"Me?" I said, again giving him the chance to fix his very obvious screwup.

He smiled, and I knew it was no mistake. "Yes, you."

Red-hot anger boiled up inside me and I set my jaw, ready to let him have it. I was fixing to have a hissy fit with a tail on it. Then I saw Taylor out of the corner of my eye, her hands over her face. I reminded myself that this was live. Matthew was off somewhere watching. I couldn't let her get fired. Sisters before killing misters who made promises and then broke them.

I stalked over to him, trying very hard not to glare. "Lemon, will you accept this piece of my heart?"

"Sure," I said, smiling falsely and as sweetly as I could. He handed me the pin, and I didn't hug him. I went back over to my spot. He looked a little uneasy at the expression on my face.

Like he knew I was planning on giving him a Krav Maga crotch kick later.

Harris wore an appropriately sorrowful expression. "Ladies, I am sorry for those who did not receive a piece of Dante's heart. This means you will be going home tonight. Please take this opportunity to say good-bye."

I heard a couple of sobs behind me, and then everyone was hugging the girls who weren't chosen. It seemed really unfair that women who wanted to be here would be sent home, and he had put me in a position where I had to stay. I held the pin so tightly in my hand that I worried I might draw blood.

If we could just get these women to leave without someone begging Dante to reconsider, this would be over faster and I could let him have it. Fortunately, there were no beggars. Some of the cameras followed the rejected competitors out the door while an assistant handed out champagne flutes to those who remained.

I passed on the drink and saw that he took one. "To finding true love," he said, holding his glass aloft. The other girls all clinked their glasses against his before taking a drink, but Dante set his flute down on the bar behind him.

"Cut!" someone shouted, and a collective sigh of relief went up from both cast and crew. Things had gone flawlessly, and I hoped Taylor appreciated the sacrifice I had made.

Stalking over to Dante, I said, "Come with me. *Now.*"

We went into the kitchen, the reflective surfaces of the stainless steel and quartz countertops making it feel even brighter. It was a direct contrast to my murderous mood.

"What is wrong with you?" I asked as I tossed my pin onto the counter. He watched as it bounced and jumped before settling in one corner.

"*Limone*, let me explain . . ."

I actually stomped my foot. Like a three-year-old. "Don't you '*Limone*' me. You made me a promise. You said you would send me home."

"I never promised to send you home. You asked if I would, and I didn't say anything back."

"You . . ." That made me stop short, as I recalled the conference room. Taylor had agreed to my plan, but Dante had just smiled at me and said nothing. He had tricked me. I should have made him put it in writing. Signed in blood.

"I would never make you a promise that I wouldn't keep." That made me a little less mad, until he reached for my hand. I smacked him away. He was not going to use his charm and magic touch against me.

"I need your help," he tried again. "Please."

He sounded so serious, and he looked exhausted. He sat down at the counter, picking up my pin.

More of this serious Dante. I didn't know what to do with real emotion from him. It kind of freaked me out.

"I've watched enough of this show to know that half of the women who sign up are here to become famous and they lie to the suitor about their true intentions. You could help me by being my inside woman. My spy. Like that movie you loved as a child."

He was talking about *Harriet the Spy*. I had wanted to be her when I was little. Except nicer. Only I didn't think the nicer part had worked out. "I never should have told you about that."

"*Limone*, I would very much like to make your fantasy come true."

Which sounded sordid and steamy and made me a little woozy.

"It's a childhood *dream*, not a fantasy."

There was that grin. "Sorry, sometimes I get words in English confused."

Words in English confused, my butt.

Dante always seemed to know where my weak spots were. The idea of being a spy did appeal to me. Sneaking around, taking notes, and keeping a spy journal. I had spent so many hours doing just that when I was younger, and to think that I could do it now for real, and for an actual purpose, was way too appealing.

But I was too old to be making decisions based on a little girl's wishes.

"You're already engaged. You've found the person who makes you happy, and you want to spend the rest of your life with him. I respect that. But you're my friend, and the only person here that I trust to have my best interests at heart. Stay and help me choose my wife."

My heart beat furiously, anger bubbling through my veins. Then my throat suddenly felt thick, like I might start crying. And I felt stabby from the jealousy.

Mad, sad, and jealous. None of which made sense.

Because I didn't have any right to those feelings. I looked down at the counter, picking at a raised fleck. I didn't want to look at him.

I couldn't believe that he was taking this show so seriously. "Don't you think you're a little young to be getting married?" It was an argument we'd had multiple times before. Dante was two years younger than me, which was another reason I could never be with him. I wasn't into cradle robbing.

He sighed, and I could practically feel him rolling his eyes. He would say that he was so much more worldly and sophisticated than me that it balanced itself out. Then he'd say, "When you're sixty and I'm fifty-eight, you won't care."

"But I'm not sixty. I'm twenty-four," I'd reply, and we'd argue about it more.

"I guess Nico's had a bigger impact on me than I realized," he said. "He's the happiest I've ever seen him, and it made me realize that I want what he has. Creating arbitrary restrictions because of age seems foolish to me."

Maybe he really was ready to settle down. He'd definitely had a chance to sow plenty of royal oats. There was certainly enough photographic evidence of it.

Not that I cared. He could run off and marry whoever he wanted and have lots of babies and it wouldn't affect my life one way or the other.

Yeah, I wasn't buying the lie either.

But, forgetting about my own personal drama, he was right about one thing. He was my friend. I did care about him and his future. And I couldn't let him be snowed by some awful reptile like Abigail. "You really think the woman you want to marry is here?"

He reached over and put his fingers on my chin, turning me to him. "I really think the woman I want to marry is here."

His eyes were so intense, so honest. The world stopped. Time ceased to exist. The oceans had dried up for all I knew. There was only me, Dante, and that current that tugged me to him, begging me to kiss him.

Which I could never do again.

Letting out a shaky breath, I tried to joke. "Every other man is terrified of getting married, and I know the one guy who thinks it's the best thing ever."

I turned my face away for my own sanity. His fingers lingered for a second and then dropped.

"Does that mean you'll help me?"

"Does a one-legged duck swim in a circle?"

He sounded adorably confused. "I don't know."

"It does. It means yes, I'll help you. I'll stay. For a little while. That's what friends are for, right?"

I really, really hoped I wouldn't live to regret it.

"So we are friends."

"Of course we're friends."

"With benefits?" he asked hopefully.

I raise a scornful eyebrow at him. "Um, no. No benefits whatsoever. Benefitless."

Then he laughed, and I suppressed the desire to laugh with him. Because every time I did, another one of my defenses fell down.

He took the backing off of the pin. "May I?"

All of the oxygen left the room. I was playing with fire again, and I was definitely going to get burned. But stupidly I said, "'Kay."

He tugged my jersey lightly and pushed the pin through the fabric. He reached inside to attach the backing, and as his fingers brushed against my heated skin, I hoped that when I passed out I wouldn't hit the edge of the counter on my way down.

Then he adjusted the pin, making sure the heart pointed the right direction. My actual heart beat so fast I anticipated a visit to a hospital in my near future.

He didn't help the situation when he put his hand on top of mine. I could just imagine the doctors' conversation. "She ended up here how again?"

"The prince touched her, apparently."

"Thank you, *Limone*." His voice sounded husky and full of emotion as he interrupted my ride on the crazy train. "It means the world to me that you would stay and sacrifice to help me. *Grazie*."

Serious, emotional Dante again. He was making all my feminine parts overload.

"And if I get to surround myself with beautiful women in the process, what's the harm?"

I let out a sigh of relief. This I understood and could deal with. "There's the Dante I know and lo . . ." I trailed off in a panic, realizing what I'd nearly said.

"Love?" he finished playfully.

"The Dante I know and tolerate for a paycheck," I responded, and he put both of his hands over his heart, as if I had wounded him, and whirled backward. It made me laugh.

"If you stay, will you have time to do your work and plan your wedding?"

His voice was this strange mixture of casual and friendly, tinged with what sounded like sadness. But that couldn't be right. I did like that he cared about what I wanted.

"You haven't met my mother yet, but I am superfluous to her planning. She could pull off something twice as elaborate in half the amount of time. And I'll have to make some kind of arrangement so I can have access to my phone to check on Nico and Kat's press tour, but I'd set aside this time to be your liaison. I suppose it doesn't really matter whether I'm behind the camera or in front of it."

"Well, if you're on television, it might help you get some new clients. Everyone in America will know who you are."

Now that idea had merit, and it hadn't occurred to me. He was right. This might open doors for me to build my business. We just couldn't tell anyone about our little scheme or else everyone on the show and across Internet message boards would be talking about how I wasn't there for "the right reasons."

Taylor entered the room, still looking panicked. I was pretty sure this job was going shave ten years off of her life expectancy. "Dante, Chris needs to interview you in the interview room."

"Of course," he said. He nodded at me before leaving, and I smiled back.

The anger had been sustaining me, and now that it was gone, I felt drained and exhausted. I was ready to find my room and go to sleep. "Where am I staying?"

"Not yet," Taylor said, not quite meeting my gaze. "Matthew Burdette wants to talk to you."

Chapter 6

HRH Dante:

I'd like your permission to slightly exaggerate our relationship.

"Why does he want to see me?" I asked, my heart in my throat. "What's wrong? Where are we going?"

Taylor chose the last question to answer. "Everyone calls it the 'Bat Cave.' It's the studio where the production team lives and obsesses over everything on the show." She took me outside, and it was now light enough that I could see a small guest cottage positioned just south of the main house. I knew they had a room inside the mansion where the story producers would stay with monitor feeds, and that the garage served as their control room.

It seemed rather ominous to go somewhere called the Bat Cave. If this were a scary movie, the audience would be screaming at me not to be stupid enough to go in.

She opened the door and ushered me inside. I hesitated for a moment, and then went in. The house was dark, because someone had put blackout curtains on all the windows. It took my eyes a second to adjust, and I recognized Matthew Burdette before Taylor led me over to him.

He seemed very average—average height, average appearance, brown hair, brown eyes. Your eyes would skim over him in a crowd.

But the anger he radiated was not average, and was wholly intimidating. I instinctively realized that he was meaner than a wet panther, and I would be a fool to cross him.

"Tell me," he said, his voice low and dangerous. "What is the name of your company again?"

I felt the urge to lie to him in order to protect myself, but I was a terrible liar and it would be very easy for him to find out.

"Lemon Zest Communications, sir."

I hadn't meant to add the *sir* on the end. All my life I'd been raised to say "yes, ma'am" and "no, sir" to adults. I'd had a hard time dropping the habit in my college years as it had been so ingrained, and this man was bringing it back out in me. That abject fear that I'd endure something terrible if I didn't show the proper respect.

"You're filling in because of the girls we had to send home, correct?"

"Yes, sir."

"And you didn't want to fill in?"

"No, sir. I didn't." He was pee-your-pants scary.

"And you thought, what, you'd sabotage my entire show by dressing up like this and ignoring Dante?"

Ignoring him? I felt like I'd spent the whole evening doing nothing but talking to him. Well, I probably hadn't talked to him that much, but I'd definitely spent the entire party thinking about him when I wasn't talking to him.

Which was a disturbing realization.

"You thought you'd just disrespect my entire show and everything I've worked so hard to accomplish here?"

There were easily twenty people in the room with us, but not one made a sound. They were also all motionless, as if moving would draw his attention and his wrath. "I didn't mean any disrespect to you, sir."

He leaned forward, both of his hands clenched up like he was fixing to punch me next. "Then I'll tell you what's going to happen. Unless you want to be blackballed from this industry for the rest of your life, you will never pull another stunt like you did tonight, where you acted angry and put out. You will act like Dante hangs the moon and as if you can't wait to be his wife. Do you understand me, or do I need to use smaller words?"

I could feel the sweat beads forming at my hairline. "No, sir. I mean, yes, sir, I understand you and you don't need to use smaller words. Sir."

Then he slammed his hands down hard on a nearby table, making everyone jump in fear. "And no more logos! Didn't anyone explain that to her? No shirts with logos on them!"

I fought back the urge to cross my arms across my chest, like I could hide what he'd already seen.

"Now get out."

He didn't need to tell me twice. My heart pounded in my throat, and a silvery, metallic taste filled my mouth as I sprinted out the door and across the yard before anyone could catch up with me. I ran like a scalded haint.

The Monterran royals were my only clients. I'd been so busy with the engagement announcement and the show that I hadn't had time to try and find anyone else. And no one else would ever even speak to me if I angered Matthew Burdette. How could I help a potential client if no talk show hosts would e-mail me back, or if no reporter would return my calls? I could never get anyone any publicity. I had no fallback plan if Burdette carried through on his threat to blackball me.

And if that happened, I would have to go home to Georgia, tail between my legs, proving everyone right. Like the bosses from my summer coffee-fetching internships, who immediately assumed I was nothing more than a dumb blonde and predicted that I wouldn't be able to hack it in the real world, or my family, who thought I didn't need a job.

I had worked so hard to prove myself. I couldn't fail miserably. I reckoned I would do whatever I had to do to keep my company afloat.

Even pretending to be falling in love with Dante whenever a camera was pointed at us.

I headed straight for the kitchen and threw open the door of the stocked pantry. There was mostly quinoa, granola, and dried fruit, but I did manage to find a box of Keebler Mini Fudge Stripes in the one-hundred-calorie packs.

Ripping the box apart, I sat in the middle of the pantry and started hoovering up cookies as fast as I could get the packages open. I had always been a terrible stress eater, and I knew I'd be kicking myself tomorrow.

Or later today. After I got some sleep.

I didn't feel tired anymore though. I was so wired. Like I was mainlining coffee.

My cheeks felt wet, and I realized that I was crying angrily. I wasn't the type to run away from anything. My daddy used to say that in a fight between me and a grizzly bear, he'd put his money on me. And now I was cowering in a pantry. I hated that I'd been so weak in front of Matthew Burdette. But he held all the cards, and I had none. I never liked feeling powerless and out of control.

It was in this state that Dante found me. Sitting on a pantry floor, streaks of black mascara running down my face, surrounded by crumpled-up empty packages.

"*Limone*, what's wrong? What happened?" He crouched down next to me, his expression of concern too much for me. It made me want to cry more.

Instead I sniffled, ordered myself to stop crying, and wiped the tears from my cheeks. I tried to calmly and dispassionately recap my run-in with Burdette. Dante sat down next to me and put his arm around me. It took all the willpower I possessed not to turn and cry on his very broad and very comforting shoulders.

"Do you want me to go and talk to him?"

"No!" I barked, startling him. "That's the absolute last thing I want you to do. I'm a big girl and I don't need you to protect me. I can do this on my own, even though nobody else thinks I can."

"What do you mean?"

"I told you how my parents and my grandma don't want me to work. My momma wants me to come home, marry Sterling, and go volunteer at the Junior League with her. Sterling thinks it's pointless for me to have a job since he can support us. But this is important to me. I want to work. I want to succeed on my own, on my own merits and talents, and not ride somebody else's coattails or be somebody's accessory."

I was perilously close to crying again. I drew in a big breath and continued.

"This is important to me. I can't mess it up. Does that make any sense?"

It was pathetic how desperately I wanted him to get it. Nobody else seemed to.

"It does," he said, his arm tightening around me slightly.

Relief crashed into me, and I wanted to cry yet again. I blamed the lack of sleep.

"It's a good thing these cookies come in these hundred-calorie packs, because now it's easy to count the thousands of calories I just demolished." I shook my head. "Such a mistake."

"This is why you should spend more time with me. I don't make mistakes."

"Oh, really?"

"I thought I did once, but I was mistaken."

It felt good to laugh.

Taylor wasn't laughing, though, when she found us sitting on the floor. "Dante, we need you to get some rest before the group date later on today. They've set you up in the master suite. Lemon, I think you and I need to have a discussion."

This time I let Dante help me to my feet, which turned out to be a mistake. Once I was upright, he tugged my hand and pulled me a little too close. "I'm glad we're friends," he said.

Friends. Yes. Friends. That was all we were, I told my prickly skin and racing heart.

I needed to remember that.

Despite being upset, Taylor was a woman with a pulse, and so she watched Dante until he left the room. "So you're staying?"

"I'm staying."

"I'm assuming you don't have the right clothes."

I ran my fingers through my short, blonde bob, certain I looked terrible. "Sure don't."

"Okay," she said, taking out her phone and typing. "You're going to need some dresses and shoes and accessories."

"What about the stylist?" He had offered me dresses at the hotel.

"You only get him for the first Heart Celebration and the last one. Other than that you're on your own."

"For hair and makeup too?" I could do my own everyday makeup fine. My own evening makeup. Pageant makeup too. But I'd never done television makeup. I didn't want to put on too much or too little.

She nodded.

"It's fine. I'll go out later and get some things."

"You can't. You can't leave this house unless you're on a date with Dante or we're traveling to a different location. No shopping, no movies, no gyms, nothing. You have to stay here on the estate."

"What?" I hadn't realized that I'd basically be a prisoner. It was a gilded cage and all, but I wasn't down for being locked up.

"Sorry. Look, I'll go out and get your stuff today, okay?" Taylor and I were the same dress and shoe size and had often shared clothes in college.

Looked like I didn't have much of a choice. "My things are back at the hotel. I'll reimburse you when everything gets here."

She nodded.

"And I have a condition."

That made her look up. "What?"

"I am going to need access to my phone. I will need to call my fiancé and my family. I will also need to keep on top of Kat and Nico's engagement press tour, so I can't be completely cut off from civilization." I could just imagine my poor little phone blowing up with incoming texts and e-mails. People were probably wondering why I'd fallen off the face of the earth.

"The problem is that this show relies on total lack of communication with the outside world. It changes things if the contestants know what's happening when they're not around." She started chewing on one of her fingernails, a terrible habit she had when she was worried. An older sorority sister had once tried to cure her of it by adding cayenne pepper to her nail polish. It hadn't worked.

"I understand, but this is nonnegotiable."

"How about this? You can periodically check your phone, but not every day. And I have to be in the room when it happens to make sure no sensitive information is leaked. Either by you or to you."

I sighed. The paranoia was ridiculous. But she was serious about her job, and I had to respect that. "Fine. I agree. Now where can I go to sleep?"

"Follow me."

She explained that the mansion had eight bedrooms and nine bathrooms. Which wouldn't be fun at first since we'd all have to share, but would get better as time went on and people got sent home. Taylor explained that we would have to double up, and, in a couple of cases, triple up. She led me into a darkened room where I could see Genesis sleeping in one of the twin beds. "She claimed you as her roommate. Have a good nap."

I nodded, so tired I could barely keep my eyes open. I heard the door close behind me as I kicked off my shoes, pulled my jersey and jeans off, and climbed into bed.

And prayed I wouldn't have any dreams about Dante.

Genesis gently shook me awake. "Sorry, Lemon," she said in a soft voice. "They want us to go outside to the pool because they're announcing a group date for this afternoon."

Showtime. I sat up and rubbed my eyes. Genesis looked pretty and natural. She'd put her hair up in a ponytail and her face was makeup-free, and she was the kind of woman who looked nice even without it on. She had on a green one-piece bathing suit under a sheer cover-up.

My luggage had been brought over and was at the foot of my bed. Just beyond that were shoe boxes and dress bags hanging up in my closet. I ran over to take a look and was glad that Taylor had such excellent taste. She chose dresses I would have chosen myself.

I had two swimsuits with me, and I knew how much of this show took place poolside. I held my bikini up, and Genesis said, "They have swimsuits downstairs. Apparently we'll be wearing them a lot. You should probably hurry, because I think you're the last one up."

I told her I'd meet her there and to go on without me. I jumped in the shower, dried off, put on sunscreen, and fixed my hair. I put on one of my bikinis, a pair of shorts and sandals, grabbed my sunglasses, and went to inspect what else they were offering.

What they had were barely there suits that would leave little to the imagination. I would have had more coverage if I'd slapped on a couple of Band-Aids.

But beggars couldn't be choosers. I tried to pick the least offensive ones of the bunch and decided America could get over it if I wore the same bikini more than once.

I came out to the pool where the girls were all sunning themselves, angling their bodies just so to make sure that they didn't look fat or flabby. I wondered if their backs hurt from arching them like that.

There were bottles of liquor and glasses everywhere. I guessed that production assistant hadn't been kidding when she said our job was to interact and drink heavily.

I grabbed a lounge chair next to Genesis, who smiled at me as she slathered on more sunscreen. "I have to wear like SPF 9000. I have two shades. Pale white and bright red."

"Me too," I told her, putting my sunglasses on. I never liked the way spray tans looked. Although, considering the women surrounding us, I was alone in that sentiment.

We couldn't wear our mike packs because of the water and the bikinis, so there were several sound guys holding boom microphones over us. There were also cameras everywhere, and I wondered how they all managed to stay out of each other's shots. They were fixated on the girls in the bathing suits, filming their conversations. I didn't understand this because presumably the show's target audience was women between eighteen and thirty-four. Women who weren't all that interested in watching other women in their swimsuits. Now, shots of a half-naked Dante, on the other hand—that I understood.

There was some giggling and splashing, and I turned to see a bunch of girls getting into the pool. They had deigned to do so because Dante had shown up and, as if he'd read my mind, was taking off his shirt to join them.

His shirt hit the ground, and he flashed his very muscular and defined torso, and I melted. I was so, so shallow and grateful for my sunglasses that allowed me to watch him without him knowing. "I wish I didn't like that so much," I murmured to myself.

Fortunately Genesis was distracted by him too, so she didn't say anything in response. He dove in and everyone squealed in delight. I noticed that all of the girls were careful to keep their heads above water.

I wished so badly for a magazine. Or a computer. Or my phone. Watching Dante flirt with the masses was not my idea of a good time.

He surfaced and waved at me. Then he swam over and came up to the edge, crossing his arms on the side of the pool. Which obscured my view of his perfect chest.

As Pepé Le Pew would say, *le sigh*.

I felt hyperaware of every detail—how his muscles flexed in his forearms, how the water droplets clung to his dark hair, how his smile seemed brighter and more blinding than the sun.

And I was hyperaware of how much I liked it.

"Come in. The water feels nice." I could actually feel nineteen sets of eyes boring into me.

"I'm good. Thanks, though."

"Your loss," he said, flinging some water at me. I refused to be goaded into responding.

Genesis started to say something to me, but we were interrupted by Harris's voice. "Good afternoon, ladies. I hope you all got a good night's rest, because this afternoon Dante would like to take everyone out on a group date. You'll be going horseback riding. Cars will be out front waiting for you in one hour."

Everyone practically sprinted back in the house, nearly trampling Harris in the process. I wondered if an hour would be long enough for them to get ready. "You're not going in?" Dante asked.

"You've seen me without my makeup. I don't need to impress you."

"You don't," he agreed.

But Genesis was gathering up her things, so I decided to go inside after all. I didn't want to be left alone with Dante when we had such little clothing on. Bad things might happen.

And I wanted to kick the part of me that got excited at that prospect.

Chapter 7

HRH Dante:

Those gorgeous eyes, that amazing body, that incredible brain, that earth-shattering smile . . . but enough about me. How have you been?

"When did he see you without your makeup?"

"What?" I was just delaying for a second until I could think of something. "Oh, last night. After the Heart Celebration. It wasn't a big deal."

Technically he had seen me last night without my makeup on because I had cried it all off. But if I told her that, then I'd have to explain everything, and I didn't know if she could keep a secret and I couldn't risk my career.

I was still lying to her though, and I did not enjoy it. Another girl might have seen right through me, but Genesis just accepted what I said.

Fortunately, I had my red cowgirl boots with me, and some comfortable black leggings. I put on a soft T-shirt, one I wouldn't mind the horses chewing on if they got affectionate. I hadn't packed a hat, not knowing there'd be a need for one. The show had given us bathing suits; maybe they'd give us some hats so we didn't burn.

Genesis put on a similar outfit, including well-worn boots. That surprised me. "Where are you from?" I asked her.

"Iowa," she said. "Farm girl." Which explained it.

There were indeed hats downstairs by the front door, and we picked up a couple.

We were also the first ones down. There were two twelve-passenger vans waiting. We climbed into the first one, where I asked Genesis more about where she grew up.

Just as it was time for us to leave, the other women arrived en masse. And most of them were wearing Daisy Dukes, tank tops, and high heels. They all had cowgirl hats on as well, and a couple had even tied bandannas around their throats. Like they were doing their own slutty interpretation of what a real cowgirl would dress like.

They were going to be sorry later when the inside of their legs had been rubbed raw from saddle burn. The high heels were the stupidest part though. They would be sinking into the ground left and right, and they would slip in the stirrups.

It wasn't my job to babysit them though. Just to find out which one was the least vain and the least stupid and point Dante in her direction.

When we got to the ranch, Dante was already there, and everyone spilled out of the vans, racing toward him. And, as I'd predicted, they very nearly broke their ankles on the way. One of the ranchers called everyone over and asked who knew how to ride a horse. Genesis and I were the only ones who raised our hands. He told us a couple of basic commands that they used, and then sent us over to the stables to choose a steed while he taught the other girls how to control their horses.

A ranch hand showed me the horses, and I saw a beautiful caramel-colored palomino in one stall that made me homesick. I saw the name "Butterscotch" on the door. "Hello, Butterscotch." I petted her on the nose, and she whinnied at me. I let myself in and saddled her, cinching it tight, making sure I left two fingers between the girth and her side. I adjusted the stirrups to the right length.

As I led her out, Dante came up behind me with a large black stallion. "Who's this handsome fellow?" I asked.

"Dante." He winked.

And, against my better inclination, I laughed. "I meant the horse."

"This is Prince, believe it or not."

"So why did you choose horseback riding?" I had wondered if he chose it because of me. I had told him once how much I loved my horse Honey back home.

"Genesis grew upon a farm and is studying to be a veterinarian. We thought she would like it. The show originally wanted to have you all mud wrestling in order to win a date. I vetoed it."

Why did that make my heart sink faster than a lead balloon?

"That's nice," I said. The lady in question came out of the stables with a white mare, and she mounted her horse quickly and easily. I went to Butterscotch's left side and did the same. Dante followed suit.

We rode the horses over to the rest of the group, where they were passing out riding helmets. I heard several of the women complain about how it would ruin their hair. I thought of telling them that if they fell on their head, ruining their brain would be worse, but in some cases that probably wouldn't be true.

Several mounting blocks were brought out to help them get on top of their horses. The head rancher went down a path and told everyone to follow. There were multiple handlers who stayed off camera. They were necessary because it was like herding cats. Apparently nobody had listened to their instructions, and now the horses were meandering off in different directions.

And even that wasn't enough to keep them safe, because Genesis had to race off after a girl whose horse was trotting toward a small creek.

"Want to race?" Dante asked me, once it looked like the chaos had been contained.

"You're on," I said. Momma always said I was too competitive for my own good.

I kicked Butterscotch lightly with my heels and yelled "Yah!" and she was off. I heard Dante laugh behind me as Prince galloped to catch up. I leaned close to Butterscotch's neck, crouching above the saddle to encourage her to go faster.

But it didn't matter. Dante easily caught me and surpassed me, winning the race. I admired him as he left me in the dust. There was something unbelievably appealing about a man who knew how to handle a horse. I called out "Whoa," and Butterscotch instantly and obediently slowed down, coming to a complete stop. I led her over to where Dante waited for us.

"About time you got here," he said.

"I don't think that was very chivalrous of you." I actually liked that he didn't let me win. That he made me fight hard to get what I wanted. Because if I ever beat him at something, I would know that I had earned the win.

He took me seriously. Very few people did that.

"You wound me to the quick, my lady! I am always the master of chivalry. I actually wanted to be a knight-errant when I was younger."

He led Prince over to the creek to let him drink. I urged Butterscotch to do the same. It was so beautiful where we were. Flowing water, wild, high grass, and bright green trees surrounding us.

"Poor you. Born a prince instead of a knight. It must have been a terrible burden to bear."

Dante laughed, patting Prince on the side of his neck. "I got in big trouble when I was eight and I stole a set of armor from the great hall. And then it didn't even fit and I could barely move or see. But my mother read us fairy tales from countries all around the world, and I loved the idea of finishing quests and tasks like the knights-errant."

He had that intense look in his eyes again. "A true knight-errant must always finish a series of tasks to prove his chivalry and love."

I remembered the party the night before, when he'd accepted my "challenge" and said he wouldn't drink. "Was that what you meant when you said you accepted my task?"

"Something like that." I could hear the disappointment in his voice. A disappointment that I wanted to soothe and make better, but I couldn't. I shouldn't. I wouldn't.

At some point I really would figure out how to be in control of my feelings and my reactions to him.

"I can't believe you liked fairy tales."

"You didn't?"

"Not so much." Now I was the one who sounded disappointed. "They're totally unrealistic. I mean, except for that one time my best friend fell in love with an actual prince and is living a real Cinderella story. But other than that, no."

His face looked like he was struggling with something, and then he gave me one of those smiles that didn't quite reach his eyes. "Have you had a chance to speak with any of the other women so far?"

"I like Genesis. She seems sweet. Sincere. Normal."

"She does," he agreed thoughtfully.

Jealous, stabby pangs.

Voices came up over the ridge behind us, and the high-pitched, excited sounds that followed when the girls caught sight of Dante caused a small frenzy among the horses. It was all the handlers could do to calm the animals down.

I was annoyed that we'd been interrupted.

"You could probably talk to them easier if you weren't glowering at everyone."

"I am not glowering. I do not glower."

"You're not going to be much of an inside woman if you keep ignoring everybody. If I didn't know any better I'd say you were jealous."

He very smartly rode off before I had the chance to smack him with my reins.

Before the party started, I would see if I could call Kat. And Sterling. And I would remember why I was here and what I needed to accomplish.

I hoped that getting back in touch with reality would put me in the right headspace.

But I wouldn't have bet on it.

There would be a nightly cocktail party before each elimination, giving everyone another chance to talk to Dante and make an impression. It would also give everyone another opportunity to get embarrassingly drunk and make a fool of themselves on national television.

Win-win either way for the producers.

Just like I'd thought, several of the girls were complaining about saddle burn, and some medics were brought in to clean their wounds, leaving the women to walk around bowlegged.

It would have been really wrong for me to laugh, right?

But pain didn't stop anyone from getting ready for the party, which reminded me of my beauty pageant days. There was boob tape, Vaseline, flat irons, makeup, and enough fake eyelashes to outfit a millipede with a whole set of prosthetic legs.

I had just finished putting on a knee-length, dark blue cocktail dress with matching beads that made me shimmer, and applying my dark red lipstick, when Genesis came back into our room.

I gasped.

She had on neon green eye shadow, coral lipstick, and a hot pink shade of blush. Not to mention bronzer that made her face and neck different colors, and mascara tinged with purple that was layered onto false lashes so long and so thick I wasn't sure how she could see.

"Who did this to you, sugar?" I really, really hoped she hadn't done it herself. She looked like a cross between a televangelist's wife and an unskilled drag queen.

"Abigail." That actress. "She said she knew who I was and wanted to make amends. I'm such a fan that I was flattered, you know?"

I did know, and apparently so did Abigail.

"I don't really know anything about makeup, and she offered to help." Yeah, Abigail was going to help Genesis the same way that a snake helped a mouse.

By swallowing it whole.

I wondered if Abigail had unhinged her jaw before she made this mess.

"Do you like it?" She sounded so hopeful.

"Let me just lighten it up a little. You have to remember that Abigail is an actress and they tend to put it on a little heavy for the cameras." I took out a makeup remover cloth and scrubbed everything off. I started from scratch, putting a pale violet eye shadow on her lids to make her green eyes pop, and using a dark brown eyeliner to give her a soft cat eye. I removed most of the lashes, and put black mascara on those that stayed. After some light powder and a light pink lipstick, she looked gorgeous.

"Much better," I said. She went over to the mirror. "That does look better! Thank you!" She gave me a giant hug, and I tamped down any residual jealousy and reminded myself that we were friends.

And that I needed to keep a closer eye on Back-Stabigail so that I could make sure Genesis was safe. She was like a newborn fawn being released into a lion's den. I had thought that once I'd told Dante the truth about each girl I could leave. But now I'd have to stay as long as Genesis did so that I could protect her.

Darn my overdeveloped protective instincts.

We went downstairs together, and I looked for Abigail. I wanted to keep her far away from Genesis. I didn't see her. I stepped outside to check the pool area, but she wasn't there. I did find a dark-haired woman staring up at the full moon.

I should get started. "Hi, I'm Lemon."

"I'm Tiffany."

"Funny how something made out of a bunch of dusty rocks can be so pretty, don't you think?"

She turned to look at me. "Are you talking about the moon?"

"Yes?" I didn't mean for it to sound like a question. But what else would I be talking about?

"I'm pretty sure that's made out of cheese. Like in those cartoons."

She had to be kidding. "I'm pretty sure it's made out of rocks."

"I don't think that's right." No one could be that stupid, could they?

"Seriously?"

"Is what serious?"

"What you just said about the moon being made out of cheese."

She looked at me like *I* was stupid. "Yes."

The beautiful babies that Dante was sure to produce could not be infected by this gene pool. I refused to allow him to have idiot children.

Things didn't get much better from there. There was bubbly Michelle, who thought everything in life was So Awesome. And Ashley S., who said meanly, "You're talking to me why, exactly?" I wanted to retort that it was my job to figure out what kind of person she really was. She had spent all day smiling and being sickly sweet to Dante, and that one sentence told me everything I needed to know about her.

Then there was Ashley M., who giggled at everything everyone said. And Lisa, who spent two hours complaining about her ex-boyfriend and how their relationship had gone so wrong and she didn't know why. She never even took a breath so that I could excuse myself and leave. I started imagining forms of suicide that would be less painful than this conversation, and decided all of them would be, including dropping myself into the tiger enclosure in the zoo and being slowly eaten alive.

Jessica R. wasn't drinking. I thought I had found a kindred spirit, but then I saw that she wasn't getting drunker than a peach orchard boar only because "all the empty calories in alcohol." She told me that she wanted to start a modeling career and hoped the show would launch it.

When she asked, I told her that I wanted to get into PR, and she said the show could help me, as well. "You're not the first person to say that to me," I told her.

Abigail had already found herself two acolytes, women named Cece and Heather. They followed her everywhere, brought her drinks, and made sure not to "stand in her light."

Genesis came up and stood next to me. "Abigail tried to sabotage me, didn't she?"

"She did. Sorry."

"Don't be sorry. I can't believe she already has minions."

"I wonder if they get dental."

"Only henchmen get dental. Minions are out of luck."

"Yeah, they're basically glorified interns."

I *so* liked her. We were on the same wavelength. Dante would like her too, much as that thought made my stomach twist itself into knots.

She was tapping her fingers against her leg. "Nervous tic?" I asked.

"What?" She followed my gaze and looked down at her hand. "Oh, no. I think I'm going through withdrawal."

Maybe I had to reevaluate her as the front-runner. "Withdrawal?"

She must have heard the alarm in my voice. "Not that kind of withdrawal. I don't drink or do drugs or smoke or anything. That strict upbringing of mine has sort of stuck with me. I'm missing *WoW*."

"Wow?"

"*World of Warcraft*." I must have had a very confused expression, because she continued. "It's a massively multiplayer online role-playing game?"

Still nothing.

"It's a computer game." That I understood. "I miss it, like in an it's-my-crack kind of way."

Too bad she didn't know she was trying for the wrong twin. Rafe played video games the way other people drank water. He went to MIT and earned a software engineering degree and spent a lot of time in the MIT Game Lab in order to learn how to design video games. But I couldn't tell her about Rafe because I wasn't supposed to know Dante already.

More lying. I was becoming an evil person.

Taylor came over and asked to speak with me in private. When we were alone, she said, "Now would be a good time to make your phone calls. All of the other producers are focused on the party. Follow me."

She took me into the downstairs bathroom and handed me my phone. She sat on top of the closed toilet seat, texting.

I called Kat first, needing the support. It was very early morning in Monterra, as they were nine hours ahead of us, and there was every possibility that she would sleep through the phone ringing. Thankfully, she picked up on the first ring. "Hey! Do you have any idea what time it is?" She mumbled the words groggily.

"Hey, darlin'. I'm sorry for calling you so early. Dante sort of forced me to stay on the show." Kat knew that he had promised to send me home the first night.

"Oh frak." She sounded panicked and wide awake. "Did you murder him? Do you need me to be your alibi? Because I totally will be."

I so missed my friend. "I haven't killed him yet, but I make no promises."

"Totally understandable. What's up?"

I explained that everything she needed to know had been put into her calendar, and both her and Nico's event secretaries had a complete copy of their schedules as well. I told her about the no phone or device rule. I gave her Taylor's number and told her to use it if she had an emergency and absolutely had to get a hold of me.

"Don't worry—you know everything here is like a well-oiled machine. We'll be fine. You should just, you know, enjoy yourself. Maybe give Dante a chance."

Kat did not like Sterling. She knew all about our past and thought he was a slimeball. Nothing I said or did would change her mind. She really wanted me to marry Dante so that we would always be sisters and part of the same family.

But that wasn't going to happen. Dante wasn't serious about me, and I was very serious about not ending up with a guy who would break my heart.

I hung up with her and called my parents. It was about 11:00 p.m. in Atlanta. After I apologized profusely for calling so late, I told my mother that it would be more than one episode; that I had agreed to stay for a little while. My mother fretted about what to tell my grandmother, and then she asked if they'd get to meet him. "Only if I'm one of the last people left on the show, and I'll be off long before that."

"Well, that's a disappointment. Think of everyone's face at the country club if we walked in with a real-life prince!"

"This is all just pretend, Momma."

"I know that. But it would still be worth it just for the bragging rights alone."

I asked about the wedding preparations, and there was a pause. Her voice sounded fakely cheery and bright. She said it was well under control, and not to worry. Everything would be just the way I wanted it to be. My right temple started to throb. She pretended like everything was fine, but I could tell she was worried. Worried that I would let her and Daddy down again and embarrass them somehow. I sent my love and pressed the "End" button.

I was dreading the next phone call the most.

I had to call Sterling's cell twice before he answered. "Brown."

"Hi! It's me!"

"Me who?" I thought he was teasing, but realized after some dead air that he was not.

"Your fiancée? Lemon?" Who else would be calling him this late? It made me uneasy.

"Oh! Lemon! Sorry. I'm so swamped right now. Is this important?"

I gave him a brief summary of what had been going on, and braced myself.

"Well, you do whatever you think is best." He sounded so distracted. I knew he wasn't really listening.

"I just want you to know that if it looks like I'm flirting with Dante or anything, I'm only doing it because the producer is making me."

"Sure, sure, fine. I really need to go."

He hung up before I could tell him good-bye or that I loved him. He acted like he didn't care. Shouldn't it upset him? Shouldn't he be even a little bit jealous?

And why did it bother me so much that he wasn't?

Chapter 8

HRH Dante:

Where are you? I have put you on text probation.
I expect prompt and witty textual responses posthaste.

After giving Taylor my phone back, I was leaving the bathroom when someone opened the door to the story producers' room. Matthew Burdette was in there. I scurried back to the party before he realized that I wasn't where I was supposed to be.

Time to put on a show.

And I told myself that it had nothing to do with Sterling's lack of reaction.

Dante stood in the middle of the room, talking to four different women at once. He wore an expensive custom Armani suit and looked mouth-wateringly good. I walked up to him, put my hand in his and gave him my best come-hither look. "I need you," I said.

His hand tightened around mine as I led him out back. A cameraman had been filming a conversation between a girl who was crying and the one who was comforting her, but he came over when he saw us.

I stood too close to Dante. I ran my hand up his arm and bit my lower lip before looking up at him through lowered lashes. "I forgot how strong you are," I said to him in a low voice. I was trying to give the show what they wanted, but instead it was making me crazy. Being this close to him; him smelling so, so amazing; touching him without feeling like I shouldn't.

I was liable to be reckless because I was mad and disappointed.

It was not good.

"What's happening, *Limone*? I don't understand."

I got even closer to him and stood on tippy-toe in an attempt to whisper in his ear. His breath was hot on my neck and it made my stomach do gymnastics and my head feel light. He instinctively moved a hand to the small of my back and I wanted to sigh. "Burdette ordered me to flirt with you." I should have moved away, but I didn't. I stayed put, loving the way it felt when we were pressed together. Like I belonged there. Like it was right. I contemplated nibbling on his ear, remembering how much I'd liked it when he'd done it to me.

But before I could do something dumber than a bag of hammers, he stepped back, anger flashing in his eyes. "Don't. You should only do something like that if it's really the way you feel."

He went back inside, leaving me alone and extremely confused.

Dante flirted with me constantly. Did that mean *that* was how he actually felt?

Emily B., a girl I hadn't spoken to yet, got sent home amidst more tears and promises from the other contestants to stay in touch.

We turned in for the night, and Dante had barely looked at me. When he called my name, he couldn't have sounded more unenthusiastic. Had I really upset him outside?

Some of the other girls stayed up to party after he and Harris left. Genesis and I agreed to call it a night, only we didn't manage to do much sleeping. It was like being back in college with Kat our freshman year, staying up laughing and whispering and finding out everything about each other.

Well, almost everything. I had no intention of telling her about any possible residual feelings for Dante.

No one needed to know that.

We did make a promise that no matter what happened, we wouldn't ruin our friendship and we wouldn't talk about our time alone with Dante. I didn't want to hurt her if she ended up really liking him, and I worried that her stories might hurt me.

The next day was much like the first. We cooked and ate, put on our mike packs, hung out by the pool, found out about the date we'd go on that day or night. Sometimes we got pulled for formal interviews with the field producers. Other times we had ITMs, or "on the fly" interviews that happened right there, right then.

Some of the girls took to running laps around the pool as their exercise, since we didn't have a gym. I decided my exercise was having to walk up and down the stairs in the mansion every day to get from one floor to the other.

There was a heart-shaped card that came a little after two o'clock with Abigail and Heather's names on it. Dante invited them both out to dinner.

Abigail read the card loudly and slowly to the group out by the pool, and then came into the house where I was teaching Genesis how to make homemade pecan pie, and read it again.

She wanted a reaction, and we didn't give her one. Jen L. was already outside crying. Abigail wasn't going to find anybody to be upset in here.

"I'm glad Dante invited me out alone." Did she forget that he'd asked Heather too? "That's what America wants to see. I suppose I'd better go and start getting ready for my date."

"Yeah, I bet it takes a while to shed that skin." Genesis tried to muffle her laugh, but Abi-fail glared at us as she walked slowly up the stairs, swaying her rear end for the camera's benefit.

The camera guy's shoulders shook as he tried not to laugh at what I'd said. I wanted to offer him some pie, but we weren't allowed to talk to him.

And the person I should be giving pie to was Dante. I owed him an apology. I had sort of used him, and it wasn't cool.

Carefully carrying a slice upstairs, I looked around corners, making certain the way was clear. I tiptoed past the bedrooms, in case anyone was taking a nap as a way to kill time. At the far end was the flight of stairs that led up to Dante's room. His master suite took over the entire third floor. I was envious of all the space and that he had his own bathroom.

There was a rope barrier and a sign, but, not seeing any crew members or cameras, I decided to risk it. My heart beat quickly as I ducked under the rope. It was exciting sneaking around. More real-life *Harriet the Spy*.

I gently knocked on the door to the master suite. Too bad we didn't have a code. Dante opened the door, gorgeous as ever, and I handed him the piece of pie.

"Sorry I was being insane last night. Burdette is making my life miserable."

"Thank you, and I understand." A big, heartfelt smile, and I knew all was forgiven. Another thing I liked about Dante. He never held grudges. Me, I could hold a grudge like nobody's business.

He took the pie and stood to one side, offering to let me into his room. I didn't think that was a great idea. Particularly given how very tempted I was to accept.

And what had happened the last time we were alone in his bedroom.

"I just wanted to tell you to have fun tonight, and to please be careful."

He knit his eyebrows together. "Careful?"

"Yes, Timmy. Stay away from the well."

Now he looked even more confused.

"That's a *Lassie* reference. You can look it up later. Abigail is not to be trusted."

"I'll keep that in mind."

"Okay, well, I'm going to go do, uh, a whole lot of nothing. So, see you later."

"Thank you for the pie."

He closed the door and I was glad that I'd finally had the chance to do my job. Now he knew Genesis = good, Abigail = bad.

What he chose to do with that information was entirely up to him.

Most of the girls had gathered in our room, where we were having a grownup slumber party. Painting each other's nails, braiding hair, that sort of thing. I had suggested it as another chance for me to check out the girls and their personalities. Which so far seemed mostly nonexistent. Most of them were the type of women who'd always been pretty, and so they didn't ever need to try very hard at school or, you know, at life.

"I think he has money. Do you think he has money?" Emily F. asked.

"He wears expensive suits. Maybe he does, or maybe the show is trying to trick us into thinking he's rich and then we'll find out at the end that he's really poor so they'll see if we loved him or his money," Jessica T. offered.

I pressed my lips together. I would *not* smile. I also would not tell them that he was the kind of rich that would buy a new yacht because the old one got wet.

"Who cares if he's rich when he looks like that?" Ashley M. giggled, and to be honest, I could not disagree.

"I don't think money matters. I think you should be with someone because you really like them," Genesis said, and about half the girls side-eyed her like she'd just announced that spray tans would cause cancer.

A peaceful ceasefire and weird camaraderie existed, but the strangeness was compounded by the fact that all of these women wanted the same man. They'd all be dating him and possibly kissing him and maybe more, but I didn't want to think about that part.

My evil witch senses started tingling, and sure enough, Abigail came floating into the room looking entirely too smug.

I wondered how she could breathe in a dress that tight.

"In case any of you were wondering, he is amazing. In every physical sense of the word." She slowly and carefully enunciated each word in her last sentence.

She pivoted on her heels, leaving a cloud of floral-scented perfume behind. How did she know what to say that would piss me off the most?

Everyone sat silently, probably wondering, like me, if what she'd said was true. Had she and Dante actually . . . he wouldn't, would he? That was foul.

I would seriously lose all respect for him if he had. He would be tainted. Because that girl was so stuck-up, she'd drown in a rainstorm. I decided to ignore the waves of jealousy that threatened to choke me. Even though they were also making me want to choke her.

There were cameras pointed at me. I refused to dignify her vileness with a reaction. I wished I could telepathically communicate with the other girls to tell them not to react either, but most of them already looked so disappointed.

An assistant brought in another heart-shaped card. This one had my name on it.

And only my name.

I opened the card, and saw that the "audience" had selected me to go on a "Fairy Tale Come True" date with Dante.

Just me. And Dante.

Oh, *sugar sticks.*

It was one thing to be "on" for a few minutes at a time. It would be another thing entirely to act that way for a whole evening.

"What does it say?" someone asked, but I couldn't deal with the other contestants right then.

I jumped up and ran down to the production room, looking for Taylor. She was there. I wondered when she ever slept.

All the producers and their assistants looked at me funny. "Can I talk to you for a second?"

She followed me out of the room, closing the door. We went back into the bathroom again. It seemed like a strange meeting place, but whatever.

"I know I told Burdette I would do what I could, and I want to help you out, but what is this?"

"They've screened the first couple of episodes for focus groups, and you were overwhelmingly picked as the favorite."

"Me? Why?" I wasn't even really in the running. I was not supposed to be the one the focus groups liked.

"They liked that you wore your jersey the first night. Said it made you seem relatable and down-to-earth. And there were a lot of words thrown around about you and Dante. Like, chemistry. Heat. Obvious attraction."

I could think of some words to throw around too. Like, engaged. Off the market. Never going to happen.

But my opinion apparently didn't matter. I would do what I'd been doing—stay quiet, do as I was told, and make Matthew Burdette happy.

And all I could do was hope to keep my real life as intact as possible.

The show provided a dress for me, a strapless pale blue ball gown that made me feel like I was going to somebody's prom. It cinched in at the waist, and it had an overlay of delicate silver flowers. I had matching silver heels. I had also spent more time on my makeup and hair than I would care to admit.

I was going to be on television. I had to look good.

And as long as I kept believing that was the reason, everything would be okay.

Genesis watched me get ready. "I don't need a purse, I have the dress, the shoes—what am I forgetting?"

"The mice? The pumpkin? Fairy godmother?"

"Ha-ha," I said as I touched up my lipstick.

"Looks like you're all ready for your hot date."

I was planning on more lukewarm than hot. But I smiled at Genesis and told her I'd see her later.

When I left my room, an assistant was standing by with a cameraman and some other people, and I wasn't really sure what they did. Someone asked, "Is it a go?" into their headset, and then nodded at me.

The production assistant told me I could go down the stairs. I wondered if I should walk down slowly or normally. I settled for somewhere in between.

Dante stood at the bottom, in another tuxedo, holding a bouquet of lemon lilies for me. I didn't know if he was deliberately using the flowers to make a pointed reference to what had happened between us on my graduation day, but I decided to give him the benefit of the doubt.

"Flowers, huh?"

"I know, clichéd. But they were easier to carry than what I wanted to bring you." He handed the flowers to me and I took a deep breath, inhaling their scent. Like a cross between lemons and orange blossoms.

"What did you want to bring me?"

"A Tuscan villa."

I laughed, and one of the PAs took the lilies to put them in water. I twirled around once and asked, "So, what do you think?"

His light brown eyes appraised me, and I could tell he liked what he saw. "You expect me to be able to think when you're wearing that?"

Suddenly I regretted asking him. It was what happened when you were an only child. I was so used to constant attention and affection from my parents that I often sought it out in others. Which wasn't the best idea given my current situation.

"You look . . ."

I stopped him. "Don't."

"Don't what?'

"I don't think you should say whatever it is you're going to say. I think it's better for both of us if you don't."

"I was going to say you look awful."

"Awful?" He had me back to laughter again.

"Just terrible. I'm not sure I can be seen with you in public." He offered me his arm, and I put my hand on the crook of his elbow. It was supposed to be a polite, chivalrous gesture. Instead it made all my nerve endings tingle as my pulse did a two-step.

"You look awful, too."

"Thank you."

We had a short limo ride where he refused to tell me where we were going. You would think it would have been weird with all the cameras and people watching us, but honestly, after a while I started to forget they were even there.

The limo pulled up in front of an adorable restaurant that overlooked the ocean. Dante helped me out of the car and then escorted me inside.

Where there was only one table for two, set up with candles and more lemon lilies. Very beautiful. Very romantic. Very intimate.

Very terrifying.

I'm engaged, I'm engaged, I'm engaged.

He helped me to sit, and after I had scooted in, he handed me a menu that had been left on the table for us. "Do you like sushi?"

"Where I'm from we call that bait."

He laughed as he picked up his own menu, and we fell into a comfortable silence. I figured this probably made for boring television. Two people choosing what they wanted to eat.

Especially because there was no way we would actually eat.

A waiter came out, and I ordered lobster risotto and the salmon entrée. Dante said that it sounded delicious and that he'd have the same. When the waiter left, we were alone.

With six people watching us.

He reached over and put his hand on top of mine. "There's something I've been meaning to ask you."

A million different things ran through my mind. What had he been meaning to ask me? Would it be inappropriate? Would I be embarrassed and unable to ever hold my head up in public again after the shame?

Would I be tempted to say yes?

"How did you get your name?"

That was *so* not where I thought that was going. I pulled my hand away and put both of them in my lap. I couldn't be trusted while he was holding my hand and giving me all the feels. "My great-grandparents met at a barn raising, and started dating or courting or whatever they called it back then. They shared their first kiss under a lemon tree on the family ranch. They named their first daughter Lemon, and my parents named me after her. My grandparents and parents all shared their first kisses under that tree."

"It's still there?"

"It is."

He looked thoughtful. "You'll have to show it to me sometime."

The skin on the back of my neck felt hot. I prayed that my cheeks weren't blushing, too. Because the idea of showing him the lemon tree made me think things that I shouldn't be thinking.

I hoped he couldn't tell.

Chapter 9

HRH Dante:

Quick, lemon tarts or lemon meringue?
I need something sweet to tide me over until I see you again.

"Favorite color?" he asked.

"Red. You know that."

"I certainly do." He winked at me, and I was glad he didn't elaborate. America did not need to know about the time I'd given him a pair of my red underwear.

"What about you? What's your favorite color?"

"It used to be green, but I'm more partial to red now."

I turned my head slightly away from the camera because I was sure by now that I was definitely blushing.

He saved me from further embarrassment by asking another question. "Favorite way to spend your free time?"

"Watching old movies. You?"

He leaned back in his chair with one of his playful smiles. "Being with you."

"Be serious."

"You always think I'm not being serious. I am serious. I love being with you, and you are you, so it works out well for us to spend time together."

For the nine billionth time, I reminded myself that he was just a flirt and a flatterer and it meant nothing.

My heart, unfortunately, was not on the bandwagon.

"Your turn to ask me a question."

I shouldn't have said it, and it was probably a clear indication of where my mind was. "Who was your first kiss?"

"Frederica Antonelli." He pronounced it in that Italian way, rolling his Rs. "I was at boarding school and I was twelve. She kissed me, I'd like to state for the record. I was a helpless victim."

"Oh please, I bet you were a charming heartbreaker even back then."

"I don't break hearts. I am very fond of hearts."

Okay, now that definitely wasn't true. It still made me smile, though.

He didn't ask me about my first kiss. Probably because I'd already told him, and he didn't seem keen on bringing the ghost of Sterling into this conversation.

Our waiter reemerged with a man who introduced himself as the restaurant's sommelier, who said he wanted to recommend a wine based on our menu choices. Dante held up his hand. "We won't be drinking tonight, thank you."

From the expression on the poor sommelier's face, it was like Dante had said, "We just murdered your entire family, thank you." The waiter put his arm around the sommelier when they left. Like he was trying to cheer him up.

A few minutes and a few questions later, our food arrived. It smelled divine. "Should we?" Dante asked.

"We can't. Nobody ever does."

"What do you mean?"

"You constantly see dates on this show that involve food, but no one ever eats it." I glanced over at the crew. "It looks like the couple are so busy talking that they just don't have the time to eat, but I suspect it's more that people don't want to be caught on TV with a mouthful of food, or to end up with spinach stuck between their teeth. I know I don't want to be filmed eating."

He sat for a minute, looking at me. "That's ridiculous. Life is to be enjoyed, and food is an essential part of that. It should be savored and eaten. Not just looked at. Quest two, begun."

"Quest two?"

"Where you get to eat this delicious food before it gets cold without having it being filmed. Just follow my lead."

He started mouthing words and paused. I caught on to what he was doing, so I mimicked him and it looked like we were having a conversation with no sound.

"Cut! Cut!" the director called frantically behind us. "Somebody go out to the van and get a fresh pair of mike packs! The batteries on those have died!"

"Eat fast," Dante whispered before he shoveled a huge portion of salmon into his mouth.

"Doesn't eating fast negate that whole 'food should be savored' thing?"

"Shh. Hurry."

So I started eating as quickly as I could, but I kept laughing and practically choking. He even reached over to help finish off what I couldn't.

By the time the crew returned their attention to us, dinner was gone and we were both laughing with food in our mouths.

"What happened to the food?" the director asked.

Dante cleared his mouth first. "It was delicious. Thank you. Oh, look at that. It would appear my mike pack is working fine."

I swallowed the last bit. "Mine seems to be working now, too."

The director sighed and said to clear away the plates and to have the kitchen send out more. "Why?" I asked.

"The audience will want to know what happened to the food."

"Tell them we ate it and it was fantastic," Dante offered.

"It doesn't work that way. They have to see you eat it."

"Maybe they won't notice."

"Oh, they'll notice. They'll make memes and YouTube videos in slow motion where they circle the table. Don't talk until the food comes back. We don't want to miss anything."

"Have I proven myself, my lady?" Dante whispered. He had that dangerous twinkle in his eye. The one that made me forget myself.

"Most definitely." He reached over to hold my hand again, and this time I let him.

The newly delivered food sat while we talked more. It was always so easy with Dante. I could carry a conversation easily by myself (Kat was never much for talking), but I never had to with him. Even the silences didn't seem awkward.

"Should we ask to see the dessert menu?"

"Really? Sterling never lets . . ." I stopped. I shouldn't compare. It wasn't fair.

Dante's eyes narrowed. "Any man who denies you dessert should be horsewhipped."

I felt like I should defend the mutual decision to stay away from sugar and all related carbs. "I don't want to get fat." He still looked skeptical. "Please. You wouldn't want me to get fat, either."

"Then there'd just be more of you to love," he said conspiratorially, that devilish gleam in his eye making me very glad I was already sitting down.

"Said no man ever," I retorted, trying to ignore the sound of blood rushing in my ears. "You know, in fairy tales, every time somebody's trying to fatten you up it's because they want to cook you and eat you."

"I bet you taste delicious."

Serious heart palpitations. "I'm probably all gamey. Or maybe, true to my name, I really am sour."

"Sweet and tart. I already told you what you taste like, as I recall."

I recalled. I recalled very, very well.

"The limo is here," one of the PAs came over to tell us. Dante stood up and went over to help me out of my chair. He offered me his arm again, and I was very grateful that I had sworn off drinking for the time being. Because impaired judgment would make everything worse.

Even without it, was I was fixing to do something stupid before my brain caught up.

He told me that we were going to a charity ball. He didn't know who was running it or what it was for, but the show wanted footage of us dancing surrounded by other people in formal gear.

"Haven't we already done the ball thing to death back in Monterra?" He was sitting closer to me in the car than he probably should have been. I should have moved. I shouldn't have been playing with fire. I liked him being close. I liked the warmth that he radiated. I liked the way it made me feel.

"I know. This is out of my hands. I would have taken you somewhere else, if it were up to me."

"Like where?"

The passing streetlights occasionally lit up his striking profile, and I quickly turned away when he looked at me to say, "You'll see."

I both liked and didn't like that.

The event was like every other charity ball my parents had ever dragged me to. Too-rich people spending too much money on mediocre dinners, and then drinking and dancing the rest of the night away.

"I have to tell you, it's nice to be here and not have anybody know who I am."

It was one of those things where you wanted to say, "Poor little rich boy," but I really did feel bad for him. It couldn't have been easy to always be noticed and always be photographed everywhere he went in Europe.

And once this show premiered, it would start happening in America, too. My heart went out to him. I wanted to be there for him. To protect him. To make his life easier. To make him happy.

The realization shocked my system like a lightning bolt hitting a rod. The physical attraction was one thing, but this was emotional. Obviously, I cared about him. He was my friend. But this was something more.

It made me feel like I was about to have a panic attack.

"Let's dance."

"I don't know if that's a good idea."

"Why not?"

I didn't respond. I couldn't. I had just had a major life epiphany, and he wanted to dance and hold me close, his strong arms wrapped around me, my hand in his, and it would be more than I could take.

"Sometimes I think you're afraid to touch me, *Limone*."

"Afraid?" My voice hitched when I said it. I hoped he didn't notice.

The self-satisfied smirk on his face let me know he had.

"Yes, afraid. Like you think you'll lose all control if we touch."

That irked me. I wasn't some kind of deranged wild woman who would ravish him on the dance floor.

At least, I thought I wasn't.

"I promise to be a gentleman as long as you promise to be a lady," he said. I hated him teasing me, but I hated knowing he was right even more. Because when he touched me, held me, it was like dropping a blazing torch on a field of dry grass.

We moved into position, and Dante stepped back as I stepped forward. I knew all the waltz steps perfectly, having had them drilled into my head at a very young age, but he was unlike any other partner I'd ever been with. No other man had danced with me and made my heart want to beat out of my chest, or made my stomach flip and flop, or made my whole body tighten up with anticipation.

I was in serious trouble.

"*Limone*, I want to ask you for a favor."

The last time Dante had said those exact same words to me had been the second time he kissed me. We were in Monterra, and he was getting ready to play a game of snow polo (horses running on a frozen lake—I was shocked by it too) and he sent me a text and asked me to meet him in his room.

I had spent the entire morning in meetings with various press secretaries as I went over my plans to expand the brand and online presence of the royal family.

Given what had happened the previous night, I was glad for the distraction.

I had knocked on his bedroom door and he called out, "Come in!"

"Are you decent?"

"Depends on who you ask."

I rolled my eyes, even though he couldn't see me. "I meant are you dressed yet?"

"Come in and find out." Which caused a fluttery feeling in my stomach I didn't want to acknowledge.

He was in his snow polo uniform, which was a long-sleeved red polo shirt, knee-high black boots, and tight white pants that showed off a drool-worthy amount of his muscled legs. He was in the middle of making his bed.

"Want to lend me a hand?"

It was probably not a good plan to go over to his bed. "I'd love to help out, but I can't. I once killed a man in a bed-making accident."

"Sounds serious."

"I don't really like to clean."

He turned to look at me as he organized his pillows. "I heard you were a bit of a slob."

"Who told you that?" He smiled in response, and I wanted to guess he'd heard it from Kat, but seriously, anyone who had ever stepped foot in my room would have been able to tell him. It made me uncomfortable that he was talking with other people about me.

He pulled his comforter into place. It wasn't very neat looking, but I had to give him props for making the bed himself and not relying on the palace staff to do it. He sat down on his bed and faced me. I found an armchair across the room and settled into it.

"So . . . things with Salvatore are . . ."

I should have known he'd bring it up. I just wanted to forget. "Over." I don't know why he asked. He had been with me when I caught Salvatore having sex with a woman behind the nightclub. When, yet again, I had chosen a man who cheated on me the first chance he got.

"He didn't deserve you."

"Probably not. But you can't really help who you're attracted to, can you?"

"No, you can't help that." I knew he was talking about me, and I suddenly found my shoes fascinating. "I just wanted to see how you were doing." He looked so concerned.

"I'm fine. Keeping busy. Is that the only reason you asked me to meet you?" I wanted to sound calm, even if my insides were all churned up.

"No. I wanted to ask you for a favor."

"Sure. What?"

He smiled. "No, a favor. When knights used to joust, ladies would give them their favor. Some kind of token, like a ribbon or scarf, that was usually the colors of the lady's house. Knights would put it on their lance; I want to put your favor on my mallet."

That was a weird thing to ask for. "My house doesn't have colors."

"Maybe your favorite color then?"

"Okay. Give me a second." I went back to my room. I never wore ribbons, because I wasn't six, and I had never been all that into scarves. But I needed something small that could fit around a handle.

I literally had nothing that would work. My shirt was too big. I didn't have red socks. My lipstick wouldn't work. The only thing I had was . . . I picked up a pair of red lace underwear from my drawer.

I wasn't naïve enough to believe that if I took these back with me nothing would happen. I knew if I handed these over to Dante, that he would definitely think it meant something.

And I couldn't say it didn't. I was feeling depressed and bad about myself and the world in general. Not because I'd had any feelings for Salvatore, but because of what he represented. Another cheating man. Who wanted someone other than me.

I wanted to feel wanted. Dante wanted me. We had already kissed once, and I knew he would kiss me again.

He was very tempting. Like in an Eve-introducing-Adam-to-apples kind of way. Gorgeous, masculine, charming, smart—all the things I loved in a man. It would be fun.

Maybe it was wrong to use him that way. It was another bad habit of mine—some loser would cheat on me, and I'd find some random guy to take my mind off of it for a few hours. After which I would feel sick and gross for treating myself so badly, and always promised that I would change. That next time I would do better.

But this time I wouldn't let things go very far. I would keep it casual and under control. A few kisses never hurt anybody, right?

I decided to ignore the fact that it made no sense that I had dated Salvatore to stay away from Dante and now I would use Dante to feel better about myself. I never claimed to be totally logical. Or sensible. As I was about to prove.

I came back into his room and shut the door behind me. He looked up at me expectantly, and I walked over to where he sat on the bed, pulling the underwear out of my pocket and handing them to him.

He quickly realized what I had done, and said, "I don't think I understand."

"Don't you?" I stepped closer to him so that my legs were positioned in between his, and I rested my hands on his shoulders. I liked the way my heart went into a free fall whenever I was this close to him. How my whole body seemed to hum with anticipation.

He put both of his hands on my waist, and I let out a little gasp. My pulse slowed and thudded loudly.

Being near him was like that moment before you stepped out on stage, waiting in the wings for your cue, nervous and excited and giddy, adrenaline pumping through your veins, your nerves crackling with excitement. Kissing him before had been like doing the best routine of your life in front of a packed theater, with everyone standing and applauding you.

I wanted to feel that again. Putting my no-kissing-guys-first rule aside, I started to lean in and he stayed put, waiting for me to come to him. "There's no one here to get jealous over this kiss," he said in a low voice.

"I don't need an audience," I whispered back.

I moved in slowly, inching my way closer to him, letting the anticipation grow.

Chapter 10

HRH Dante:

Have I ever mentioned that red is definitely my favorite color now?

But just before I kissed him, he said, "*Limone*, wait."

Wait? What? I straightened back up.

"I understand that you have issues with men."

"Right now I do!" What was his deal? I mean, other girls kissed toads to find a prince. I kissed a prince and he started acting like a toad.

"I don't want you to feel like you're making a mistake."

That did it. I let go of him and felt sadness well up inside me over my constant poor decision-making. I plopped myself down on the bed next to him. "You're right. I always get into these meaningless hookups with guys who say everything I want to hear but then never call me again. They think love is a four-letter word, and I'm dumb enough to pretend that getting physical means they'll magically change. I'm getting too old for it. I like myself too much."

"I like yourself too much, too."

I let out a laugh that was edged with unshed tears. "There's something to be said for respecting yourself and waiting until you think it's right. Kat's never had to feel this way, and I envy her that. Passion just gets you into trouble. I think I'd rather have a man who treats me well than a passionate physical relationship."

He cupped my cheek with his hand and turned me toward him. "There's no reason you can't have both."

Yeah, right. I wanted to laugh or maybe cry again. That hadn't been my experience, ever. "You were right, though. I don't want to use you just to make myself feel better."

"I have no problem whatsoever with being used in any fashion you see fit."

If he didn't stop, I was going to start sobbing when this laughter became a hundred percent tears. I couldn't keep it at bay for much longer.

His hand moved to the back of my head, and his gaze was focused on my mouth. "Now that we have decided that I won't feel used and you shouldn't feel bad, it seems to me that when a man and a woman are alone together, in his room, on his bed, that there's only one logical outcome."

"It is possible for a man and a woman to be alone together and not kiss." My breathing had quickened, and I could hear his rapid, short breaths too.

"That may be true for some people, but we're attractive."

I closed my eyes, loving the funny and indescribable things his touch did to my insides.

"I've actually been wondering if that first kiss was a fluke. It registered on a magical scale."

That made me open my eyes, where his heated, intense gaze caught me and made me willing to do whatever he wanted. Like if he wanted to club me over the head to take me back to his cave, I would have let him. "Magical?"

"If I'd been a frog . . ."

"You would have turned into a prince?"

Then his mouth was finally, finally on mine. Gently claiming, promising. I had that tantalizing, floaty sensation mixed up with my adrenaline and endorphin cocktail. If I could have bottled that feeling, I would have been a millionaire.

He was tentative and soft, and usually a kiss like that just seemed sweet and nice, but there was nothing sweet or nice about his kisses. They were hot and—what word had he used?—magical. Definitely magical. He gave me every opportunity to pull away.

Instead I wrapped my arms around him and deepened the kiss. Which he had no problems with as he responded in kind.

There was a mindless need, and I felt and knew nothing but his kiss and his touch. His kisses grew deeper and firmer, and then needier. My heart beat faster than a hot knife cutting through butter, every sensation heightened, every touch explosive. It seemed like we had been kissing for hours, but it wasn't enough. It would never be enough. He finally let me breathe, and I was glad my lungs remembered how to work, even if all I could manage was short, shallow breaths.

He lowered me back onto his bed, and I went willingly, loving the feeling of his weight against me. He moved his lips along the column of my throat, giving me chills at every spot where he stopped to plant a kiss, stroking the other side of my neck with his hand. I felt his hand move from my neck to the top button of my shirt.

And despite my decision earlier to keep things casual and under control, they were very serious and very out-of-control, and I wanted them that way.

I dragged him back up to my lips, not able to have him away from me for even a second longer.

"Why is everybody kissing all the time now?"

We broke apart and sat straight up to see his seven-year-old sister, Serafina, standing in the doorway. She had her hands on her hips and looked disgusted. I felt mortified. If she had walked in only a few minutes later, she would have found something very different and probably traumatizing.

"Serafina!" I said. My mind was not currently capable of any other words, but her presence was like a bucket of ice water being dropped on top of me. My mind cleared, and I realized how quickly things had escalated, and what exactly I had been doing.

And who I had been doing it with.

"Kat asked me and Chiara to find you, so that she could ride over with you to the match. I'm going with Mamma and Papa."

She walked back out of the room, leaving the door wide open.

Dante rested his forehead on my temple. "I'd say that qualified for a worst-timing-ever award." Then he captured the bottom of my earlobe with his mouth, and a series of fireworks exploded up and down my spine.

Somehow I managed to pull myself clear. It wasn't easy.

He went still. "What is it?"

"We can't do this. I can't kiss you and . . ." And not have it lead to more. I liked him too much as a person and a friend. Even if he said I could use him, he meant more to me than that.

I couldn't tell him that. He'd insist I was being ridiculous and that we were just having fun. That I shouldn't take things so seriously. I'd probably let him talk me into picking up where we'd left off.

But how would I ever change if I kept making the same stupid mistakes over and over again?

"I'm sorry." It was the only pathetic thing I could say before I left.

My eyes darted over to the crew who silently filmed us. "What kind of favor?" I somehow mustered up the courage to ask. I hoped he didn't take any detours down memory lane like I had.

He had to whisper in my ear so that the mikes didn't pick up our voices. I told the shivers running across my skin to stop. "Meet me at midnight out in the gazebo. I want to talk to you about what you've discovered about the other girls."

It had started off romantic and ended up some place practical. *Which is good*, I reminded myself. The crew finally let us go home, and Dante kissed me good-night on the cheek, and it felt like he had branded me. I had to consciously refrain from touching where he had kissed me. I thanked him and headed upstairs.

Half of the remaining girls waited in my room. "So? How did it go?" Genesis asked.

"It went fine. We had a nice time," I told them as I kicked off my shoes. I started to unzip my dress and realized that everyone had gone silent and was staring at me. "What?"

"Are you really not going to kiss and tell?" Jessica R. asked.

"There was no kissing and so no telling." Their expressions looked like a cross between disappointment and relief. "Look, Genesis and I already have an arrangement, and maybe we should make one as a group. If somebody does kiss him, nobody talks about it. It will just hurt everyone's feelings."

Several of the girls nodded. I said it like I was concerned about the group's feelings, which I was, but the honest truth was that I didn't want to hear about somebody else making out with Dante. I knew what he was capable of, and I didn't want to imagine him doing all of that with someone else. I decided not to consider the reasons why too closely.

I wished Abigail was in the room, but it probably wouldn't have made a difference. She couldn't wait to tell us about what she'd done with Dante. Which reminded me that I needed to ask him about it when I saw him later.

Yawning, I told everyone I needed to turn in. I took off my makeup, got into some yoga pants and a T-shirt, and climbed into my bed. Someone in one of the production rooms turned off the overhead lights, plunging the room into darkness. Just a couple of hours until I had to sneak out.

Normally I would have been worried about falling asleep, especially since today had felt emotionally exhausting. But I was so afraid that I would fall asleep that I was wired and ready to go. The party girls downstairs were doing their nightly falling-down-drunk routine, and I had already decided to head to the first-floor bathroom and climb out the window instead of trying to get past them.

But by midnight, most of them had fallen asleep on the couches and floor. One girl was even lying on the kitchen island. I didn't want to risk anything, so I followed my bathroom escape plan. It was a low window, making it easy to get out.

I had a blanket wrapped around me, although I didn't need it. It wasn't cold. It would have been back in Colorado.

Dante was in the gazebo, lying on a blanket and propped up by a bunch of pillows. He had something in his hand that looked like paper. He stood up when he saw me coming and smiled, making my heart thud uncontrollably.

I am engaged, I am engaged, I am engaged.

Right when I got to him, I accidentally stepped on the edge of my blanket, propelling myself forward. He caught me, thanks to his athletic reflexes. And nicely formed biceps. And . . .

"Are you clumsy because you're finally starting to fall for me?"

I straightened up, ignoring the jolt that made my pulse go haywire. As far as he knew, I had zero feelings for him. So presumptuous. A little bit right, but presumptuous. "As if. I am not clumsy—and how long have you been waiting to use that line?"

"A while now. You'd be surprised by how few opportunities I've had to use it." He always managed to make me laugh, even when he irritated me.

"I got these photos for us to go through," he said. He was holding a head shot of each remaining contestant. "It took some convincing, and based on the look I got, I don't want to know what the PA thought I needed them for."

He sat back down, and I took a spot across from him. Sitting next to him was just asking for trouble.

"First one. Jessica."

"Jessica R.," I corrected him. "She wants to be a model, and she's on the show because she thinks it'll make her famous. Even though it almost never, ever does. Every time somebody thinks they're the exception I want to be like, *Here's a lance, there's a windmill, have at it.*"

"Literary humor," he said. "I like it. So, not here for the 'right reasons.'"

"Definitely not."

The next picture was of the emotional Jen L. "Hair extensions. So fake."

"If that isn't the pot calling the kettle blonde."

I hit him with one of the pillows while he laughed, fending me off. "I may color my hair, but it is all mine. It is totally different."

"Oh, obviously," he agreed.

"Next picture." I ground the words out, ignoring his fading laugh. He held one up.

"Ashley S. She's meaner than a skilletful of rattlesnakes. She keeps trying to insult me, but I don't respond. I refuse to have a battle of wits with an unarmed woman. There's no sport in it."

He looked puzzled. "But she always seems so nice."

"I'm sure she does. She's not."

"And there's the other Ashley." I pulled her picture out of the group. "She giggles at all of your jokes, and we both know there has to be something wrong if someone laughs at *your* jokes."

"You laugh at my jokes!"

Yes, and there was something very wrong with me because I was getting married in a few weeks and I was here at midnight with another man in a gazebo thinking impure thoughts, and having more fun and feeling more alive than I had any right to.

"Tiffany." He held the picture up so I could see it.

"Let's just say science isn't her forte. Like Grandma Lemon would say, cute as a button, and nearly as smart as one."

"You're saying she's dumb?"

That seemed so mean. "*Dumb* is probably too harsh a word. Suggestible, maybe? Logically flexible, perhaps?"

"Science isn't my forte either. Our final year in boarding school Rafe took my final science exam for me." I swear, half my holiday in Monterra had been filled with stories about all the times Rafe and Dante had switched places and the mischief they'd caused.

"Where were you?"

That devilish gleam was back. "Indisposed."

Translation? With a girl. Of course. "It isn't just that she isn't great at science. If her brains were dynamite, she still wouldn't be able to blow her nose. She literally thinks the moon is made of cheese."

His eyes got big. "Pass."

I thought so.

I took the stack of pictures from him and showed him Michelle's head shot. "She's, um, bubbly."

"I don't want bubbly. I'd like a noncarbonated woman."

Abigail's picture was next. Even a two-dimensional rendering of her made me frown. "You should just send Darth Abigail home."

"The producers love her. I made an agreement with them to keep her around in exchange for getting to choose who stays and who goes. She creates drama with everyone, which keeps the audience at home watching. They keep telling me there are three people the audience will remember—the girl who wins, the girl they wanted to win, and the villain. It wouldn't be much of a show if we sent the villain home."

I wondered if I specifically asked him to send her home, if he would. I suspected he might. Just to make me happy. He was a really good friend, even if he couldn't be a great boyfriend.

"Speaking of the devil, did you kiss or do other stuff with her?"

He had that teasing smirk on his face. "Define 'stuff.'"

Of course he would have to make this hard. "You know what 'stuff' is."

"I do know what 'stuff' is. I am a fan of 'stuff.'"

"So, did you?"

He stayed silent for a moment, like he was trying to figure something out. "No," he finally said. "I didn't kiss her or do 'stuff' with her."

Ha! I knew she was lying. Dante might be a manwhore, but I had always hoped he had some standards. It was nice to find out I had been right. I grabbed the next head shot. "Cece is pretty in an obvious kind of way." I flipped the picture around to face him. "If you like that sort of thing."

He took the head shot from me to study her more closely. "That is annoying. I much prefer having to really search for something to find attractive about a woman."

"Be serious!" I laughed. We'd never get this done if we just kept cracking jokes. I thumbed through the next few pictures. "Did you specifically request shallow and dumb women?"

"They asked, but I told them I didn't care who they chose. Because you're the only woman I want to be with." He waggled his eyebrows at me, making me stifle a giggle.

"You mean today?" Now it was his turn to laugh.

Then his face went serious. "I am joking about wanting to be with you. Because I could never live with a hoarder like you."

"I am not a hoarder! I am sometimes disorganized in my personal life with a small side of slob."

"Small side? Where did you find your shoes this morning?"

I glared at him. "In my closet, thank you very much."

"And the other one?"

I had to hesitate, knowing the truth would give him way too much satisfaction. But if I lied, he'd know it.

"The backyard." He laughed so loud I worried he might wake up the entire house. I was going to shush him myself, but he had that look in his eyes when I leaned toward him, the one that made my knees go hollow, and so I refrained.

He took the remaining pictures back from me. "What about Lisa?"

I was glad he put us back on task. "She spent most of one evening telling me about her last relationship without a pause. She kept saying, 'I don't even know how to describe it,' and yet she spent two hours doing just that. So boring. Like, if I wanted a sleeping aid I'd pop an Ambien."

"She's out. I need someone that I can talk to the way that you and I talk." His intense, hot gaze was back. "Do you sit and talk with him like this?"

No need to clarify who "him" was. I wanted to say yes. I opened my mouth to say yes.

But I realized it would be a lie. I loved talking to Sterling, but it wasn't like this. I often watched what I said with Sterling. I let whatever stupid thing I was thinking fall out of my mouth when I was with Dante. I had a connection with him that I'd never had with anyone else.

Including my fiancé.

"I shouldn't be doing this," I said, pointing to the pictures, but also referencing what was happening in that moment. I was turning out to be a huge fan of avoidance. "Grandma Lemon always says not to treat other women disrespectfully because it gives men ideas. But when I'm with you, apparently I have no filter."

He put his hand on my knee, and I never knew knee-touching could give you goosebumps. "I like that you're honest with me. Right now I'm pretty sure you're the only person on this entire show who's telling me the truth."

Another one of those charged, connected, electric moments passed between us, and this time he was the one who broke it off by looking away. "I think that's almost everyone. You fulfilled your promise, so I should probably send you home tomorrow night."

Unexpectedly, that was the last thing I wanted. The thought of being sent away made my stomach tie itself up in knots. "You can't."

He looked shocked.

"Abigail is out to sabotage Genesis, and she's so sweet and innocent, I . . . I want to stay and protect her. So you should keep me for as long as you keep Abigail."

"Is that the only reason you want to stay?" His voice sounded low and seductive. His eyes glittered dangerously.

What was I doing? He had given me the out I wanted, and I'd told him no. What was wrong with me? And why did I have to keep lecturing myself? I could blame Abigail and Matthew Burdette all I wanted, but the reality was that I was the one taking things a step farther than I needed to. Burdette had only asked me to pretend, and I wasn't just pretending. I'd always had feelings for Dante, even if I didn't want to acknowledge them. I had always been attracted to him. I had been able to quash those things down, deep inside, where they weren't a problem. It had been even easier when he and his dangerous lips were not in close proximity. But being with him here, like this . . .

I didn't want it to end.

I told him good-night, failing to answer his question. I had to get my mind straight. I had to make the right choice.

I needed to talk to Sterling.

Chapter 11

HRH Dante:

Thou art to me a delicious torment.

Another day passed, filled with boring sunbathing and trying to make conversation with women who only wanted to talk about themselves, while Dante went on a morning date with Tiffany and Michelle. It was one of those dates where one girl would get a heart pin, and the other one would be sent away. Poor Dante. It would be like being stuck between a rock and a moron.

I managed to track Taylor down. It seemed like she had been avoiding me, but I didn't have time for that. "I need to ask you for a favor."

"You don't know me very well. I don't enjoy doing those."

I ignored her prickly and sarcastic response and figured something was not going well on the show. I knew it wasn't me she was upset with, so I didn't take it personally. "I need to call Sterling. Like right now."

She narrowed her eyes at me, and I hoped she would say yes. I needed to talk to him. I was dangerously close to chucking it all and believing Dante. I hated to admit it, but he had breached my defenses and was getting so close to making me really and truly fall for him.

"Come with me."

She led me into the first-floor bathroom again. "Why do we always come in here?"

"No cameras." She gave me her phone, and I hoped Sterling would answer. Sometimes he didn't pick up when he didn't know the number.

"Can I speak to him alone?"

"I'm sorry, you can't. We have a deal."

I nodded and hoped that this bathroom would be like a Catholic confessional, and that she would keep anything she heard to herself.

I dialed Sterling's number, and after a couple of rings it went to voice mail. I tried it again, and thankfully, this time he picked up.

"Sterling Brown."

"Hi! It's me. Lemon. I'm using a friend's phone to call you." It was a little bit sad that I felt the need to identify myself, but it was understandable given our last phone call. It would have been the straw that destroyed the camel's back if he'd failed to recognize me again.

"I'm walking out of my office right now for a deposition. What's going on?"

"Could you just stop for a second and listen to me? This is important." I thought of everything I wanted to say to him. *I'm having feelings for another man. I'm considering breaking off our engagement and canceling the wedding.*

I want something more.

"Lemon, this is a really terrible time. Can we talk later?"

"We can't. I need to talk to you now." My lower back felt sweaty and my heart was stress-beating. I sat down in the tub and pulled my legs up to my chest.

"What is it?" He sounded angry and put out.

This was not the time for him to act this way. I needed him to be understanding and kind and steady, all those things that I had fallen for. I needed him to remind me why I had said yes to marrying him.

Instead I was getting some angry, stressed workaholic. I admired ambition, but not at the expense of the things that really mattered. Like family. And fiancées.

"I . . . I have to tell you that . . ."

"What? Jiminy Christmas, woman!" (He didn't say Jiminy Christmas, but I substituted it because our pastor told us to not take the name of the Lord in vain, and it was at least one commandment I could keep.) "Spit it out and get to the point!"

All I could think was that Dante would never speak to me that way. He never had, and I couldn't imagine him ever doing it. Even when I made him angry, he was always a gentleman with me.

I couldn't find the words to tell Sterling the truth. About my doubts and fears. How far away he seemed, and how I needed him to help me reconnect. I needed a reason to be with him, and all he was giving me was reasons to go. "I'm staying on the show for a while. I just thought you should know."

"You wasted my time for that? Next time send me a text." He hung up on me. I don't know that I'd ever had a man hang up on me before.

For a few minutes I just sat there, shocked. I considered calling him back and letting him have it. Telling him it was over. I shouldn't do anything while I was this upset, though. I might regret it. I climbed out of the bathtub. I handed the phone back to Taylor and caught a glimpse of the pity in her eyes. I didn't cry. I was too angry to be worried about crying. I thought about calling Kat, but I knew she could be right in the middle of an interview. I'd have to try her later.

Because I had no one else to talk to about it.

You have Dante, said some evil, scheme-y voice inside of me. Dante did know about Sterling, but that was probably the worst thing I could do. It would create more of a bond, there would be more emotions, he'd convince me to dump Sterling, and then I'd have to face reality—that Dante had never wanted a relationship with me and was only chasing me because I hadn't given in.

We were friends with an attraction, but that was it. He'd never said that he wanted more than that. He'd been pretty clear that he wanted to mess around, but nothing beyond that. Which wasn't surprising, given his past.

I didn't need a crystal ball. Dante had proven who he was. And he would cheat on me.

Remember that part? I told the evil little voice. *Dante will cheat on me. He will.*

I said it so often that it probably should have been my meditation mantra. *Dante will cheat on me. Dante will cheat on me. Ohm.*

And when it happened, I would be devastated. Totally destroyed. I knew it would be the worst thing that had ever happened to me.

Because I could handle it from the other men. I knew how to cope and how to get over it.

Just like I knew that it would be different with him, and I couldn't bear it.

I turned a corner and nearly ran into him. He must have just come back from his date. I wondered which girl he had kept. I could use the distraction. I pasted a smile on. "Michelle or Tiffany?"

"I sent Tiffany home." He started to return my smile and immediately stopped. "What's wrong?"

How did he do that? I had been struggling to keep my emotions in check, to appear normal. I didn't want to answer a million questions from the other girls, and I most definitely did not want to tell Dante. It would just give him more ammunition. "It's, I was, um, talking to Sterling." The truth just came out of me.

"And how is your insignificant other?"

I gave him A Look.

"What? Did I say that wrong?"

"Significant other," I corrected him.

"Right. Sorry. English." He didn't sound even a little bit sorry.

"Things are . . . well, they're . . ." How could I tell him? It wouldn't be fair to either man.

He put both of his hands on my upper arms, in a very soothing and calming way. Too bad it didn't make me feel soothed or calmed. "I'm here to talk, if you need it. I only charge three hundred dollars an hour."

It was a sweet attempt at making me laugh, but it felt like my whole world was a gigantic mess and I didn't know how to fix it.

"It's probably not okay for me to talk with you about it," I admitted.

He still looked so concerned. "I understand if that's how you feel. But it doesn't change anything for me. I'm here. Anytime and anything you need. Always." He leaned forward to kiss me on my forehead. It was probably the same way he kissed his sisters, but I wasn't feeling very sisterly toward him. I closed my eyes and realized how much I missed this. I was tempted to wrap my arms around his waist for a hug. I only just stopped myself.

I shouldn't compare. I shouldn't. But here was Dante, the center of a television show, so many jobs dependent on him, a member of a royal family with responsibilities that most people couldn't even begin to imagine, and he had never made me feel like I was bothering him or like he didn't have time for me.

Maybe I wasn't being fair. But it wasn't fair how Sterling had talked to me, either.

"Is that offer part of your knight-errant quests?" I asked as he pulled away from me. He stayed put for a moment, looking at me, and then he began walking up the stairs.

"A knight, Indiana Jones, whichever hero you need."

I gasped. Now that, without a shadow of a doubt, had definitely been deliberate.

New Year's Eve. Monterra. The royal family had a costume ball to celebrate. I had gone as Scarlett O'Hara, and Kat had been Elsa from *Frozen*, which had been Serafina's idea. It had been our last night in their country, and we were scheduled to return to the United States the following morning.

I had pretty successfully dodged Dante's attempts to talk to me about what had happened in his room. I dragged Rafe along with us whenever we went somewhere and made sure that we were never alone. It all seemed particularly pointless to talk things out, considering that I'd never see him again.

Kat and I walked into the ballroom, and I saw Dante immediately. He had dressed up like Indiana Jones, including the scruff, and he was the hottest man I'd ever seen. I was so glad a fan was part of my costume, as I immediately tried to cool my flushed skin.

Rafe had dressed up as Dr. Who—the Eleventh Doctor, he made a point of telling me later that evening—and Nico had on a Mr. Darcy costume that made Kat more excited than I'd ever seen her.

"There's Dante," she pointed out, after Princess Caitlin, who was married to England's crown prince, had joined us in her geisha costume. As if I didn't know exactly where he was and exactly which girl he was flirting with at that very moment. "He looks great in his costume."

"It's all right, I guess." I was striving for nonchalant.

Kat saw through it and said, "Please. Like you wouldn't let him raid your lost ark."

I wanted to protest, but we started talking about Nico instead. Then Nico came to claim Kat, swirling her onto the dance floor.

At some point in the evening everyone seemed to have disappeared. Leaving me by myself.

I couldn't believe how sad I felt about going home. I had thought I would be fine, but I had come to care about the entire family, and I would miss them.

Much as I didn't want to admit it, I would miss Dante the most.

I started searching through the dancing couples to see if I could figure out where everyone had gone. I didn't see them.

At least the time spent in Monterra had been fruitful professionally. I had finished everything up, and there were no more meetings, nothing that I had to do. I just had to get on a plane back to Brighton University, where I would complete my very unique and sure-to-be-amazeballs thesis, and then graduate. No more distractions for me.

But I wished for those distractions when I accidentally found Salvatore. The noble *Duca di Brista* sat in a darkened corner with one girl in his lap, and another kissing him. Ugh. He was repulsive. I couldn't believe I ever let him touch me.

Salvatore, as a man, didn't matter to me. I'd never really cared about him. It was more of what he symbolized. He was every stupid guy who got my pulse racing and turned me dumb. Every jerk who didn't know how to be faithful. Every dog who pursued me relentlessly to get what he wanted and then moved on, leaving me brokenhearted.

It made me feel old and tired. I wanted so badly for things to be different. I didn't want to keep falling into the same trap over and over again. I was like Charlie Brown, running down the field toward that football, and even though Lucy had yanked it out of my way a million times before, I convinced myself that this time would be different. This time she would let me kick it.

I needed to stop running for the ball. She'd never hold it in place. I would always, always fall flat on my back.

I was going back to my room, packing my things, and vowing that it would all be different when I got back to Colorado. No more of this. No more letting men treat me like dirt. No more mistakes.

Dante stood on the other side of the massive ballroom doors. "Why are you crying?"

I reached up to feel a couple of tears on my face. I hadn't even realized that I was crying. "It's dumb, and it doesn't matter," I told him, wiping them away. I couldn't explain that I wasn't crying over Salvatore but about how my life was turning out. He took me by the hand and led me over to an alcove, where a stone bench was covered by a red seat cushion. We sat down.

"It matters to me." He took both of my hands in his. The concern in his eyes was enough to make me start crying again. Which made me inexplicably angry, and something shattered inside me.

I didn't want him to touch me, and I pulled my hands away. "You were right, okay? I should have listened to you when you told me about Salvatore. Do you know how humiliating it feels? To be constantly cheated on? What's wrong with me?"

He grabbed me and made me look at him. "There is *nothing* wrong with you. You're amazing."

I was taken aback by the force behind his words. "Then why do I keep letting this happen? Why do I keep choosing men who will hurt me?"

"Because you haven't found the right man."

I let out a laugh. "Much like *Babbo Natale* and *La Befana*, he doesn't exist."

"He does. You need someone like me. I would be your hero, if you'd let me. I would never, ever hurt you." I wanted so badly for him to be telling the truth. I wanted to believe him.

I just couldn't.

Without warning, he kissed me. I should have stopped him or told him no. But his kisses were to comfort me, to reassure me. His thumbs wiped the leftover tears from my cheeks, soft and delicate in a way that made me want to cry all over again. I felt an aching sweetness that made me want to surrender. A melting tenderness that turned my insides to jelly.

"You are so beautiful," he said before he kissed me again. "So smart, so wonderful, so beautiful." He kissed, nibbled, and teased me in between each phrase.

"You said beautiful twice," I murmured against his mouth.

He pulled back with a dazzling smile. "That's because you're extraordinarily beautiful."

Said the prince who dated the most beautiful women in the world. I mean, I knew I was pretty, but in comparison? "Uh-huh," I replied.

"You are." That definitive tone was back. He held me close. I loved when he touched me like this, the electrical current buzzing between us, making me forget everything else. He smoothed my hair, caressing my face. "You are. Inside and out. I wish I could show you. That you could see yourself the way I see you."

No one could have denied that Dante had game. That he always knew the right thing to say and when to say it. But before I could call him on it, he set out to prove his words true and the world exploded as he pressed his lips forcefully against mine.

If he had been gentle and reassuring before, that was all gone. Now there was only heat and need and desire. Wanting to taste and be tasted. It was like being caught up in the most intense lightning storm, as the flashes of electricity crashed inside me over and over again. My heart beat so hard in my chest, like it was struggling to get closer to him.

A mixture of hormones, all that pent-up passion and frustration, had been swirling around inside me, as if waiting just for this moment, and they burst to life, racing through my bloodstream, making my stomach feel hollowed out. I really did want to swoon.

The stubble from his unshaven beard moved across my jaw and my cheek, stinging as he went, but I loved the way it felt. He smelled so good that I took the chance to press kisses to his strong neck, breathing his cologne in deeply. Yummy. His skin tasted like faint salt and . . . Dante. I moved up to his earlobe, and it was like pouring kerosene on a fire.

He made a noise like a combination of a growl and a groan—right before his mouth ravaged mine, escalating the already intense kissing that had been going on. I started shaking, overwhelmed, clinging to him like a raft in a storm. He was the only solid thing in a world that had gone hazy. His lips enveloped my lips, like he owned them. And me.

My stupid hoop skirt kept getting in the way of me getting closer to him. It was all I wanted, to be as close to him as possible, in every way imaginable. He had possessed me with his hands and his mouth, and I wanted more.

We kissed and kissed as the blood roared through my ears, as I dissolved from his tantalizing promises, worried that I might never feel satisfied again, that it wasn't enough—it could never be enough.

Then he somehow managed to make the kiss deeper and more intense, and tremors rocked my entire body. I felt like I might suffocate from the lack of oxygen, but I didn't care.

When he kissed my throat, down to my collarbone, I finally said in a strained voice, "I can't remember how to breathe."

"You're not supposed to," he said before his mouth returned to mine.

All those girls in my sorority who had talked time and time again about the earth moving and time stopping had annoyed me. I had never understood what they were trying to explain, until that very moment. Because the earth most definitely moved, and time most definitely stopped.

There was only me and Dante.

He broke off the kiss, and I opened my eyes to see him staring at me, the desire in his eyes unmistakable. We were both breathing hard as we looked at each other. Why had he stopped? My body urged me forward, wanting me to keep kissing him. My lips literally tingled in anticipation.

"*Limone*, come upstairs with me."

Chapter 12

HRH Dante:

Had a dirty dream about you last night. You got stuck in the castle moat and were tracking mud everywhere. What? What did you think I meant?

There was no mistaking what he meant, or what he wanted. My heart beat even faster, and more intently.

It was what I wanted, too.

"Yes."

It was all he needed. He stood up and then pulled me to my feet. He kissed me again, his hands flat against my back, holding me close. I held on to his shoulders, excited and happy.

He stopped long enough to take me over to one of the elevators. He pushed the button a bunch of times. "Come on, come on," he muttered.

I giggled and couldn't help but kiss his shoulder. That made him hoist me up, holding me so that our faces were level. He kissed me again and I loved his strength and masculinity and I wanted to thank whoever had taught him to kiss like that.

Laughter came from somewhere behind us, and I turned to see a group of costumed men pointing and laughing.

At us.

I realized how ridiculous we must have looked, in our costumes, my hoop skirt flipped up in the back as he held me.

When I saw myself the way others could see me, my mouth filled with a sourness and disgust.

I had just finished making plans and promises to change, and here I was. Doing the exact same thing I always did.

Again.

"Stop."

Confusion on his face. "What is it?'

I pushed against him. "Put me down. Now."

Stepping away from him, I buried my face in my hands. I was a mess. I was always going to be a mess if I didn't stop the pattern. "I can't keep doing this. I can't keep making the same mistake over and over again."

I felt bad, I would find someone who would make me feel good, and then I would feel even worse when it was over. I would feel numb and hollow. Something had to change. Something had to give.

That something was me.

He looked shocked. I was sure he had no idea what was going on. I didn't know how to explain it to him, but I at least owed him that.

"I won't be pathetic and desperate," I told him. "I won't be the kind of girl that people laugh at for all the stupid things she keeps doing."

"This isn't like that."

"Isn't it? Isn't it exactly like that?" I gestured to where the men had been a moment before. My self-loathing was quickly turning to anger, and I started to take it out on him. "I mean, part of me thinks I should just sleep with you so you'll leave me alone. Because that's what this is about, right? The conquest? What was it you told me in your club? 'Men only want what they can't have.'"

The elevator doors dinged as they opened, and we both turned to look, but we didn't stop them from closing again.

He finally spoke. "*Limone*, you can't mean that."

"I do mean it! I don't want this. I want it to matter. I want to be in love with the next person I sleep with. I want to be with the man that I'll spend the rest of my life with. And you . . ." I let out a short bark of laughter. "You are most definitely not the kind of man I'll end up with."

His expression was as stunned as if I had just slapped him. "Why would you say that?"

"Look at you! Do you take anything in your life seriously? You've had the world handed to you on a platter, and are you grateful for it? I've seen the articles online. I know what you're like."

"What I'm like?" He finally got angry.

"You are such a womanizer! And you are never going to have a career."

"Being a prince *is* a career." His words were terse, like he was trying to keep his anger in check. I noticed he didn't deny the womanizer part.

"In fairy tales! You could get an actual job. You could be working for something instead of partying it up in your castle every night with a different girl."

My anger finally spent itself, and I felt sick at the look on his face. "I can't believe you're saying this," he said.

I couldn't believe it had taken me this long to say it to him. I should have said it the second I saw him for who he really was.

"I want to be with someone who will be my partner and my equal. Who wants to work hard for what they want in life. Who is faithful and loyal to one woman. Someone who doesn't think that monogamy is a tree."

It all felt very final. Finished.

"I'm sorry. I'm sorry this happened, I'm sorry I led you on. But I'm done. This is done."

Another long silence stretched between us. He put his hands in his pockets, looking down at the floor. "You're leaving tomorrow and . . ."

"And it's for the best. Good-bye, Dante." The pain on his face when he looked up at me was almost unbearable. It even managed to make me cry. I told myself that he was an excellent actor. He was a player. He knew just how to pull at my heartstrings.

But I wouldn't let him play me any longer.

I pushed the button, and the elevator doors opened. The tears fell fast and furious, and it blurred my vision. I got inside, watching him as the doors slid shut, closing off that chapter in my life.

I had no intention of ever seeing him again.

He, on the other hand, had other plans.

I found out later that when everyone had disappeared from the costume party, it was because they were staging an impromptu intervention for Princess Violetta, Dante's eighteen-year-old sister. Which made me feel even worse. He was dealing with something serious like his sister using drugs again, and I was having a hissy fit about my stupid choices.

Sometimes I didn't understand why he stayed my friend.

Kat had had her own drama on New Year's Eve with Nico, and so my focus had been totally on her and her problems. It was a good distraction. Kat had asked me once what had happened with Dante, and I'd told her that we had a close encounter of the catastrophic kind. I didn't elaborate on our gland-to-gland combat, and she didn't ask, too wrapped up in her own misery.

Now, here in California, I was the one who was miserable, with Dante making that crack about being my hero. It was to remind me, to let me know that he hadn't forgotten, and neither should I.

As if I could.

Overly emotional Jen L. was sent home that night, and the next day we had another group date.

Soccer. Or as Dante would mistakenly call it, football.

I hated playing sports. I was not a fan of glistening, which was what we called sweat back home. Once upon a time, I hadn't minded it, but ever since I gave up ballet, I'd avoided unnecessary exertion. I didn't like hiking or throwing things or catching them.

I put on a pair of tennis shoes, shorts, and a T-shirt. Half of the girls came out in sports bras and shorts that looked more like underwear. I didn't understand dressing so impractically. But I wasn't the one who'd be embarrassed when something sprang free.

Genesis's hair kept flying out of the rubber band she used to hold it back. I offered to French braid her hair to keep it down, and she agreed. In the middle of doing that, some of the others asked if I could French braid their hair too.

Dante arrived on the field that the show had set up in the backyard with goals and lines. The girls called out a greeting to him, and he waved as he walked over.

It was easier to control my physical reaction, because I was annoyed at him. Only a small heart murmuring this time.

"So the den mother now does hair."

Den mother? I was hot. I was not a den mother.

I wrapped the last elastic at the bottom of Jessica T.'s hair, and she left, giving Dante a lingering and flirtatious look. I would not roll my eyes.

"Part of the pageant thing. You learn how to do hair pretty quickly." I didn't have a brush, so the hairstyles didn't look as nice as I would have preferred, but they were going to be running around so it didn't matter.

"Always taking care of everyone else," he mused. "Who takes care of you?"

I shrugged.

"I would, if you'd let me." He ran out onto the field and started kicking the ball around with the women as they decided on teams.

What was I supposed to do with that? He sounded serious, but I knew he wasn't. Right then, he was flirting with tons of other girls. He managed to confuse me, give me false hope, and make me wish for things that just wouldn't be.

Even if his offer to take care of me had been legit, I needed to take care of myself. I needed to protect my heart from him.

It was time for the match to begin. The show had even sprung for a referee. I was put on the pink team versus Dante's purple team, and we wore bands on our arms to tell everyone apart. I couldn't believe we were playing soccer. It was like a soul-crushing wade through a river of misery. How did anyone think this was fun?

I was glistening more than I wanted, and sort of moved back and forth instead of trying to actively play. Genesis was on Dante's team, and she was killing it. She scored so many points that they called the game before it got much more embarrassing. Dante high-fived her, and she hugged him. He glanced over at me with a shame-filled expression, before disengaging from her.

That was weird. I thought he liked Genesis.

I found some shade and wished for water. I was too tired to get up and walk back to the house to get it. Some assistants were setting up a table, putting a tablecloth over it, and I hoped they were putting out food and water.

Genesis joined me. "Good game."

"You had a good game. I had a minor stroke."

She laughed. "I didn't know he was so good at soccer. Kind of impressive."

"Everybody in Europe is good at soccer. He's nothing special."

Ashley S. strolled past right then and stopped to glare at me. She put her hand on her hip and said, "Why are you still here if you dislike Dante so much? There are lots of us here who do like him, and we're getting sent home while he keeps you around. If you aren't here for the right reasons, why don't you just step aside?"

Right then I was tempted to do exactly what she had said. I would just leave. Then there would be no more temptation, no more Dante, and no more putting up with these women.

And I would go back home to . . . what exactly? Things were not great with Sterling, and I was peeved that he still hadn't tried to reach me to apologize. He should apologize, and he should suffer a little for it.

I didn't think he even missed me.

I was too tired to come up with a retort to Ashley. She could suck it.

After I didn't reply, she walked away.

"Do you think maybe she has a point? You don't seem like you like him all that much." I could tell how hard it was for Genesis to say that to me. I had the impression that she didn't like conflict, and it must have taken a lot for her to confront me.

"It's hard to explain, but I promise I will fill you in on all the details someday. And how could I leave you? Somebody has to stay here and be your bodyguard against Crabigail."

She gave me a weak smile, but I had the distinct feeling that this was not over. "I'm going to get a bottle of water. Want one?"

"Yes, please. I would love one," I said.

She brushed the grass off her shorts and went inside.

Dante was on his phone, off standing by himself. I thought I glimpsed Marco in the bushes behind him, but I couldn't be sure. He was like a stealth ninja. I wondered if Marco had been around when we were out at the gazebo. That was more than a little disconcerting, to imagine that we had been watched the whole time.

Although, how could I be upset about that? I was being watched around the clock thanks to those cameras.

Dante saw me looking at him, and he walked over to me, still on his phone. He was speaking in Italian, and finished up his conversation. He slid his phone into his shirt pocket.

"Totally unfair," I complained. "How come you get your phone?"

"I'm not allowed to call family or friends. This phone will only dial the numbers that have been programmed into it. I told the show that I needed it because I was near the end of a deal that might fall apart if I couldn't make phone calls."

"What kind of deal?"

I noticed that he didn't look at me. "I'm building a club."

"Like a 'no girls allowed' thing?"

He let out a short laugh. "No, a nightclub."

Wait, what? "A nightclub? When did this happen?"

Now he looked directly at me, all intensity and hotness, and I practically fell over. I blamed the dehydration.

"New Year's Eve. When you talked about the kind of man that I was, I realized you were right about one thing. I hadn't ever tried very hard at anything because I didn't have to. I knew I'd never have to get a job, and there are a lot of responsibilities that come from being part of a royal family, so I figured, what was the point of doing something else?"

I had been so terrible to him that night. It was more about me than it was about him. I started to apologize, but he kept talking as he searched through the grass and pulled up a clover. "No one had ever spoken to me that way before, and it changed everything for me. I looked at what I was good at, what I enjoyed. I love putting together mixes, but there aren't a lot of DJ princes."

"There's the Fresh Prince," I said, stunned by what he was saying.

He smiled. "I don't think he's an actual prince. Anyway, I decided to open a nightclub in Monterra. I'm using some of my trust fund and money from investors. We're hopeful that if it does well we can franchise it across Europe. I'm calling it 'Inferno.'"

"I see what you did there. Dante's Inferno. Literary humor. I like it." I echoed his words back at him, and all the annoyance and animosity I had been feeling had somehow just dissipated as he laughed.

When his laughter subsided, he reached over and squeezed my hand. He said, "*Limone*, you were the first person to ever really challenge me. You made me want to be a better man. Thank you for that."

What on earth was I supposed to say to that? My chest swelled up and I felt giddy and excited and amazed and touched and shocked and . . .

Won over.

It was one of the things that had always bothered me about him. I was from a rich family, but I wanted to work hard. I didn't have much respect for people who didn't care about doing their best and used their parents' money to coast through life.

Now he was building his own nightclub. A possible franchise.

Had he done it for me?

My heartbeat was up in my throat. I was so glad he couldn't read minds. I couldn't settle on one thought or one feeling. My brain jumped like a frog on crack, too bewildered to make sense of his announcement.

It didn't change everything.

But it did change some things.

"Any advice before I go 'once more unto the breach'?" He was the only man I knew who quoted dead playwrights.

"With the girls? Go talk to them. Act like you're really listening and interested in what they're saying. Women love that."

"And here I was wasting my time buying them jewels and flying them to Paris."

I couldn't help but laugh as he walked off and started a conversation with Emily F.

Genesis returned with our water and handed one to me. It was cold and perfect and I thanked her.

"That looked serious," she said.

I didn't really respond to what she'd observed. I didn't want to explain. That moment had been between Dante and me, and wasn't anyone else's business. Even hers.

"Sorry about earlier. I was feeling a little depressed."

"Know what helps with that?"

"If you say exercise, I will punch you."

"I was going to say chocolate and Valium, but exercise really does help."

Abigail chose that moment to slither past and stopped in front of us. "Do you mind if I join you?"

I did, on so many different levels and at a staggering intensity.

But before I could tell her to get lost, Dante announced that he had set up a sundae bar for everyone. The table was loaded with all kinds of ice cream flavors, with whipped cream, fudge, caramel, bananas, nuts, anything and everything you could think of to make ice cream taste even better.

Finally, something besides Dante that made my mouth water. Nothing sounded better than ice cream on a hot and glisten-y day like this one.

He might as well have put out bowls of cyanide and arsenic, though, given the women's reactions. He looked let down. I was sure he had thought this would be a sweet gesture and that the girls would enjoy it.

"Any woman with even a smidgen of self-respect would never put such poison in her body. It says she doesn't care about herself," Abigail announced loudly, projecting her voice so that everyone would hear.

I had a brief fantasy of force-feeding Abigail ice cream, one scoop at a time, before deciding to help myself. I grabbed a bowl and made a show of filling it up with chocolate marshmallow and cookies-and-cream flavored ice cream. I put some whipped cream on top and managed to spray some on my hand before I got it in my bowl. I licked the excess off of my fingers, and caught Dante's gaze.

The way he looked at me made my heart stop.

"Have I ever said how much I adore a woman who isn't constantly on a diet?"

It felt like he was talking just to me, but there was a mad rush to the table to pile up the ice cream and toppings.

Even poor Jessica R., who hadn't consumed actual food the entire time we'd been in the house together, took delicate bites from her bowl.

"Lemon! Look!" Genesis came running up behind me, waving something in the air. "I got a one-on-one date!"

I should have been happy for her, but the ice cream in my mouth turned sour.

Chapter 13

HRH Dante:

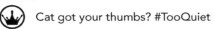

Cat got your thumbs? #TooQuiet

Probably the worst part of being on this show was the thumb-twiddling boredom that led to too much time to contemplate what was happening when Dante was out with other women.

When Genesis showed me her date heart, I had been mind-numbingly jealous. Jealous, jealous, and then more jealous. I had to rein it in, calm down, and remind myself that we were friends.

I even helped her get ready for her date.

Yes, I thought it was awfully big of me, too.

Taylor grabbed me for an interview. At least it would make it so I could stop wondering what Dante and Genesis were doing. If he took her dancing and held her close. If they laughed while they scarfed down food. If he held her hand or kissed her or . . .

Augh!

She indicated where I should sit, and then sat in a chair across from me. A camera was pointed directly at my face, and a green screen had been set up behind me.

"Has Sterling called or texted for me?"

"Not yet. I'm sure he will. When he stops being so busy with work." I didn't like that he hadn't reached out yet and tried to apologize. Especially since he didn't know how much his behavior was driving me away.

"Other than that whole situation, how are you doing?"

"I'm sore. I hurt everywhere. Dante made us play soccer yesterday, and I think I tore my everything. Is that thing on?" I gestured at the camera.

"Not yet. I wanted us to have a chance to chat before we got to what you should say on camera."

What I should say? Taylor had her tablet in her lap, and she typed something and then pointed it at me. She had typed in big letters "MATTHEW IS WATCHING. DON'T LOOK." She pointed up at a camera in the corner of the room behind her, which I could just see out of the corner of my eye.

I nodded slightly, and she put the tablet back in her lap. I would have to play along and say what they wanted to hear when the camera went on.

"How are you?"

"Finer than a frog's hair split four ways."

Her eyes lit up. "I wish we'd filmed that. That would have been a fantastic sound bite. Remember that one. I'll probably ask you to say it again later. Now, before we start filming, tell me what you really think about Dante. And this is me, Taylor, talking. Not Taylor, field producer."

I sighed. These days I couldn't tell the difference between Friend Taylor and Producer Taylor. "Don't get me wrong—in a lot of ways he is an amazing man. He has a lot of good qualities. And then there are some bad ones that I think are insurmountable."

She slid her finger across the tablet screen. "So you don't see a future with him?"

"To be honest, I don't. You've seen him back there on your monitors. You know what he's like. A total player. I bet he's made out with every woman here."

She looked up at me, pausing for a beat. "You'd be surprised."

How would I be surprised? I knew how he was with girls.

She stopped for a minute, putting her hand over one ear. When she removed her hand, I realized she was wearing an earpiece. I wondered who was feeding her questions. "I wanted to let you know that the first show has premiered."

Now that was unusual. I knew from my initial talks with the producers that they would spend weeks filming, edit it, and then release the show. "Why so soon?"

"Something about the show feeling more alive instead of being edited to death," Taylor said under her breath. I could barely make it out. "How would you feel if I told you that you were the audience's favorite? By a landslide?"

"Landslide?" I echoed, not sure where she was going with this.

"Almost every e-mail, tweet, and Facebook post we get is about you and how much they want Dante to pick you. The ratings are the highest they've ever been. I told you. Mad chemistry. What's between you is real. All of America can see it."

"But we're just friends. I'm engaged."

She tilted her head to one side in a sympathetic gesture. For some reason, it made me feel like I was getting played. "I know. But if Dante were different, if you knew he could commit and be faithful to you, would that change how you would feel?"

I started inhaling and exhaling a bit too quickly for my liking. "Off the record?"

"Of course."

I gulped down the emotion in my throat. I couldn't lie. Not about this. "Yes. It would change how I feel."

I saw a brief triumphant smile, and then she was back to her sympathetic face. "Can I tell you what I think?"

"You're in the driver's seat. Have at it."

"I think you're in love with him."

"I am not . . . not . . . there's no way that I . . . You don't know . . ." Had this room always been this hot? Why was I glistening so much?

"Sentence fragments? You can say you disagree, but your speech pattern proves otherwise."

"It means that I'm so shocked by how wrong you are that I can't even think of a dignified response," I retorted.

She shrugged. "It was just an observation."

Fan-freaking-tastic. Hooray for Taylor being so observant. Maybe I should just slap a dome on her head, give her a telescope, and call it good.

When had I become so moody? My feelings were more unpredictable than a twister in a trailer park. One second I was mooning over Alternate Reality Dante, the next I was ready to knock out my own sorority sister.

This place was literally making me crazy.

"Back to you being the clear favorite. Matthew is thrilled. We all are."

As cynical as the producers on this show seemed, they all had one annoying and unbelievable trait in common—they really and honestly believed in true love. They wanted a couple to fall in love and get married and have babies. The fact that they had repeatedly failed at this attempt did not seem to deter them. Taylor had told me once that Matthew Burdette's fondest wish for this show was that at the final Heart Celebration the couple would be so in love that they would ask for a justice of the peace right then and there. It hadn't happened, but he kept trying.

They might be helped in that desire if the producer stopped deliberately making half the contestants crazy, and encouraging the other half to be evil.

"Which means what, exactly?"

She had that pity expression on her face again. "Which means you're not going anywhere. I think the success of the show depends on you sticking around. I'm sorry."

I felt my lungs deflate. I couldn't even blame her or anyone else.

This was my fault. Dante had offered to send me home, and I'd said no under the pretext of helping Genesis, who was doing just fine on her own, truth be told. Now I was stuck.

At first I had stayed because he asked me to. Then I stayed because some part of me wanted to. But now I would have to stay because Matthew Burdette wanted me to stay.

And what Matthew Burdette wanted, Matthew Burdette got.

More days passed, more girls were sent home. Heather, Cece, both Jessicas, and Emily F. all were gone. Dante spent almost all of his time on single dates as a chance to really get to know the women better. And true to our pact, nobody shared. I had no idea who he liked or which girl he was getting closer to.

There were still too many secretive and all-knowing smiles for my liking.

Harris announced a new series of theme dates called "Get to Know Me." Each girl would be in charge of creating a date that would tell Dante something about herself. We had no budgetary restrictions and could travel if we wanted. One was going to take him to Las Vegas, another wanted to travel to Europe. Abigail decided to take him to the set of her soap opera and impress him with, and I quote, "how popular, talented, and amazing" she was.

I threw up. In my mouth. Twice.

I had been trying to figure out a way to keep my job and make the audience not root so hard for me. This date would be another chance to do that. While the other women went full-throttle, I would do something simple. Hopefully everyone would think I was boring.

Sterling had finally texted. Taylor showed it to me in passing. One word.

Sorry.

Unfortunately, it didn't seem like enough. I didn't ask to call him, and he certainly hadn't tried to call me.

There needed to be a serious conversation in our future, or I didn't see this wedding happening. Which I couldn't bear to tell my mother, because she sent constant e-mails, which Taylor let me read (after she deleted anything that might influence my actions with regards to the show), and all my momma could talk about was the wedding and how excited she was that her in-laws were already her best friends.

I spent so much time not being the woman my parents wanted me to be, and I couldn't bear to disappoint them in this too. Not yet, especially when I wasn't sure what would happen.

Dante went on all his "Get to Know Me" dates without sending anyone home. I missed him because he was gone all day every day. The with-someone-else part bothered me as well, but I decided to put a pin in that crazy for another day.

I sent word to him through an assistant to dress casually and meet me in the backyard at eight thirty. I put on my favorite light blue sundress and a pair of open-toed wedges.

He waited for me, his black hair still slightly damp at the ends, and wearing a tight black T-shirt and a pair of blue jeans that made me want to pen a thank-you note to Their Royal Highnesses, King Dominic and Queen Aria, for passing along such fine genetic material.

I felt like I was thirteen years old again, standing there, giddy just to be in his presence.

He caught sight of me and walked across the lawn. "*Buonasera, Limone.*"

My pulse went wild from the way he looked at me. It didn't help things that he had spoken Italian to me, either. That made me want to collapse into a puddle of Lemon. Then he greeted me hello as he had a million times before, a soft kiss to the left cheek, then one on the right.

Where he, again, lingered for a half a second longer than he should have, and I, again, enjoyed it much more than I should have.

He also didn't move away, and stood entirely too close to me. "What have you planned?"

That was the question of the ages, wasn't it? What did I have planned? For Dante, for Sterling, for my wedding?

But for tonight, I had something boring and easy. The show had brought in a giant outdoor movie screen and set the whole system up. All I had to do was press "Play."

They had taken things a step further than what I'd asked for, surrounding the area with more lit candles. The team had also laid out a blanket and had beanbags, pillows, and throw blankets in case we got cold. Or, more likely, they'd added the blankets so they might give us some privacy if we decided to make out. Which made my blood start heating up, just thinking about it.

I had to clear my throat. "This is my favorite movie ever. *Gone with the Wind*. I figured you'd never seen it, and it's important to me, so I thought you could get to know me a little bit better by watching it with me."

The movie was nearly four hours long. We would sit in silence and watch the adventures of Scarlett O'Hara and her idiotic life choices, along with her amazing ability to survive, and then the date would be over. We'd never even have to speak.

I wanted to pat myself on the back.

There were movie treats as well—Red Vine licorice, Junior Mints, M&Ms, massive cups of soda, and actual movie tubs of popcorn. Dante set up a little nesting area for us to sit together and watch. I debated. It would look more romantic for the producers if I sat there, but there might be some serious negative consequences if I did.

I decided to risk it.

It was only once the movie started that I realized what I had accidentally done. Scarlett started off the movie in the exact same costume I'd worn on New Year's Eve. If it was possible to have a panic attack followed up by a heart-attack chaser at twenty-four, I would have been the prime candidate for it.

Dante didn't say anything though. Or look at me. He just put his arm behind me on the pillows, like this was a real date, and watched.

I finally started to relax after the men got called off to fight in the Civil War. The moment had come and gone and it looked like he wouldn't tease or remind me about it. I hadn't chosen this movie to bring up the costume ball. It really was just my favorite movie. I hoped he didn't think there was some hidden double meaning.

We finished off most of the snacks with Dante doing the bulk of the work, and we somehow managed to scoot closer to each other so that by the end, my side was pressed to his. This was both exhilarating and nerve-racking. He was playing with the ends of my hair as I pressed "Stop." The movie screen went blank.

"Well, what did you think?"

"I liked it." His voice was a murmur. He didn't have to speak very loudly, because we were so close together. "Why is it your favorite?"

"Well, the South, Atlanta. But I love Scarlett. I know I should like Melanie better. Scarlett is selfish, immature, and unaware of the damage she causes, while Melanie is good, kind, and forgiving. But I so wanted to be Scarlett when I grew up! I'm not sure what that says about me."

"She was also brave, loyal, hardworking, and determined like you."

He would never know the thrill he gave me when he compared our strengths. "But she has terrible taste in men. Another thing we have in common."

"Hey!" he yelped, looking insulted. I laughed.

"She just chose the wrong guy," Dante said. "She should have loved Rhett from the beginning. Ashley was all wrong for her. She would have frustrated him and he would have bored her. They would have been miserable."

There was something there, something he wasn't saying. I felt it. It was too deep and too serious for the moment. "From the beginning, huh? Don't tell me you believe in love at first sight."

He raised both of his eyebrows in response.

"You do! How can you of all people believe in that?"

"The men of our family fall hard and fall fast. There is a legend—my great-grandfather was kind to a group of traveling Romani. He granted them safe passage through Monterra and welcomed them to stay for as long as they wished."

I must have looked confused, because he clarified. "People also call them gypsies, and it was at a time when many others were being cruel and enslaving them. And as a thank-you, the leader of the group granted him the desire of his heart—he had several possibilities for a queen and wasn't sure which one to pick. The leader said that he and all the sons born in his line would know the very moment they met their true loves. And it happened. My great-grandfather met my great-grandmother at a ball, proposed later that night, and they were very much in love their entire lives."

"That's sweet. I still can't believe that *you* believe in this sort of thing."

"I didn't. Until . . ." He trailed off. He did have a real-life example of it, though.

"Until Nico and Kat?" I tried to finish off his sentence.

He stayed still for a moment, and that feeling returned. The one that said something important was happening and that I better pay attention. The one that made all the hairs on the back of my neck stand up. He looked at me. "No, I didn't believe it until the first time I held you in my arms. Comforting you after Kat's accident. That's when I knew it was true."

He couldn't be serious. He couldn't. I waited for a wink, or one of those flirtatious smiles that would let me know it was all a joke. Ha-ha, so funny. Because I knew him, and this boy was so slick he could steal the sweet from sugar without touching a grain.

I waited. And I waited.

It didn't happen.

I finally expelled a deep breath that I hadn't even been aware of holding. This was too much. I became painfully aware of how fast my heart was beating, and of the camera crew standing ten feet away.

This was not real. Nothing that had happened since I'd been drafted into this situation had been real. Maybe the show had told him to manufacture a romance with me, too. If they had, I wished he had warned me first.

Because he was a little too convincing.

Despite what he'd said to me about wanting to get married, I wanted to laugh at the idea of it. The day that happened I would have to start ice-skating home from work because hell would have frozen over. It was that ridiculous.

So why was he doing this? Tormenting me? Had I actually hurt his feelings? It was probably more like a bruised ego.

"Say something," he said, holding me with his gaze.

"I can't do this with you. I just can't."

I got up and stormed off toward the house. I didn't appreciate being toyed with, or how it would look on the show.

It wasn't hard for him to catch up with me. He grabbed my upper arm, turning me around. Even when I was angry and hurt by him, his touch still managed to make my knees go floppy. "Just tell me this one thing. Is it like this with him? Does he make you laugh?"

I stared up at him, my eyes glassy and full of unshed tears. "Maybe not. But at least he doesn't make me cry."

He looked stricken when he let me go, and I walked inside without looking back.

Chapter 14

HRH Dante:

I think once we have our first fight we should definitely kiss and make up.

Dante found me at breakfast and asked to speak with me. I couldn't say no because every other girl was gaping at us, and two camera crews stood nearby, capturing every word.

I didn't want this preserved for posterity. So I took him by the hand and led him into the bathroom, locking the door shut behind us. Someone banged on the door loudly, and a man's voice said, "Come on, Lemon! This is the kind of stuff the audience eats up! Let us in!"

The knocking continued as Dante took both of my hands. He looked so sad. "I hate when you're upset with me, *Limone*. You're my best friend. What can I do to apologize and make this right? I'll do anything."

My mouth literally dropped open. I was his *best* friend? I'd always considered us friends, but best friends?

Then I realized that it was true for me too. He had become one of my best friends. On par with Kat.

I also realized that there was no rational excuse for my behavior last night. If a man hinted that he had feelings for you, you thanked him for it, told him you found it flattering, but you really just thought of him as a friend. You let him down gently. You definitely did not reciprocate it.

You did not freak out and storm off and say something you knew would hurt him. There was only one reason that I would have acted that way.

Because I had feelings for him, too.

I'd been unable to sleep last night. And I decided how I felt didn't matter. Even if Dante imagined himself in love with me, it wouldn't last. I knew from the start that I had to keep him at arm's length to keep my heart safe. Now I would have to do it for both of our sakes.

I had to. It was the only way to stay sane.

"There's nothing to apologize for," I told him, trying my hardest to make it look like I was smiling for real. "You're one of my best friends too. Sometimes friends fight, but then they get over it."

Before he could respond, I opened the bathroom door, and nearly ran into the crew who stood there waiting with the camera pointed at us. Taylor approached from the side with her phone. "Lemon, the phone's for you. It's Sterling."

She had done that on purpose, and I didn't know why. I took the phone, but now the crew stood in the doorway, leaving me nowhere to go.

Dante was gone.

I only had a second to wonder what his disappearing act meant before I walked back into the bathroom. "Hello?"

"My case settled and I only have a light workload this week before the Belmont case ramps up. I finally have a chance to talk. When are you coming home?"

This was what he called me for? "I told you I was staying."

"You did? When?"

"The last time we talked. You know, when you were a complete and total jerk to me."

There was a pause. "What? I don't remember it happening like that."

How convenient.

"I didn't even realize you were this upset. Maybe I shouldn't have said some of the things I did, and I wish I hadn't. But in my defense, I told you I was busy, and I did text your friend Taylor to say that I was sorry."

And again, I was comparing. Two men had just apologized to me in the space of five minutes. One had made my heart flutter with his sincerity and promises to do whatever he needed to make it better, and the other was shifting blame to me. One always knew when I was upset, and the other didn't even realize it. I sat down on the side of the tub and put my forehead in my free hand.

What a mess.

He sighed. "I shouldn't have said that either. I am just screwing everything up. I am trying so hard to do everything right. I was caught up in proving myself to my father."

Now that was real and understandable. I knew what it was like to get caught up in trying your hardest to prove yourself to your parents.

"Can you forgive me?"

I supposed that depended on what I wanted. Something I had to figure out and decide, once and for all. Nothing had really changed with Dante. To be fair, he had changed and grown in some ways, but it had not altered who he was at his core. He was still a charming womanizer who could make any female weak in the knees and willing to throw her life away for a chance with him. It was why he had been such a perfect choice for this show.

And why it was so easy to get sucked in by him.

"Lemon? Are you still there?"

Did I want to put myself through it? Did I want to walk away from a lifelong friend and partner who planned to build a life with me? The kind of life I truly wanted? Was I really willing to risk everything for something I knew was destined to fail miserably?

"Yes, I can forgive you," I said. I'd made a commitment to him. A promise I intended to keep. And I needed to be better about not comparing him to an ideal man who didn't exist. Sterling had his flaws, but I knew him. He was real. I trusted him.

"Are you still my girl?" It was the phrase he'd always used growing up when we made up after a fight.

"I'm still your girl," I reassured him, and a soft tenderness flooded through me. "I'm glad you called me."

"I didn't call you. Your friend Taylor called me and said that you needed to talk."

Why would Taylor do that? What had she been trying to accomplish? Something was going on and it made me uneasy.

He asked me some questions about the show, how it was going, and when I thought I would return home to Atlanta. I explained the circumstances and what the producers wanted, and how I couldn't risk my career by just up and leaving.

Someone must have come into his office because he put his phone on mute and I heard a voice say something before Sterling started speaking again. "I need to go. I love you. See you soon."

He hung up before I had the chance to tell him that I loved him, too.

But some part of me wondered whether I would have said it back.

The "Getting to Know Me" dates ended, and Dante sent Lisa home. Apparently she couldn't shut up on their date either, and Dante had gotten to know more than he wanted. Jen K. was next, followed by Ashley S., who swore at everyone on her way out and apparently during the entire limo ride to the airport, too. The other Ashley was sent home after that, and I hoped she and her giggles had a nice flight home.

Which left me, Genesis, Abigail, and carbonated Michelle.

At this point we were scheduled to go on exotic mini-trips with Dante. In other years the girls had traveled together to each location, but this year the producers decided to continue the one-on-one time with the remaining girls. Dante chose where we would go.

I was left until last, again. When I complained to him, he winked at me and said, "You always save the best for last."

Genesis pulled me aside before her trip and asked if she could talk to me. I wasn't sure that I wanted to, but the nicer part of me prevailed. She sat on her bed, and I sat on mine.

"They just told me that we're going to Cozumel. That's in Mexico, apparently. This is my first time traveling out of the country," she confessed. "And I've never gone alone anywhere with a man before." Her eyes were downcast, and I got what she was trying to tell me.

Why did I keep making friends with virgins? It wasn't like I had good life experiences to share and guide them with. I was the last person they should seek advice from.

"First of all, you are never going to be alone. You will have a camera crew with you at all times, and production assistants who will show you where to go and what to do." I realized how that sounded. "I mean like at the airport and customs and stuff. And for the other part, you don't have to do anything you don't want to do. Or anything you aren't ready for. And if you get really freaked out or worried, you call Taylor and she will find me. Don't put any pressures or expectations on you or on him. Okay?"

She hugged me. She was such a sweetheart. I had to find a way to be okay with her and Dante. If he could really see who she was, how kind-hearted, how loving, how fun, he could have a real relationship with her.

And since we shared a room, I was often subjected to the happy glow and private smile that she carried around with her constantly. I knew they were hitting it off. Or at least she really liked him and he was being Dante and couldn't help making her fall in love with him.

Genesis gathered up some last-minute things and asked if I had any advice about Mexico. I told her not to drink the water and not to get kidnapped.

Abigail stomped by our room, apparently upset that she hadn't been chosen to go first. She hovered in our doorway, looking angry. "What brings you by, Abigail?" Genesis asked.

"Cloven hooves?" I offered.

She only glared at me as Genesis and I dissolved into laughter. She went off in a huff, and I probably should have felt bad, but I didn't. Genesis had told me about how Abigail had crashed her last date with Dante, and he'd had to send her away. Abigail had told him that they belonged together and it was what everyone wanted and was waiting to see. Genesis had been impressed by how much of a gentleman he was, and he promised Abigail he'd talk with her more when it was her turn. But at the same time, Genesis had been pretty furious that Abigail tried to sabotage her date.

"I don't know why he keeps her around."

I did, but I couldn't tell her. So instead I said, "She's the kind of girl who would make a preacher mad enough to kick in a stained glass window."

Someone called her name downstairs. "That's my ride. I'm off." She hugged me again with that excited smile, and I felt terrible.

Why couldn't I just be happy for my two friends?

He took Genesis to Mexico, Michelle to Puerto Rico, and Abigail to St. Croix. He wouldn't tell me where we were going. I couldn't wait to see what beach he planned on taking me to. It would be so, so nice to escape this house and lie out on some white sand somewhere. I decided to think of it as a pre-wedding getaway.

As the days passed, my wedding date drew closer and closer. I sometimes pulled my invitation out of my purse and looked at the picture of Sterling and me. We looked happy. We were happy.

But it felt like I shouldn't have to constantly remind myself of that fact.

I packed my bathing suits, shorts, and T-shirts, along with my sandals. I so needed this break.

I was driven to the airport and put on a private plane. It was not the royals' private plane, and it wasn't nearly as nice or as big. The crew assigned to me, men that I now knew as Mike, Steve, and John (only because they called one another by name), also came on board. They continued to film, although I didn't think hours of me perusing a copy of *SkyMall* I'd found on one of the seats would qualify as entertainment. I wondered if Dante would be joining us, but the flight attendant told me to fasten my seatbelt and we took off without him.

A couple hours later, we were preparing to touch down. I pushed the button next to my seat, and the attendant appeared. "Yes? How can I help you?"

"Are we having troubles with the plane? Is that why we're landing?"

"Not at all. We've reached our destination. I hope you enjoy your time in Colorado."

Colorado? I turned to the crew, wanting an explanation, but they were how they always were—silent, stone-faced, and nonparticipatory.

Why were we in Colorado? This wasn't exactly exotic.

A car waited for us and drove us to my favorite ski lodge, the Rocky Mountain Red Lodge. The one where I spent all my free time skiing during the winter when I was still in college. I wondered the entire way what I was doing here and why Dante had chosen to take me to the mountains instead of a beach.

He waited for me outside the lodge, and I was both happy to see him and thoroughly confused about what was happening.

After he kissed my cheeks hello and made my toes curl, I said, "What is going on? How come everyone else gets the beach and I'm here?"

Then he made everything better by saying, "We've skied my slopes, so I thought it was time to try yours."

"Um, it's May. Most of the snow is gone."

He got a huge grin. "Leave that up to me."

The lodge was empty of any other visitors, as they had closed for the summer. The woman who checked us in said they had a skeleton staff—she'd given us suites with their own kitchens as room service wouldn't be available and the restaurant was closed. She kept trying not to look at the cameras directly. She wasn't successful. They'd probably cut every shot she was in.

"I don't have anything to wear for skiing. I only packed swimsuits," I told Dante as we went to our rooms, which were side by side.

"You can ski in those. I won't complain."

I hit him for laughing, and when I opened my door, I saw all the equipment and clothing I would need. I looked back at him with a grateful smile and let my door close behind me. The room was large and luxurious, dominated by a king-sized bed. As promised, there was a small kitchen with a fridge, stovetop, and a microwave. There was an adjoining door between my room and Dante's. I started toward it to check the locks, when I heard his door slam shut. He was already dressed! I hurried and changed, eager to get to the slopes.

He was waiting in the hallway for me. "Let's go."

We went outside the lodge and headed toward the medium difficulty slopes. I put my hand up to my eyes and realized the entire run was covered in snow.

"How did you . . ."

He pointed and I saw three snow cannons pumping out man-made snow. "I can't believe you did this!" It must have cost a fortune.

"Let's go!" He sounded as excited as I felt.

We spent the entire day going up and down the slopes, over and over. I absolutely loved having the place practically to ourselves, with the exception of our camera and sound guys. When they picked the crews to come with us, someone had failed to find out whether or not they could ski. They spent more time in the snow than skiing on it. Dante and I had to keep helping them back to their feet. We laughed and skied and laughed some more.

As it started to turn dark, I felt exhausted physically, but emotionally and mentally I was recharged and refreshed.

"It's been a long time since I've seen you this way," Dante said, right before we walked into our separate rooms.

"What way?"

"Sparkly. Alive. Happy."

He was right, and we shared another one of those emotionally laden moments that scared me like a long-tailed cat in a room full of rocking chairs.

"Skiing always makes me happy," I said, a little too brightly. "I'm glad we came."

"That's what I'm good for. You need someone to remind you to not be so serious all the time. To have fun. Life is too short."

There was no answer to that other than hiding in my room from him. Like the yellow-bellied coward that I was. I took a very long shower, putting on one of the resort's fluffy white robes when I finished and towel-drying my hair. I wondered whether there was any food in the kitchen as I hadn't eaten in hours, and was relieved to find that there was. I had started putting together a salad when a large black spider, which bore more than a passing resemblance to a tarantula, began running across the floor.

I screamed and grabbed my salad bowl, putting it over the spider, trapping him in place. I snagged a wooden spoon and climbed up on the counter, not sure what to do next.

Dante came barreling into the room through our adjoining door. If he'd been a cowboy, he would have had his six-shooters out. "What's wrong?"

"Spider," I managed, and pointed to the bowl. It barely registered that he too had just come from the shower and only had on a pair of jeans. I had to be terrified if I couldn't even enjoy his gorgeously sculpted chest and arms.

He immediately relaxed and came into my kitchen, looking at the bowl and then back at me. "How did you imagine this standoff would end?"

"Shh, don't talk," I whispered. "He's the size of your face. I think he might even have a knife. I don't want him to hear my voice and come back and get revenge by laying spider eggs in my ears while I'm sleeping."

"I can't believe you're afraid of spiders. I didn't think you were afraid of anything."

"Oh, be quiet, funny man. I need you to do your manly duty and kill the spider, please."

He went over to the bowl and I closed my eyes. I heard paper towels being ripped, a scraping noise of the bowl being moved and then silence. "All done. You can open your eyes. I have vanquished the spider for you. Quest number three completed."

"Are you sure he's dead?"

"Very sure."

I jumped off the counter and ran to him, hugging him tightly. He put his arms around me, holding me close. Fear and adrenaline had been coursing through me, and now they were turning into something else.

Something even scarier than the spider.

Chapter 15

HRH Dante:

I have developed a deep-seated jealousy of your mirror and all the time it gets to spend looking into your eyes.

He didn't have on a shirt, and there was only my bathrobe between us. I gulped as my pulse pounded all over my body.

Even though my hair was wet, I felt a wave of heat blast through me. I finally looked up at him, and he had a roguish grin that turned my legs to rubber.

"Are you thinking what I'm thinking?" he asked.

"Not even sort of," I lied, and hoped he wouldn't see through it. This all felt so deliberate, like he knew he made me crazy and he thought it was hilarious.

Dante smiled like he knew something I didn't, and then said, "I was thinking it would be fun to go swimming. They heated the pool for us. Do you want to come with me?"

Right then I probably would have done anything he asked. "Is the pope Catholic?" I blurted out, something my daddy often said.

He had a slight frown. "Last time I checked. Oh!" His frown went away. "That means you'll come swimming."

"I, um, just need to get my bathing suit on."

"You don't have to," he teased, and we still just stood there, locked in each other's arms, neither one of us moving. It didn't seem to be an issue for him, but I was liable to have a case of the vapors.

"I think swimsuits are necessary."

I knew he had been joking, but I definitely didn't need to add skinny-dipping into this situation. While I kept swallowing and trying to keep my breathing even, he studied me. "I'll meet you in the hallway in ten minutes."

Then he let go of me and went back to his room, closing the adjoining door behind him. I leaned back, gripping the counter for support.

I should tell him I'd changed my mind. That us swimming together, alone, was not a good idea. I shoved some lettuce into my mouth. Now I could invoke the "no swimming for an hour after eating" rule.

I looked at the door. I had to figure out a way to overcome my attraction to him. Yes, this show and experience would end, but my contact with him would not. I would still be doing PR for his family, which he happened to be a part of, and soon Kat would be a part of it, too. She would invite me to events and special occasions. Dante would keep being in my life. I could not be married to someone else and still react to him this way.

Maybe the answer wasn't hiding from him and avoiding him, but spending more time with him. Kat had told me once about something called exposure therapy, where kids overcame their fears and anxieties by constantly being around the thing that scared them. Supposedly, this would desensitize them and lessen their reactions. At this point I was willing to try anything to get him out of my head.

After eating a bit, I chose my most modest bikini—a red and white polka-dot 1950s-inspired suit that always made me feel like Marilyn Monroe.

Putting the robe back on over my suit, I grabbed a towel and went out into the hallway. Dante gave me a gorgeous smile, which I concentrated on rather than his half-nakedness, and we started walking to the pool. He told me a story about breaking his left arm that involved his six-year-old belief that he could fly if he just really put his mind to it.

He stopped at the gate of the fence that surrounded the pool. There was a rule sign posted, and he studied it.

"What are you doing?"

"Acquainting myself with the rules. Okay, I'm ready."

We went in, and he threw his towel onto a nearby chair and dove into the pool's deep end. He resurfaced quickly. I slipped off my sandals and took off my robe. I could feel his eyes on me and the tension that it caused for both of us.

Repeated exposure, I reminded myself. *Keeping my company alive by making Matthew Burdette happy.* Those were the things I needed to concentrate on.

Ignoring my pounding heart, I went over to the stairs and descended slowly, acclimating myself to the water. It was warm and inviting, and if I closed my eyes I could almost imagine that I was entering some tropical ocean instead of a pool at a ski lodge.

I got to a place where I could touch the bottom and keep my head and shoulders above water comfortably. He swam to a point across from me.

"I heard that the men who star on this show keep a running bet on who can make out with the most women. Where are you ranked?" It was a good thing to ask him. Him messing around with other girls was still the one thing I could hold against him. The one thing I couldn't abide in a man.

He smiled and stayed quiet. I was about to ask him again when he said, "I invoke my Fifth Amendment right against self-incrimination."

I knew it. "You're not a US citizen. The Constitution doesn't apply to you."

"You could always rectify that by marrying me."

I narrowed my eyes at him while he laughed at his own joke. "Pass. And thanks for not answering my question."

"Why do you care if I kiss anyone else?"

"I don't!" I said, a little too quickly.

He treaded water, watching me. "You really want to know how many women I've kissed from this show?"

I did, desperately and inexplicably. "Yes."

"Including you?"

I nodded.

"One."

Which filled my heart with both glee and disbelief. "I find that hard to believe."

He shrugged one shoulder. "I've never lied to you, so I don't know why you wouldn't believe me. I haven't kissed anyone. Out of respect for you."

I couldn't have adequately described to anyone the twenty different things I felt when he said that. It was overwhelming, terrifying, and made me tremble.

"I know you better than that." I had meant to sound playful, but I came across as accusatory.

"You don't know me as well as you think you do."

"Really? Fine. Tell me something I don't know about you."

"You've stolen my heart."

That made the million different swirling emotions kick up into overdrive. I tried to laugh, but it came out weird. "Something real and not flirtatious," I told him.

A strange expression crossed his face, and then his smile returned. "I don't keep secrets from you, *Limone*. You know that."

My heart palpitations were making me jumpier than a cat on a hot tin roof.

"But in the interest of full disclosure, I have a terrible credit score."

"How can you be rich and have a terrible credit score?"

His muscled arms moved back and forth in the water, keeping him in place. I wondered how long he could tread water. I was extremely impressed by his endurance.

"I don't get my trust fund until my twenty-fifth birthday, and I used to be terrible with money."

"Used to be?"

His eyes twinkled with mirth. "I'm still working on it."

"Me too," I admitted.

"What made you more careful?"

"Meeting Kat freshman year. I felt bad being so extravagant when she had nothing. I could see myself through her eyes and how I wasted my money, so I economized."

He cocked his head to the side. "You spend a lot of time worrying about how other people see you, don't you?"

I crossed my arms, ready to let him know just how wrong he was, but he kept speaking. "I am impressed that you're able to handle your money so well."

"You should be," I retorted. "It sucks."

He held his arms up in a "look who you're talking to, I get it" gesture.

Before I could ask him to clarify, he said, "Tell me something I don't know about you."

There were probably a lot of things he didn't know about me. A lot of things that I thought and felt that were better kept private.

I remembered his story about breaking his arm, and thought broken bones were probably a safe topic for conversation.

"I broke my ankle skiing right before my last solo ballet recital."

He raised both eyebrows at me. "I didn't know you were a dancer. Given your hatred of all things exercise-related it should be unexpected, but I guess it's not that surprising. I've danced with you often enough to know that you know what you're doing."

"Grandma Lemon wanted me to compete in beauty pageants, but I couldn't sing, and she said twirling a baton was beneath me as a Beauchamp, so I started taking ballet and I loved it. I miss it so much."

I had enjoyed it, the exactness and grace of it, and at the time, I wanted nothing more than to earn a solo and become a professional ballerina someday.

"Did you stop because of your ankle?"

"I stopped because when puberty hit, I no longer had the right figure for ballet."

He waggled his eyebrows at me suggestively. "Ballet's loss was my great gain."

I shook my head. One-track mind. "My sophomore year, I finally got my solo. Madame La Grand let me know that it would be my last performance with them. My company was performing excerpts from *The Nutcracker*, and I won the part of Clara. We had rehearsals every day, and then I would go home and practice for hours every single night. I wanted it to be perfect. Then my family went skiing in Utah the weekend before the show, and that was it. I never got to perform it."

"That's so sad, *Limone*. I'm so sorry that happened to you."

I could feel the tears welling at the back of my eyes at the emotion in his voice. "Speaking of sad, I still remember every single step of my routine even though it's been almost ten years."

"Couldn't you go back? Do ballet for fun?"

"Sometimes you need to know when to let go of impossible dreams and be real about your life."

He slowly swam closer to me. "So you think you have to settle for less?"

We were no longer talking about ballet, and Sterling needed to be off-limits. "It's not settling to be with someone who I know won't cheat on me."

Even closer. "This isn't about cheating or getting hurt. It's about control. You think you can control your life if you choose a certain kind of man. But you can't control anything. If that's the one thing in my life I've learned, it's that everything is out of our control."

From the timbre in his voice, I knew he was talking about his father. The king had become a quadriplegic after a boating accident.

"You should be choosing a man who loves you so much that he could never even conceive of hurting you. A man who would always put you first, above everything else."

He was close enough to touch me, but he didn't. I couldn't drag air into my lungs fast enough as that zing of electricity crackled between us.

Speaking was pretty much out of the question when he looked at me like that.

"*Limone*, there's something I need to say to you."

That loosened my tongue. I couldn't let him continue. "Stop. Don't say it. If you do it will ruin everything. I'm engaged."

"And yet you're here with me."

"I'm here because I don't have a choice," I snapped.

"You've always had a choice," he said, his silky voice making my stomach flip repeatedly. "And if you were mine, I could never go this long without seeing you. Without touching you. Without kissing you."

He was going to kiss me. And I just stood there frozen, unable and unwilling to move.

"Is it magic between you two the way it is with us?" His seductive voice was almost more than I could stand.

And even then, I couldn't lie to him. I needed to, for my own self-preservation. For the preservation of my upcoming wedding. To keep my heart intact.

So I did the only thing I could think of to put some distance between us.

I splashed him.

He wiped the water from his face slowly, with a grin that promised retribution. I should have known he'd take it as a challenge.

Maybe that was why I did it.

"There are rules," he said. "You can't simply splash me. Did you not see the sign?"

"Oh, I saw the sign." I splashed him again.

He turned his head this time, as if he'd been expecting it. "As a member of the household of a reigning monarch, it is my duty to report this. Who do you call for pool violations?"

I splashed him again, and kept splashing him. We were both laughing when he reached through the mountain of water for me, restraining my arms. He held them up in the air, which made the rest of me slam into him.

The laughter died quickly, and he let go of my arms. They fell to my sides, but I didn't move. I couldn't. I could feel his heart rapidly beating against his chest. We were both breathing hard and fast, and it wasn't from the splashing.

I stared at his mouth, willing him to kiss me. My tingly lips and racing pulse throbbed. But he didn't move. We stood, pressed together, surrounded by the warmth from the pool and each other. I wanted him to make that first move so that I could blame it on him later. Just one kiss wouldn't hurt, would it? If it wasn't my fault? What could I do if he just grabbed me and kissed me? I had to make the show happy, right?

Thinking about the show made me remember the camera, and I turned to see them still filming. This would look so bad. So, so bad.

"Are you sure we can't . . ." he started to say as I backed up, and I knew then that he wanted it just as badly as I did.

Heart in my throat, suddenly angry at my own behavior and wanting to take it out on him, I said, "In your dreams, Dante."

He didn't get upset though. He just looked at me in that way of his and said, "Every night, *Limone*."

There was nothing to do after that but excuse myself and hurry back to my room before he got any ideas.

Or before I got any.

I practically ran back, making sure to lock every single door. I didn't know what was wrong with me. Why I was so willing to ruin my entire future for lust.

But I did know one thing for sure.

The exposure therapy was not working.

I heard him return to his room. I thought he might knock and try to talk to me, but he didn't. I didn't know whether to be relieved or upset. I just kept rerunning our conversation over and over in my head. What he said, how he said it, what it meant, and whether it was real or just some kind of game that he wanted to play.

Mostly I thought about what he'd said regarding me.

It was probably three o'clock in the morning when I realized that my hotel room had a phone with a landline. I'd been without a phone for so long that it hadn't even occurred to me that I might have one now.

Kat was going to kill me, but I needed her.

She picked up on the fourth ring. "Just so you know, the next time I see you, I am going to smack you."

"I know, I'm sorry. I really needed to talk to you."

"What has he done now?" She sounded exhausted and mumbled her words.

"Am I a control freak?"

She was quiet for so long I thought she might have fallen back asleep. "Is this a trick question? I feel like there's not a right answer here." She didn't sound sleepy anymore.

"The right answer is no!"

Another long pause. "Even if it's not true?"

"I am not a control freak! I don't want to control everything. I know I can't."

"You kind of do. And that's okay. People who know and love you understand and accept that about you. That's just you. Like how I'm screwed up emotionally and almost totally ruined my chance at true love. Nico and you know that about me and you both love me anyway."

I didn't know what to say. I had never, ever thought of myself that way. And now two of my closest friends were telling me that's exactly how I was.

"Are you attracted to him?"

A pain started throbbing in between my eyebrows. "That's not the issue. That has never been the issue."

"Do you like being with him?"

I did, more than I should. "Yes, we're friends. And before you ask any more questions that you already know the answer to, there isn't a future with him, and that's the problem. I need to make different choices. Be with a different kind of man. You understand that, don't you?"

She sighed. "There are no guarantees, Lemon. Even Sterling can't make you a guarantee for the future."

"I shouldn't have come here. I should have said no. Because . . . I have to tell you something that you can't tell anyone else."

I heard a noise that sounded like sheets rustling, and I could imagine her sitting straight up in bed. She did love a good secret. "I promise I won't say anything."

"I'm not missing Sterling. Like, at all."

"You know what they say. Absence makes the heart go wander."

"I think that's supposed to be 'Absence makes the heart grow fonder.'"

"Not in your case."

I couldn't even laugh. But I was glad I had finally said it out loud. I had kept it buried inside me because I didn't want to think about what I might have to do if I admitted it.

"Don't you think you should miss him?"

Of course I thought I should miss him. I didn't know if it said something about me, or something about our relationship.

Or if it said something about Dante.

"You remember how I was right after we left Monterra and I was apart from Nico."

During their time apart, Kat had been the most miserable person alive. I'd never seen anyone so sad and depressed. I had actually worried for her mental health.

And I'd never felt that way about Sterling while I'd been away from him. Not even once.

"Maybe it's because I'm just secure in our relationship," I rationalized.

"Nico's in New York and I'm in California and I feel like part of me is missing. And I'm very secure in our relationship. You know I adore him. But when we're apart, I'm counting down the minutes until we're together again."

There was nothing I could say to that.

"Look, it's late and we should both get some sleep. Just ask yourself this—when you're apart from Dante, do you miss him?"

"Good-night, Kat." I hung up the phone.

It was a question I didn't want to answer.

Chapter 16

HRH Dante:

I had a lengthy conversation with your doctor, and he thinks you need more Vitamin Me.

They kept Dante and me separate on our return back to California, and I was glad to have some alone time before returning to the house.

Genesis was excited to see me, Michelle was indifferent, and Scabigail was hostile. Genesis had a date that afternoon with Dante, and she asked if I would help her get ready. I said yes, and helped do her hair and her makeup while she told me about what an amazing time they'd had in Cozumel. There had been some kind of comic book convention at their hotel, and he'd agreed to take her. I tried to imagine Dante with a bunch of comic book enthusiasts, and I couldn't.

He must have really liked Genesis to do something like that.

Which is good. Even if it felt awful.

She left, and I had more time to think about what a terrible person I had become. How I was engaged to one man and falling for another. How I despised cheaters and was in danger of turning into one.

And how all of America could end up hating me for being such a fickle, horrible woman.

Taylor scheduled another interview, covering up the camera so we could talk candidly. I didn't tell her about Sterling and not missing him, but I did tell her pretty much everything else. It was nice to have someone to talk to who wasn't half-asleep or halfway across the world. She was so sympathetic and so kind, she even started crying. Which made me cry, and we sat in the interview room crying and hugging each other.

When we finally stopped, she told me that Matthew Burdette was not only happy with how I'd been with Dante, he had a present for me.

She handed me a piece of paper. "He had an assistant make up a list of people that he knew were looking for a new public relations company. He said as soon as the show was over he would personally put in a good word for you. You can start calling them once we're all done here."

I looked over the names, and I recognized most of them. Even just two of them hiring my company would make a huge impact, which was both exciting and disturbing. It felt like a gift or a bribe, and something to give Burdette even more leverage.

I went into the kitchen to find something healthy to snack on. Crying it out had helped to clear up some of my negative emotions, and the prospect of having a life again after this show, and of being able to grow my business, made me feel happy.

And I stayed happy, right up to the moment where I saw Dante and Genesis outside in the backyard holding hands. She rested her head on his shoulder, and he tilted his head so that they touched. She turned to smile up at him, and it looked like he was about to kiss her. My stomach hardened and I felt sick with jealousy. Doubled-over, ready-to-run-for-the-bathroom sick with jealousy.

It's okay, I told myself. *I have Sterling, and we're getting married, and I want Dante and Genesis to be happy.*

I really did want it. Even if it made me want to bludgeon somebody.

Then it was time to get ready for a cocktail party. I guessed that Michelle would be sent home. They wanted Abigail to stay to cause problems, and I saw with my own eyes how well Genesis was doing. Burdette wanted me to stay, so it seemed like the only logical outcome.

I was glad Genesis didn't come upstairs while I was getting ready. It gave me time to compose myself, so that I could be nice and happy for her when I saw her again.

As soon as I came into the family room, Dante took me by my elbow and asked to speak with me. I put on a bright, happy smile and followed him.

Then he said the last thing I expected him to say. "Do you want me to send you home? I don't want you to be unhappy. You can go back to Atlanta, if that's what you want."

Things must have been more serious with Genesis than I thought. "It's not what Matthew Burdette wants." I told him about everything that had gone on with the producer. He looked more and more worried with each word.

"Has he said anything to you?" I asked.

Now he seemed distinctly uncomfortable, which was surprising. "Just that he liked the way you and I are together."

He wasn't lying, but I could tell he was choosing his words very carefully. I thought about my list upstairs. I didn't believe for a second that Burdette didn't have his own copy, and that he wouldn't hesitate to call each and every person to tell them never to speak to me.

"Let's do this. You pick two other women for the finale. I will stay up to that point. You can come see my family, I'll go see yours. I will stay and play along and do what I have to do. But you can't choose me, send someone home that you could have loved, and then have me marry another man. It would ruin everything. The producers might try to force you to pick me, but if you promise me, I know you'll keep your word."

His jaw twitched two times, like he was gritting his teeth together. For a minute I thought he might not agree to what I asked. "If you will answer one question for me, then I will promise you."

I took in a deep breath. "Okay."

"What do you think would happen if we were together?"

The shock of that question jerked my head back and made me stand up straight. I had to clear my throat before I could speak. "I've seen the articles online. I know what you do in relationships."

"You can't know because you've never been in a relationship with me. When I commit, I commit."

He couldn't possibly think I'd be this easily fooled. "Why? Because of your knightly code of honor?"

As soon as I said it, I knew I shouldn't have. His face fell, the disappointment obvious. "Yes, I was raised to treat women with respect and honor. And that may seem stupid or old-fashioned to you, but . . ." He trailed off. He shook his head. "I suppose there's nothing I can say that will change your mind."

"This is just pretend, remember? Just for the cameras." I hated how sad he looked. And that I had caused it.

"Right. Just pretend. And Lemon, I promise you that I will not take you to the finale."

We were alone. There wasn't even a crew anywhere nearby. And he didn't call me *Limone*. That hurt worst of all. "Thank you," I said. I expected to feel relief.

Instead I felt shame and regret.

Harris came out to retrieve me and had me join the others inside. I looked back to see Dante being led in the opposite direction. I wondered if they wanted him to make some kind of big entrance. I lined up in the Heart Celebration room with the other girls, candles burning, cameras on.

Dante might very well send me back to Atlanta. We might leave things this way. I didn't want that.

"I know that you're standing here, expecting that one of you will go home. Well, as you can see, there are no heart pins on the tray. No one is leaving tonight."

Genesis grabbed my hand and squeezed it. I smiled back, and I finally did feel relieved. "Instead, I have an announcement to make." Harris looked at me specifically when he said it, and that relief dissipated as quickly as it had come. He was about to out me. I knew it. He would tell the others that I wasn't there for the right reasons and Burdette would blackball me and America would hate me. There was an ache at the back of my throat, and chills strangled my spine. The gnawing sensation in my stomach felt like a family of rabid squirrels had taken up residence. I thought I might start hyperventilating.

"As you all know, Dante is charming, handsome, and intelligent. Any woman would be lucky to be with him. But what you don't know is . . ."

Harris waited, stretching out the moment. I pressed my hand to my heart, so relieved that he wasn't talking about me.

"Dante is actually His Royal Highness, Prince Dante. His parents are the ruling monarchs of Monterra. Dante also has a substantial trust fund waiting for him when he comes of age."

It was so quiet you could have heard a rat peeing on cotton. Then the energy in the room shifted after that moment of shock and awe. Each girl had to be considering what this meant for her. The game play had to change because the circumstances did. This was no longer just about getting a hot guy. This was about getting a hot, rich prince. What girl hadn't dreamed of that at some point in her life?

Harris said, "I'll leave you to think that over, and to enjoy the rest of your evening. Prince Dante will not be joining you tonight, but he will be choosing one of you in the morning to spend the entire day with tomorrow."

As soon as Harris left the room, Michelle erupted into a never-ending round of squeals as she jumped up and down.

"I can't believe he's a prince!" Genesis said, and she sat down on the riser, putting her head between her knees. "It's bad enough he looks like that, but he's rich and royal too? I can't even . . ."

I grabbed a pillow and tried to fan her off, moving the hair from the back of her neck to help.

"I've heard of Monterra," Abigail said. "He's a real prince. Not just someone with a title without a castle or money." She tapped her fingernail against her lip. "I think this calls for a celebration, don't you?"

Michelle hugged Abigail around the waist, and Abigail allowed it to happen for a whole three seconds before pushing Michelle off. "Everyone go upstairs, get changed into your pajamas, and we'll have a sleepover downstairs. I'm making everyone milkshakes!"

"That's suspiciously considerate of you," I said. Hadn't she called ice cream poison?

"Nonsense," she replied. "I am a nice person. I can do nice things for other people."

I should have known better.

We'd stayed up most of the night gossiping and giggling, and even Abigail had seemed halfway human. She kept making us chocolate milkshakes, and we drank them until we thought we'd bust.

Harris woke us up early the next morning. We'd been asleep for maybe an hour. Dante stood next to him, dressed for a day out, looking perfect. I, on the other hand, had chocolate shake stains, crazy hair, and bags under my eyes.

I was so glad America was getting to see me at my finest.

Somehow Abigail had a ton of makeup on and her perfect hair fell in soft curls down her back.

Harris asked us to all stand up, because Dante had made his choice for the woman he wanted to spend the day with. It would be the last opportunity to be alone with him before the home visits. He would have to send at least one of us away after he met our families.

We all stood, and I wrapped my blanket around me. I suddenly didn't feel well. At first I thought it was because I was tired, but I felt sick to my stomach. It probably had something to do with the way Genesis was smiling at him. Being around him impaired my ability to make smart choices, and now it was literally affecting my health.

"These are never easy decisions," he said, and the room started to spin. It was like I was drunk, but I hadn't touched any alcohol in a long time. I was glistening heavily, like every single one of my pores had decided now would be a good time to give me a sweat bath.

"And it's not easy, because I enjoy spending time with all of you, but the person I've chosen to spend the day with is . . ."

My stomach contracted violently and made a sound I didn't know a stomach could make. He stopped for a second and looked at me, raising one eyebrow as if to ask if I was okay. I knew I was going to throw up. I ran for the kitchen sink, fearing I'd never make it to the bathroom, and I heard the other girls getting grossed out as my chocolate milkshakes raced out of my stomach.

Dante was behind me, and he said something, but I couldn't focus on his voice. Cold chills enveloped me as I just heaved over and over again.

After I'd emptied out every shake, in addition to whatever else my stomach found to toss out, my legs gave way. Dante caught me before I hit the floor.

He picked me up in his arms, settling me against his chest. Everyone gathered around me, asking if I was all right. It made my head hurt.

"I'm taking her upstairs."

I heard Harris call for the medic on staff. Then Abigail said, "That lucky girl is going to lose so much weight."

I wished I had the strength to strangle her.

Dante carried me up to my room, and he pushed the door open

with his foot. He stopped when he stepped inside. "How can you walk in here? Your floor is covered in clothes."

I started shivering. "They form a protective covering," I said, my teeth chattering together.

He eased me into my bed, pulling my covers over me. He brushed hair off of my damp forehead. "I admit, when I've imagined carrying you to bed it never ended with me leaving you there alone."

Only he would be hitting on me while I was dying. "You have got to be kidding."

He smiled a too-big smile, and I couldn't get warm enough. I just kept shivering under my covers. The medic came in to examine me, and said it seemed as if I had the flu. She said to give me lots of fluids and to keep me comfortable, and to get her if my symptoms worsened.

I must have fallen asleep, because I woke up having to retch again. I tried to get out of my bed, and there were arms lifting me up and carrying me into the bathroom. I got to the toilet just in time, and threw up bile. It was like I was trying to exorcise a demon from my mouth.

When I finished, I closed the toilet and leaned my head against the lid. The nice, cool, wonderful lid. I heard Dante's voice. "Is there anything I can get you?"

"My spleen back? I'm pretty sure it ended up in the toilet."

"You make it hard to be frustrated with you when you're sick like this." He picked me up again and carried me back to my room.

"What are you doing?" I asked. "I look terrible."

"You do look terrible," he agreed. But he sounded like that time I told him he couldn't tell me I looked pretty, and he said I looked awful instead. "Truly horrible."

"You're not supposed to agree with me when I say I look bad. You're the worst nurse ever," I told him as he put me back in my bed.

"I've never taken care of a sick person before."

"I can tell." I sighed when he put the covers back over me. He crouched down next to the bed and caressed the side of my face. "When you're up for it, there's some water on your nightstand. Let me know if you need anything."

"Why are you doing this? Why are you in here?" My voice sounded croaky.

"I want to be with you," he said simply.

"Even when I'm sicker than a white-mouthed mule?"

"Even then."

I reached out to take his hand. "I'm glad you're here. I don't want you to leave." It wasn't until after the words came out of my mouth that I realized what I'd said. His grin didn't help things.

I pulled my hand back. "I'm obviously delirious. Anything I say can't be held against me."

"Whatever you say, *Limone*."

I wanted to argue with him more, but I fell asleep instead.

Chapter 17

HRH Dante:

Flirting with you? I think politeness has become so rare that people mistake it for flirting. I just happen to be very, very good at being polite.

I woke up and stretched. I felt a hundred percent better. It was like I hadn't even been sick. I reached for one of the water bottles Dante had left on my nightstand. Yesterday, every time I so much as looked at water, I would throw it up. I took a tentative sip and waited.

It stayed put.

I heard a masculine snoring sound. I sat up. Dante was sleeping in Genesis's bed. He looked sweet. And hot. And cute.

And very alone with me.

I held my blanket up to my chest, which was ridiculous because I had my pajamas on and he was passed out.

Then a worse thought occurred to me. Had he and Genesis stayed there together? I put a hand to my forehead, ordering myself to not freak out. If he and Genesis had . . . done stuff . . . it was none of my business. It was gross and made me want to smack people, but it was still none of my business.

"Good morning."

Ack! My heart slammed into my chest. "Don't scare me like that."

"You wouldn't have been surprised if you weren't busy ogling me."

"I wasn't ogling you!" I insisted. "I was only trying to figure out where that snoring sound was coming from."

"I don't snore." He turned to face me, and I was grateful to see that he had a shirt on.

"You most definitely do. You sound like a Mack truck."

"You'd be the first to complain about it."

My skin flushed in response, and I didn't need to think about the implications of that statement. Speaking of which . . . "Where's Genesis?"

"I don't know. The producers wanted all of you in separate rooms."

I didn't examine the relief that sang through me too closely. "Why?"

He propped himself up on one elbow. "Genesis and Michelle started throwing up right after you did. They didn't want you to make each other sicker."

That was not sickness. We wouldn't simultaneously get the flu within a few minutes of each other. Something had happened.

Something named Abigail.

"Is Abigail sick?"

"Not that I know of." If he knew something, I didn't see it on his face or hear it in his voice.

I thought back to our girls' night, and how she drank the milkshakes with us and how much it had surprised me. Abigail was always careful with what little she did eat. Always organic, always proteins and vegetables. I thought she was just excited and decided to have a cheat night. And she drank and drank, up until the last batch that we had right before we all fell asleep.

Was she capable of something like that? Would she have seriously poisoned us? Was she willing to kill us all in order to win Dante?

I had a feeling she was. I would have to prove it somehow. And much as I would have loved to inflict a slow, excruciating revenge, it would be enough just to get her kicked off the show and out of our lives.

"How are you feeling?" Dante interrupted my Inigo Montoya-esque plans for vengeance.

"Totally better. I don't think I had the flu."

He pulled back the covers and sat up in the bed. "Food poisoning, maybe? That would explain why all three of you got sick."

It certainly would.

"Did you take Abigail on the last-chance date yesterday?"

"No. I was in here with you all day."

My heart stopped and melted all at the same time. The physical attraction was one thing, but the emotions threatened to drag me under. "Doing what?" My voice sounded strangled.

"Taking care of you. Watching that zombie show you like so much when you were sleeping."

It affected me more deeply than I would have cared to admit that he had spent an entire day looking after me. He didn't have to, I didn't expect it, and he did it anyway.

Maybe, just maybe, his feelings weren't as shallow as I thought they were.

I couldn't imagine Sterling doing the same thing.

What was wrong with me? It was like I was looking for reasons to be with Dante and cancel my wedding. "You mean *The Walking Dead*?"

"And I don't understand why when people fall down when running from a zombie, they scoot backward along the ground instead of getting back up and running away. They're obviously faster on their feet. Or why sometimes the zombies are loud and other times they're like ninja zombies."

Sterling also refused to watch *The Walking Dead*, even though it was my favorite TV show.

I sighed. I was doing it again.

"It does make you wonder how you'd react in an apocalypse."

That was one of the reasons I loved the show so much. I liked to imagine myself in that scenario, how I would do it better than the characters and how I would survive. I liked that he had asked the question. "I would kick butt in an apocalypse. I'm an excellent shot."

"Also useful in a revolution."

"Are you expecting a revolution?" I couldn't help but smile. The last people anyone would try to overthrow were Dante's parents.

"No one ever expects a revolution. It would be nice to know that at least one member of the royal household could shoot her way out."

"I'm not going to be . . ." I stopped talking and sucked in a breath as he stretched his arms above his head, flexing his arms and showing an expanse of his stomach that my great-grandmother could have done her laundry on.

He caught me looking and winked at me.

I could feel the blood rushing to my face, and then, to add insult to injury, my stomach rumbled so loudly I half expected it to rock the bed.

"Hungry?" he asked with a smirk.

"I know it seems weird considering what I just ate, but I would kill for some Graeter's ice cream."

"What's that?"

"It's a brand of ice cream from a company in Cincinnati, Ohio. I had a sorority sister from there and she introduced me to it. She would have it delivered for breakups."

He stood up. "Your wish is my command."

"I didn't mean for you to . . ." I said, but he was already halfway out the door.

Then he stopped and his mischievous eyes twinkled at me. "You said it would never happen, but we just slept together."

"We did not!" I grabbed one of my pillows and threw it at him, but he was already gone.

I took a shower, and it was nice to feel human again. I wondered how much of the previous day the cameras had captured. If they showed the audience that Dante had spent all day with me, it might look like he favored me over the others. Although, given the way editing worked, I could come out looking like a horrible person while Abigail seemed like the lovable heroine.

After I got dressed and dried my hair, I checked in on Genesis and Michelle. Michelle seemed fully recovered and was busy packing for her hometown date with Dante. Genesis, unfortunately, was still throwing up. She looked so miserable. "Every time I drink water, I get sick again."

"Stop drinking for a while," I told her. "Just sleep." She nodded and closed her eyes. I pulled her blanket up to her shoulder and patted her. I wished I could do more.

On my way downstairs I passed by Abigail's room. It was empty. "Abigail?" I called out. I knocked on her open door. "Hello?" No answer. I didn't know where she was or how much time I had, but I was ready to play spy again.

Her room was immaculate. Like a maid had been in to clean it. Another thing to dislike about her.

I opened dresser drawers, rummaging through them. I didn't know what I was looking for, but I hoped I'd know it when I saw it. I looked under her bed, under the pillows, and in the nightstand drawers. Nothing.

Turning on the closet light, I rifled through her dresses, checked pockets, and looked inside her shoes. I might not find anything. If she were smart, she would have gotten rid of the evidence.

Fortunately, Abigail was not smart.

I stood up and looked at the closet shelves and saw a bag of potato chips. That woman had never willingly eaten a trans-fat, sodium-infested, greasy carb in her entire life. I grabbed the bag, and saw that it had already been opened. I fished around inside it, and felt a glass bottle.

I pulled it out triumphantly and read the label. Ipecac syrup.

A former sorority sister of mine, Charlotte, had been anorexic and bulimic. After she came back from rehab for her eating disorders, she asked me to come to her room and get rid of her stash of ipecac syrup. She didn't have much of a gag reflex anymore, so the only way she could throw up was from the syrup. And it helped her to keep her eating and drinking in check, because once you'd ingested it, any other food or water would keep you throwing up.

No wonder Genesis hadn't gotten over it yet.

I ran back into her room and woke her up. "Genesis, do not eat or drink anything else. You will get better."

Groggily she said, "Okay."

"I'll come back and check on you later. It may take me a while because I have to finish killing Abigail first."

She was already back to sleep. I took the water bottles near her bed and carried them down to the kitchen in case she didn't remember our conversation.

I couldn't believe Abigail had done this. She must have grabbed the ipecac when we went upstairs to change, and had kept it on her all night, pretending to be our friend and making us shakes. She had been waiting and planning, wanting that last-chance date with Prince Dante, and was willing to make us all suffer so she could get it.

What kind of evil, sadistic person would do that?

I might actually inflict bodily harm on that woman. I was madder than a pack mule with a mouthful of bees. The vein in my forehead started throbbing, and my nails bit into my palms. I was shaking from the anger.

Stomping over to the Bat Cave, I threw open the door. "Where is Burdette?" I demanded.

Taylor looked both horrified and stunned. "What are you doing?" she hissed at me.

Before I could answer, Burdette emerged from a back room. "What is it now?"

I held out the bottle of ipecac syrup. "Abigail put this in our milkshakes during our slumber party. It's why we all got sick and she didn't. She wanted the last-chance date and got all of us out of her way."

He looked at the label and then back at me. "Go get Abigail." Some assistant scurried off to do his bidding.

Within a few minutes she arrived in high heels and the skimpiest bikini I had ever seen, followed by her camera crew. Another crew had snuck in to shoot from different viewpoints. The overhead lights were turned on and the whole room lit up.

When she came into the room, I went after her. Somebody had anticipated that, because I didn't take even one step before two men were holding me back and keeping me from her. "Of all the horrible, evil, psychotic things to do . . ."

"Shut up!" Burdette barked at me. It surprised me enough to go still. He handed her the bottle. "Abigail, Lemon has accused you of using this to make all the other girls sick so that you could have Dante to yourself."

She looked totally and utterly confused. "I've never seen that before."

Of course she would lie. I reached for her, but I was kept firmly in place. "I found it in your room!"

She turned to me, all wide-eyed innocence. I had decided early on she couldn't be much of an actress if the only role she could get was on a soap opera, but she was proving me wrong. "If you found it in my room, then you must have put it there. I don't even know what that is."

What proof did I have? There weren't cameras in the bedrooms.

But there were cameras in the kitchen. "Check the kitchen footage from that night. There has to be evidence of her adding it to the blender." I knew there had been a reason for her acting so nice that night. It was to lull us into a false sense of security.

"Pull it up," Burdette said to one of the techs.

"It had to be in the last batch she made us in the early morning." Charlotte had told me that it took anywhere from fifteen minutes to two hours to start working, depending on the person.

I glared at Abigail triumphantly, sure that her time was now done.

"Got it," the tech said.

He put it up on a main monitor, and we all watched. I saw Genesis, Michelle, and myself in the family room on our makeshift beds, giggling and talking. Abigail got up and went to the kitchen, and picked up the blender. She moved it from where it had been to a different location. The problem was, her back was to the camera and we couldn't see what she was doing with her hands.

She had done that deliberately. She knew exactly where the camera was and how to avoid getting caught.

Now she was the one to look triumphant.

I gave her a look I only gave people when there was no gun handy. "Is there a different camera angle? From a different room?"

"Not for where she's standing, no," one of the camera guys said.

She had poisoned us, and she was going to get away with it. This registered at a 9.9 on the insane and unfair scale.

"I would never hurt anyone," she said. There were unshed tears in her eyes, and she pressed a hand delicately to her chest, as if what I said hurt her.

"Oh, whatever," I shot at her.

She fluttered her eyelids gently. "What did you just say? I couldn't understand you."

"Now we're back to that? I said 'whatever.' Disdainfully and scornfully."

That had done something. I saw the anger on her face. She came and stood right in front of me, poking me in the chest. "The next time you have an accusation, don't go running to production. Come and say it to my face."

"Which face? You have more than one." The two security guys were still holding my arms so that I wouldn't strangle her, and I briefly considered spitting at her, although that would have forever shamed my mother and grandmother, so I didn't. I was most mad for what she'd done to Genesis and Michelle. They were so sweet and so nice; they didn't deserve to be made sick and to suffer the way that they had. I could fight my own battles, and I hated when people picked on those who didn't or couldn't stick up for themselves. I didn't take too kindly to people messing with my friends.

"Since there's no way of proving what happened, the show will go on," Burdette announced. I had totally forgotten he was even in the room. He looked at me. "If there is any violence or retribution done by anyone, that person will be kicked off the show and the police will be called."

It would be worth prison to mar that perfect face of hers. It would not, however, be worth the rest of my career. I knew what he was implying. The threat that he held over my head. He nodded to the two men, knowing that when they let go of me I wouldn't kill her.

"Now get out and go do what you're contractually obligated to do."

When we stepped out of the room and the door was shut behind us, I laughed at Abigail. "That completely backfired on you. He spent all day with me. It must just kill you that he likes me so much better than he will ever like you. He can't stand you and only keeps you here because Burdette makes him."

A look of panic crossed her face, and I realized there was something more there than even I'd figured out. A look that hadn't happened until I mentioned Burdette. It didn't take much to figure it out.

Two and two did indeed make four.

"You're sleeping with him," I said in shock. "That's why he insists on keeping you here."

Maybe she wasn't as good of an actress as I thought. I could see from her expression that I had guessed right. "You daft, lying little minger," she hissed. "Keep your false accusations to yourself!"

"Bless your heart. I've heard worse from better."

She stormed off then, and it killed me that I couldn't do anything with the information I had just uncovered. What I wouldn't give to be able to contact an entertainment reporter to let them know that perfect family man Matthew Burdette was having an affair with a second-rate soap actress.

But there was one thing I could do.

I could tell Dante.

Chapter 18

HRH Dante:

I used to think the best thing in the world was seeing you smile, then I realized that the best thing in the world is knowing that I caused it.

I told Michelle and Genesis what had happened (leaving out the affair part). Michelle said, "Well, maybe she didn't do it. I can't imagine anyone being like that. It seems awfully mean."

It sure did. Genesis and I exchanged glances, but she was still too weak to do much about it. I was glad at least one of the girls got it. An assistant came to let us know that the schedules had been shifted around, and Dante was going to England with Abigail first. Michelle looked so disappointed that I hugged her.

I had to see Dante. He had been gone for hours, and I was worried that I wouldn't be able to tell him what Abigail had done.

Scabigail had her bags packed and left for the airport. She stopped pretending to like any of us and didn't say a word when she walked out of the house.

Fortunately, Dante still hadn't left. He found me in my room. "Another quest done!" He handed me a sealed cardboard box.

I gave him a questioning look and opened the box. "I didn't give you a quest . . . What? You seriously got me Graeter's ice cream? How did you get this so fast?"

"Private jet and a spare production assistant." He grinned.

This must have cost him a ton of money. He was doing it again. Being romantic and sweet and irresistible.

And he looked so pleased with himself that I just had to bring him down a notch. "Then technically you didn't do it. The PA did."

He looked so insulted that I almost laughed. "But I paid for it, so it counts."

"I'm the quest giver, so I get to decide whether or not you get credit for it."

"Aha! So you admit it was a quest."

A crew member came to the door and knocked. "Your limo is waiting to take you to the airport for your visit to England."

"Speaking of evil wenches, I have something to tell you." I spilled out the whole story, telling him about finding the ipecac syrup in Abigail's room, confronting her and tattling to the production team, and how absolutely nothing had happened as a result. And that she basically admitted to sleeping with Matthew Burdette before calling me a name.

"What did she say?" His eyes narrowed. I liked when Dante was angry with someone on my behalf.

"I think she called me a 'daft, lying minger,' but don't quote me, because I'm not fluent in psychotic whore."

He put a hand over mine, making my hand tingle. "Don't worry. It will all work out in the end."

How could he not stay angry? His calmness and rational behavior made me feel worse, which could lead to bad things. Because I was still liable to choke a witch out.

"Do you want to call Kat?" He handed me his phone, and I nearly hugged him. It was exactly what I wanted. "I'll come get it after I finish packing."

I dialed her number and she picked up almost immediately. "Hey, Dante! How are things going with . . ."

"Lemon?" I finished for her.

"Oh, Lemon, hi!" She sounded frazzled. "No, I was going to say 'how are things going with the show.' You know, just life in general."

I decided not to give her grief. And I could hardly be upset if she and Dante were having conversations about me. I'd certainly had enough conversations with Nico about her.

We talked about her schedule, and how she and Nico were flying back in a few days to Monterra for the visits Dante would have with his family and the three remaining girls. Now I was glad that I was staying to almost the end, because I desperately missed seeing my best friend.

If you ended up with Dante, you could see her all the time, that stupid voice in my head said. I told it to hush up.

"How are things going with you?" she asked.

"Well, let's see. I've probably gained five pounds, there's only four of us left, and Abigail tried to poison me."

"What the actual frak?" Kat screamed into the phone. "She tried to poison you? I will hire a car and drive down there and strangle her myself! I'm pretty sure I have diplomatic immunity or something. Even if I didn't, Nico wouldn't ever let me go to prison. What's your address? I need it right now."

"You're not going to kill her, darlin'." I sighed. "That will lose me my job. But feel free to ignore her when she comes to the palace."

"I'm going to do more than that," she said, her voice angry. "I bet I could get some of the security detail to take care of her. Lorenz could make it look like an accident."

"Kat, darlin'." She needed to come back to reality.

"I know, I know. I'm just angry. I'm not actually homicidal. I'm just frustrated. This feels like Lady Claire all over again. What is it with us and British skanks?" Lady Claire was a noblewoman we met in Paris who had set out to break Nico and Kat apart.

Happily, it hadn't worked.

"You know, you and Nico never thanked me for pushing you two together and helping you to defeat Lady Claire."

"Push? You bludgeoned us together."

That was about as good as it was going to get. "You're welcome."

"So how did she try to poison you?" I told her the same story I'd shared with Dante.

She let out a sound of disgust. "We should start building an ark because it is seriously time for a flood. What is wrong with people?"

"Either she really wants Dante for herself, or it's about the fame." I couldn't blame her if she did want Dante. Even if she was literally one of the worst people I had ever met.

"And what about you?" Now she sounded tentative. I'd always had the motherly role in our friendship, and I knew Kat wanted to help me, only she wasn't sure how to go about it. "Other than the attempt on your life, how are things going? Like with the wedding?"

I lay down in my bed, looking up at the ceiling. "The wedding's on track. Momma's taken care of everything. It's just . . . I'm not sure there's going to be a wedding."

She didn't respond.

"Did you hear what I said?"

"I did. I'm just trying to figure out what to say so that you won't get mad or stop telling me stuff."

"I know what you think. I'm just . . . I might be agreeing with you. Although, maybe it's because of the situation. It's hard not to imagine yourself falling in love when you're in a place like this. Where everything is romantic and amazing and exotic. It's not real life."

"You're right," she said thoughtfully. "It's not real life. But you knew Dante in real life before this. It's not like he's changed who he is. And that's the part that matters, right?"

I closed my eyes against my oncoming headache. "Sometimes I think part of the reason why I said yes to Sterling was because if he cheated on me, I would get over it. If Dante did, I don't know if I'd recover. It kills me to be here and see him flirting with and falling for other women. I'm in this constant state of jealousy and wanting to maim people."

She paused again. "I think that says something important, don't you?"

I did. And I had spent all these weeks fighting against it, trying to stay on course and keep going down the path I had already chosen. I tried to hide my feelings under teasing or insults, but the truth was that I had fallen for Dante. I might already be in love with him. I couldn't even be sure because I didn't have anything else to compare it to. I had never felt this way about any other man.

Not even my fiancé.

And now there was a fork in the road and whichever branch I took was going to change my entire life.

"Sterling at least says he loves me. He wants to marry me. All Dante's ever done is flirt with me. I don't know if he even has feelings for me."

Another pause. "I think he has feelings for you. I think he's in love with you."

"You think or you know?" My heart leapt in anticipation, ready to burst.

"If you're trying to find out whether he's told me anything, he hasn't. I'm just basing it on what I've seen." The deflated, sinking feeling inside me had to mean something.

But was that enough? Was it worth taking a risk if I didn't even know whether Dante was capable of loving and being faithful to one woman?

I was taking him home to meet my parents, and I was going to go and see his family. Maybe I should take that time seriously. Treat it like it was real, and like we weren't pretending.

And maybe I should let Dante say whatever I'd been trying to keep him from saying all along. He might be in love with me, but it could have been just about the physical for him. I probably should find out.

I needed to know one way or the other, but was that fair to Sterling? Should I call him and tell him? What would I say? I couldn't even articulate to myself everything that I was feeling. How could I explain things to him? Was it fair to let things go ahead like normal without giving him a heads-up?

It might be a huge mistake to call him. What if when I saw him again, all of this Dante stuff melted away? What if I called off the wedding and it ended up being the worst thing I'd ever done? I might really regret it.

I also might regret walking away from Dante.

Still such a mess. "What am I going to do?"

"You're going to have to decide that. Much as I would love to take over your life and make all your decisions for you, that's not realistic. It has to be your choice. I do think that Dante will make you happier than Sterling ever will."

"Should I call Sterling?"

"I don't think you should do anything until you've made a decision. Don't talk to Dante about it, and don't talk to Sterling about it. Stay the course, keep your career intact, and figure it out when you leave the show. You do what makes you happy. I mean seriously, when did we decide to start letting boys be responsible for our happiness?"

"I was thirteen."

She laughed and said, "I was twenty-four." Which made us both laugh, and I did feel better. I told her I'd see her soon, and we hung up.

Dante walked into the room, as if he'd been waiting just outside the door for the right moment to enter. I wondered if he'd been eavesdropping. My heartbeat started a low, worried thud in my chest. I began to say something to him, but he kissed me on the cheek, took the phone, and said, "See you in a few days."

I could only pray that he hadn't heard what I'd said about him and about Sterling, because he could use it to his advantage, to keep sucking me in and making me fall for him before he walked away and left me alone.

If he knew, there'd be no way to tell if what was happening between us was real.

Genesis and I were making dinner. Michelle had left and Abigail had returned. Dante hadn't come home, which made me think he was just going to travel from one location to the next. Michelle was from New York, and then he'd go to Iowa with Genesis and Georgia with me. Genesis had already packed her bags, and we talked about how worried she was for her aunt to meet him. "We're not what you would call normal," she said.

"Nobody ever is," I reassured her.

That seemed to make her feel better. We again discussed how we imagined Abigail's family trip had gone, because we hadn't seen her come out of her room since she'd been back.

"Do you think it was a lot of tallyhos and pish poshes and hunting foxes?" Genesis asked.

"It depends on whether or not she comes from money. There were probably a lot of tea and crumpets involved, though." Neither one of us had any idea about regular English family life. We hadn't been to England and didn't really know anything about the country other than what we'd seen on TV. Which wasn't really fair, because if somebody judged Americans by our television shows, well, then nobody would ever visit our country again.

I did have one friend who was English, but she was a princess and there was no way to explain that.

"Do you think it's weird to have feelings for someone you don't even really know?" Genesis blurted out, not looking at me.

"What do you mean?" I ignored my jittery pulse, afraid of what she might say.

"I feel like there's things I should know about him but don't because we hardly get to spend any time alone together and he's always asking about me. Like, how many brothers and sisters he has. His favorite kind of car. His favorite movie or his favorite song. I don't even know what his major was in college."

"Philosophy."

She looked so sad. "You seem to know a lot about him."

I wanted to tell her why. It seemed unfair for her not to know. I kept thinking about what I wanted and how this all affected me, but what about Genesis? She really liked Dante. Should I step aside to give them a real shot? Was I confusing things for him by being there?

And how could I explain that I had found out his major the one time he visited me in Colorado, and after that was all over, I didn't know if he'd ever speak to me again?

Graduation day, Brighton, Colorado. Nico and Kat had been engaged for a couple of weeks, and he had flown out to see her graduate. She hadn't seen him since they got engaged, although they e-mailed, texted, and FaceTimed constantly, and she stood at our window in her red cap and gown, waiting for him. She offered to pick him up from the airport in my car, but he didn't want her to have to deal with the paparazzi who waited for him. No one had told them Nico was coming into the country, but it was a safe and correct bet that he would come for our graduation.

Sterling was still at his hotel. We had just gotten engaged ourselves the night before, and he planned to pick me up a bit later to take me to the ceremony. A week earlier Nico had offered me the opportunity to represent his family and their public relations interests. It had never occurred to me to start my own company, but I absolutely loved the idea. I researched online what I needed to do, and talked to some of the professors from my department and some from the Anthony School of Business. I hired my own attorney and began the process of forming my very own corporation. It was so exciting. It felt like my life was finally on track, and everything I'd ever dreamed of was finally coming true.

I had the right man, the right career path, and I was graduating from college. Everything was perfect.

"He's here!" Kat threw open the door and ran down the stairs to greet Nico. A line of paparazzi formed behind his car, and Nico's security got out first to stop the photographers. Nico jumped out of the back of the limo to meet her halfway. He picked her up in his arms and swung her around, and then they kissed. That kiss ended up on the cover of about a dozen different magazines.

I watched them, so happy to be together. I was happy for them, happy for myself, just full of happy.

I closed the blinds when they got into his limo, and locked the front door. I went into the bathroom to touch up my makeup one last time. Sterling sent me a text saying he was on his way, but that there was some traffic. I figured Nico was probably to blame for that. I texted my parents to let them know that I might be a little bit late, and my mother responded to say that they were going straight to the ceremony at the Byrd Center on campus, and they would save Sterling a seat.

I heard a knock on the door and thought that Kat had locked herself out. It didn't surprise me at all that she'd left everything behind when she'd caught sight of Nico. "Next time make sure you get your key . . ." I said, and then my mouth forgot how to talk.

Dante stood there in an expensive Armani suit, and he held out a bouquet of lemon lilies. I had forgotten how good he smelled, and how much I loved it when he smiled at me the way he smiled at me right then.

I hadn't seen him since our blow-up at New Year's Eve, and I didn't understand why he was here. I didn't think we had anything left to say to each other.

"May I come in?"

Chapter 19

HRH Dante:

Can I borrow a kiss? I promise I'll give it right back.

I stepped aside and he entered the apartment. I closed the door behind him and just stared at him. He was literally the last person I expected to see. He handed me the flowers.

"I'll go put these in water." My brain finally remembered how to use words, and I hurried into our kitchen to pull myself together.

Why was Dante here? I grabbed a vase from under the sink and filled it up. I hadn't seen him in nearly five months. He texted me almost every day, but I hardly ever answered him. I was trying to move on with my life, and thinking about him and about what had happened between us was not helping with that.

I had done my best not to encourage him, but here he was. I put the flowers on our tiny kitchen table, and he stood in our living room, waiting for me. "Thank you for the flowers. How did you know they were my favorite?"

"Knowing your commitment to your name, I took a wild guess," he said, and I wondered if he really had, or if Kat had told him. "I like your outfit."

I looked down at my red gown and felt my face flush. The color red reminded me of times and things I did not want to be reminded of.

"What are you doing here?"

"I graduated yesterday—Nico said he was coming here, and I thought I'd tag along." He didn't sound like himself. He sounded wary and unsure. It was weirding me out.

"What did you get your degree in?" Now I just sounded like the stereotypical blonde. I was in the midst of this highly charged situation, and I was asking him random things that didn't really matter. I should have been focusing on the fact that he just got his bachelor's degree. That he was too young for me. Instead I paid way too much attention to how his mouth moved.

"Philosophy."

Of course. "Underwater basket weaving was all full?"

He laughed, and he seemed more like Dante again.

"But why did you want to tag along?"

He walked over to me, and my pulse thundered as I scooted back, running into a wall.

"I wanted to see you." His voice was low and turned my brain to mush. He took my cap off and tossed it on the table. I should have moved or run away screaming, but I just stood there while he got even closer, and let out a little sigh when he put his fingers in my hair. I absolutely should not have been letting him touch me, but it felt so good.

And it was all there, all the things I had deliberately forgotten—the deep longing, that pull between us, so magnetic, so electric, so undeniable.

"I've missed you so much," he said in a whisper just above my lips. Some part of my brain turned back on and reminded me that I couldn't let this happen.

"Wait," I said, putting a hand on his chest. "I'm engaged."

He went very still. "*Ma che*? What did you just say?"

I swallowed and repeated myself. "I'm engaged. We can't . . ."

He dropped his hands from me, but he didn't move. I had thought Nico or Kat might have mentioned it to him, but they obviously hadn't. His gaze flicked to my left hand, still on his chest. "You're not wearing a ring."

"He wants us to choose one together."

A look of disdain crossed his features, and I didn't know if it was because of what I had just told him, or if he didn't think much of a man who couldn't pick out the perfect ring for his fiancée. I knew that if he were my fiancé, Dante would choose just the right one and I would love it. It had bothered me that Sterling had asked without a ring, but I wouldn't let Dante know it.

Since I was engaged, I had to remember that it didn't matter what Dante would or would not do. Things between us had ended disastrously, and he would not be in my future.

"You could have mentioned it," he said, moving my hand off of his chest.

"It was sudden," I said. "It just happened last night."

"One day too late," Dante said. He looked and sounded sad. Which didn't make sense given that he just wanted to mess around.

"He's coming to pick me up for graduation," I whispered. "He'll be here soon."

I did not want Dante and Sterling in the same place at the same time. I wasn't sure I could handle it.

"I should go."

I didn't want him to leave, but he was right. He should go.

He leaned in to kiss me good-bye, as he had so many times before, but just as he went to kiss my left cheek, I looked up because I wanted to say something to him, and our lips met.

Accidentally, torturously, wondrously, and it was just as I remembered it. Better. My lips felt like they had caught on fire.

He immediately pulled away, but he didn't go far. Our lips hovered near each other, just a fraction apart. We were both breathing hard, shallow breaths.

I waited. I was so caught up in the moment I was sure he would kiss me again. I wanted him to kiss me again, make the world fall away and to have the only thing that mattered be the passion between us.

I bit my lower lip in anticipation, and his gaze darted to my mouth, and he sucked in a breath.

Still he didn't move. Almost touching me, almost kissing me, but not.

The anticipation and want kept building inside me until I was absolutely desperate for him to make a move, do something.

Finally, not able to stand it and wanting him more than anything in the whole word, I broke all of my rules and leaned forward.

He stepped back just as quickly. Out of reach.

"Once is a mistake," he said, his breathing still just as out of control as mine. "Twice is deliberate."

Good heavens. I suddenly remembered myself. I was engaged and I had almost—I would have if Dante hadn't stopped us. I should have been thanking him, but instead I wanted an explanation that would make the feelings go away.

"Why?" was all I could say, which was stupid because I very well knew why.

"You're not a cheater," he finally said with a sad smile. "And I won't make you one."

I could feel tears, hot and unshed, just behind my eyes, and my throat felt too tight. I'd been cheated on most of my adult life, and I had just nearly cheated on Sterling. I was a terrible person, and it was so awful that Dante had to be the one to remind me of my relationship and the promise that I had made to another man. That he had to be the honorable one while I was ready to betray my fiancé and myself.

How could I ever look Dante in the face again? He must have thought

I was the worst fiancée ever. I certainly did. I sat down in a chair at the table, my knees no longer able to support me.

My voice caught when I asked, "Where does that leave us then?"

"Friends. I will always be your friend."

"And my client." I still sounded wobbly and like tears would break out at any minute.

He smiled, but it wasn't sincere. "Yes. That. I will see you in California in a couple of weeks."

Then he left, closing the door quietly behind him, and I tried to keep the tears from falling since I didn't want to explain to Sterling why I had been crying, or to let him know the kind of person I really was.

Everybody else had their hometown visits, and finally it was my turn. I was actually excited to have my parents meet Dante. I got to speak briefly with my mother before I left, and she was frantic. The show had brought twenty people to set up the house and prep them, and they were planning on being there for eight hours, even though Dante and I were only scheduled to be filmed for two or three.

My parents knew the truth of our situation, so hopefully there wouldn't be any embarrassing questions and we could all just enjoy our time together.

They didn't let my daddy pick me up from the airport, and just had one of the PAs drive me instead. A wave of homesickness hit me hard, and I couldn't believe how much I had missed being home.

Both my mother and father were waiting for me on the porch, and as soon as the car stopped, I ran to them. "My little Lemonade!" my daddy said as he hugged me tight. "I missed you so!"

"Welcome home, darlin'," my momma added, when I embraced her next. "Where's that prince of yours?"

"He should be here soon," I said. I'd brought an overnight bag, and the PA handed it up to me. I thanked him and he went to join the rest of the crew.

"Like an infestation of termites," my mother sniffed. "They have taken over every part of the house." Other parents might have been excited or thrilled to be on television. Not mine. They'd never understood why I liked movies or TV shows, as they thought an evening should be spent entertaining their friends or reading a good book.

Another way I was their black sheep.

Dropping out of beauty pageants my sophomore year had been the first strike against me. It was right after Sterling had broken up with me, I'd lost ballet, and I didn't want to do pageants anymore. They seemed shallow and heartless and I wanted to do something more meaningful. Or, at least, something I would enjoy. I knew my mother loved bragging to her friends about how well I did. She never said anything to me about it, just got tight-lipped and changed the subject if I brought it up.

Then there was the fact that I hadn't gone to the University of Georgia, and every generation of my family had matriculated there since it opened its doors in 1801. I went to Brighton University instead, and did not become a Bulldog like everyone expected me to. I still remembered the stricken look on my father's face when I told him about my college plans.

Then there was the work thing. We all kept trying to win each other over to our points of view, but it wasn't happening.

The one thing I'd done in the last ten years that had thrilled them was getting engaged to Sterling, which was one of the main reasons I had a hard time imagining calling it off. I didn't want to disappoint them again.

We went inside, letting the screen door shut behind us. I took my bag up to my childhood room and put it on the bed. I looked around at all the memorabilia, the trophies, the pictures on my bulletin board. What would the sixteen-year-old version of myself have thought of all this? Would she have liked Dante? Would she have wanted me to choose him?

I didn't know, but I was pretty sure she would have been furious with me for getting engaged to Sterling after the way he broke our heart.

Since I was planning on staying here overnight, once Dante left, I could see my fiancé. That would probably help me get my head on straight and make the decisions that I needed to make. I picked up my old princess phone and dialed his cell.

"Brown."

"Sterling! I'm in town and I wanted to see you. They're filming at my parents' house until about ten o'clock, and then I'm free the rest of the night if you want to come by." Maybe we could even stay up all night talking the way we had after our first date a few months ago.

He let out a long sigh. "I would love to, but we have a deadline for our complaint tomorrow morning, and I'll be up all night working on it with some of the other associates."

Strangely, I didn't feel as disappointed as I thought I would. My ego was a bit bruised, because shouldn't he want to spend time with me? But I would live.

"I would love to see you, but you'll be back soon and we'll be married and then I'll be able to see you all the time."

"But . . ."

He didn't let me finish. "I have to go. Talk to you soon." He hung up.

Not even an "I love you" that time. I didn't know what to make of that.

I ran a brush through my hair, put some more lipstick on, and went downstairs to wait for Dante's arrival. The show had offered to cater the dinner for us, but my mother wasn't having it. If there was entertaining to be done, she would make the phone calls herself. "Yankees wouldn't even know who to call," she mumbled under her breath as she called Dave's Barbecue to place an order. I was going to remind her that she was wearing a microphone and they could hear everything she was saying, but it wouldn't have made a difference. She would have complained out loud either way.

She was usually the picture of politeness, but not when she felt like her home was being invaded.

A half hour passed by, and my mind wandered. I probably should have been thinking about Sterling, but instead I wondered whether Dante had ever had true Southern barbecue before, what he would think of the ranch, and what he would think of my parents. I hoped they liked him.

I heard a car, and I went over to the window, but it turned out to just be the delivery driver. He left after handing my mother the food, and about ten minutes later I heard another car coming into our driveway. This time it had to be him. There was a lightness in my chest, and adrenaline coursed through me as I went out to the porch to greet him.

He was in jeans and a dark blue T-shirt today, much more casual than I'd anticipated. I wore a pale pink dress, as I'd thought he might have dressed up. He came up to kiss me hello. "You look just horrid today," he said with a grin.

"You're looking very unpleasant yourself." I smiled back.

I led him inside to the parlor, where my parents waited. My parents were slow to warm up to people, and I hoped this evening wouldn't turn into a huge, awkward disaster. "Mother, this is Dante. Dante, this is my mother, Sue Ellen Beauchamp, and my father, Montgomery Beauchamp."

My mother held her hand out to him while simultaneously glaring at me. I'd let her down yet again. She probably thought I was being too informal, given his title. "Pleasure to meet you."

Dante took her hand and, smart man that he was, kissed it hello. Like he'd just waltzed out of the nineteenth century. "This can't be your mother," he said to me. "You told me your mother was fifty-eight years old."

My mother giggled. Giggled! "Parts of me are," she said conspiratorially, which caused Dante to laugh, and my mother actually looked flustered. I couldn't remember the last time I'd seen her even a little discomposed. "Should we call you Your Highness or Prince Dante?"

I'd guessed right about the source of her displeasure.

"Just Dante, please."

My father stood up to meet him, and Dante gave him a hearty handshake. "I'm also pleased to meet you, sir."

"Likewise. Lemonade has told us so much about you. She's just gone on and on, and I'm glad we get a chance to finally meet you."

Now it was my turn to be flustered, and I could definitely feel my cheeks turning pink. Dante gave me a knowing grin, and my face got hotter.

My parents stood up, with my father offering my mother his arm. "If you would care to join us in the dining room, we've prepared one of Lemon's favorites."

Dante offered me his arm, and when I took it, he leaned in to whisper, "It's cute that your father calls you Lemonade. Maybe I should start calling you *Limonata*." I knew why he liked it. I could actually hear him thinking the words, "sweet and tart."

I told my rising blood pressure that this was neither the time nor the place for that.

And despite my decision, I still managed to say something I shouldn't have. "I like when you call me *Limone*," I confessed.

His eyes shone, like he was lit up from within. "Then *Limone* it is." While my heart tried to resume its normal beat, he turned to my mother and asked, "What is that delicious smell?"

"That? Oh, it's nothing. Just a little something I put together."

"Translation," I whispered into his ear. "My mother made her world-famous phone call to our favorite barbecue restaurant and had them deliver."

I could see him trying not to laugh as he helped me into my chair. I got the ecru linen napkin from my plate and put it over my lap. My parents had shortened the dining room table so that we could all sit close together. Momma and Daddy sat next to each other across from us, and Dante was seated next to me.

"Let's say grace." My father reached out for my hand and I took Dante's with the other, and braced myself so that I wouldn't jump or react in front of my parents. I managed to keep it under control. As my father prayed, Dante ran his thumb gently back and forth across my skin, and it was very hard to give thanks to the Lord since all I could focus on was that tingling sensation Dante caused.

"Amen," my parents said, and I threw out an amen as well. Like I'd been listening and following along.

Dante didn't let go of my hand right away, and I let us stay like that, allowing that intoxicating feeling to linger, until my father handed me the brisket.

I made sure not to look at Dante just then because I had a good idea of what I would see in his eyes, and I did not want to be responsible for giving my father a heart attack because I had pounced on Dante at the dinner table.

I had more manners than that.

At least, I hoped.

Chapter 20

HRH Dante:

Do not read the next sentence.
Aha! A rebel! I've always liked that about you.

Things were going well, until I heard a crew member complaining in the background about my father. He was looking directly into the camera as he asked my mother if she wanted the corn.

"Daddy, you can't look at the camera. It ruins the shot and we'll have to do it over again. Just pretend like it isn't there."

"Oh, right," he whispered. "Sue Ellen, darlin', would you like the peas?" And then he promptly looked into the camera again.

"Sorry," he said, and stared into the lens for a third time.

Then it was Dante to the rescue. "Mr. Beauchamp, I understand that you're a University of Georgia fan."

"Boy, I'll tell you what."

Dante looked confused. "What?"

"That's the end of the sentence," I whispered. "In this case it means he loves UGA." I probably should have given him a Southern to English dictionary.

Then it occurred to me that I had absolutely no memory of ever telling him about my father and his football. How had he known?

"I watched the Belk Bowl from last year," Dante said. "That was an exciting game."

And that was all it took for my father to talk for the next thirty minutes about UGA's win over Louisville, with all the necessary play-by-plays to make his points about what a superior team we had. Dante interjected with his own opinions and commentary, which let me know he had actually watched the game.

The game had happened not long after Dante and I had met. Had he watched it then? Or later? And why?

And when did he start liking football?

Then the discussion turned to rival schools Auburn and Georgia Tech. "We're playing the Yellow Jackets at home late November. You should come and watch with me."

"I would love that, sir."

"Any Bulldogs fan has to call me Montgomery."

And with that, he had successfully managed to get my daddy to stop staring down the camera. Then he turned his attention to my mother. "I heard that you are in charge of the Junior League's carnival this year, Mrs. Beauchamp."

"Sue Ellen, please. And I am." My mother sat up just a little bit straighter in her chair. "I have some very exciting ideas to make it the most successful fundraiser ever."

Now I knew for a fact I hadn't told him anything about my momma and the Junior League carnival, because I hadn't even known about it.

"I'm sure you're going to do a wonderful job. I would like to make a contribution or donate a prize, if that would be all right with you."

She literally batted her eyelashes at him. "That would be most appreciated. Thank you."

My father wanted to talk to him some more about the Bulldogs, and when the men weren't paying attention to us, my mother leaned in and whispered, "We should put him in the kissing booth. We'd make all the money we'd need for the budget for the next ten years."

She had no idea how right she was.

Most of dinner passed that way, with Dante knowing things about my parents he couldn't have known, and making them pleased as punch with compliments and flattery. They ate it up.

It worked so well, they didn't have a chance to interrogate him. Since I had started dating, they insisted on grilling every boy I went out with. It was humiliating and terrifying for the boy in question, but now it was almost time for dessert.

We were safe.

Or we were, right up until we weren't. "Tell me, Dante, what it is it you do for work? Will you be able to provide for my Lemonade?"

I wanted to groan and hide under the table.

Dante turned to smile at me, and I tried to smile back. "I have a lot of responsibilities as part of the royal family. Charities and events, things like that." My father nodded. These were things my parents would easily understand, as they spent most of their free time doing the very same activities. "I am in the process of opening my own nightclub, and I have hopes that it will be successful. But even if it's not, I will always be able to take care of Lemon. I will spend the rest of my life making sure she wants for nothing."

Yes, I melted right into the floor. I hoped my mother wouldn't be too mad at me for ruining her favorite rug.

"That daughter of mine has it in her head that she wants to have a career," Daddy continued. "What do you think about that?"

Now Dante was in trouble. If he agreed with my parents, I'd be furious. If he agreed with me, it would probably make them not like him as much.

"I think that's a decision between Lemon and her husband. If she were my wife, I would support her in whatever she wanted to do. If she wanted to work full-time, we would find a way to make it work for our relationship and our family. She's so smart and so hardworking, and it's very important to her to have her own career. How could I ask her to give that up?" He reached over to take my hand, and this time I just felt warmth and tenderness. It was so wonderful to finally feel understood.

He risked the parental wrath to side with me. But surprisingly, neither one of my parents seemed upset and both nodded thoughtfully. As if I hadn't explained it to them repeatedly, and Dante was the first person who'd ever presented it to them in a way that they could understand.

"And where do you see yourself in the future?" my mother asked.

"I'll be in Monterra. I'll be able to have my own suite in the palace, but it will depend on whether or not my wife wants to live there. I would like for my nightclub to be turning a profit and be successful enough for me to franchise it. And I'm from a large family, so I hope to have a lot of children, and I would love for Lemon to be their mother."

I couldn't breathe. Whether that was because he foresaw me having an ungodly number of children or because he wanted me to be their mother, I wasn't sure.

It also could have been because that was somehow the perfect thing for him to say. I was my parents' only child, but not by choice. They'd suffered at least a dozen miscarriages and two stillbirths. All boys. I was the only one who survived. My parents were both only children and had hoped for their own large family. It hadn't happened, which was one of the reasons they hovered over my life and wanted to have so much say in it. All their hopes and dreams were funneled into me. It was also why I let them down so often. There weren't any siblings to distribute the guilt among.

My eyes flickered over to the cameras. My parents would be hurt if Dante had made this up for their benefit or for the show. He had touched a nerve that he couldn't have been aware of.

"And it will hopefully coincide with Lemon's plans, because her primary client is my family, so we'll both be in the same place at the same time. And my family has a private jet, so you could come to Monterra to visit and we could come here as often as you'd like." The show was going to have to edit half of this conversation out, with the references to his family and me working for them.

That turned to a discussion of Monterra and what it was like, and how my parents had been wanting to visit after I'd told them all about it.

Obviously, I hadn't told them everything. Which was good, because if they knew the whole truth Dante probably would have had buckshot in his behind by now.

He totally and completely charmed them both. I could see it. He had them eating out of his hand. They already adored him.

My mother and I stood to clear the plates, and Dante put his hand on my wrist. "Please, allow me." More brownie points with the Beauchamp women.

He took the plates from each of us and carried them into the kitchen.

"Fine young man, fine young man," my father said. It might not have sounded like much, but coming from him that was high praise, indeed. "I'm going to see if he wants to play horseshoes."

Daddy had never played horseshoes with Sterling. It was the highest honor he would bestow on another man, one my own fiancé had somehow managed to fall short of. My father went into the kitchen, presumably to ask him if wanted to play. They came back out, and Dante had obviously agreed because they headed out front. He winked at me as they went past.

"Come help me with dessert?" my momma asked, and I went with her into the kitchen to arrange a tray. She had me get the mini strawberry shortcakes out of the fridge, while she made up a batch of lemonade.

I hoped Dante wouldn't think the drink was some kind of code.

I had thought she'd want to talk about him, but instead she told me the latest gossip from the country club. How Mrs. Delacroix caught her husband and the nanny, and how Edward Charleston was soon to become Edna Charleston. I only half listened, feeling more confused and churned up than ever. I had been worried that this evening would not go well, but it couldn't have gone any better. Dante had been, well, perfect.

We went out onto the porch and sat in side-by-side rocking chairs. I put the tray on the little table in front of us. We watched the men playing horseshoes, and I was pretty sure Dante was letting my father win. I tried to sneak bites of dessert when the cameras weren't on us because I was starving. They would have to leave soon though, because the sun was starting to set, and they were going to run out of daylight.

"I didn't want to like him," my mother said. "But I did. He charmed the pants off me."

I tried not to grimace at her choice of words, because Dante definitely specialized in charming pants off women. "He's very good at that."

"Is there something I should be doing?"

Huh? "Like what?"

She looked at me pointedly. "Like making some cancellation phone calls." Her voice sounded strained. I had done it again. Upset and disappointed her, without even trying. It made me feel like I was about eight years old.

"I'm still trying to figure it all out, Momma. I'm not sure what the right thing is to do. I love Sterling, but . . ." How could I explain it in a way that wouldn't make them even more upset with me?

"But there's something there with Dante. Anyone can see it."

Did Sterling watch *Marry Me*? Had he seen it? Had his parents? Our friends?

"Any thoughts on what I should do?" I didn't know why I asked. I could have guessed what she would say.

She surprised me, though. "Oh no, my job is to love and support you, but you are all grown up, darlin'. I don't have a dog in this hunt. You have to decide."

The one time I wanted somebody to decide for me, and everybody kept saying I had to figure it out on my own. I didn't know what to do and I didn't want to make a mistake and hurt people unnecessarily.

I also didn't want to live my life full of regrets.

"But I will tell you this. It is better to call off a wedding than it is to get a divorce. I know that from experience."

"What?"

"I was married before I met your daddy. He was a boy I'd known my whole life, and we married young before he joined the service. We were totally unsuited. Biggest mistake of my life."

I was in complete and total shock. My mother had been married before? How did I not know that?

"Close your mouth, Lemon. You'll catch flies that way."

I did what she said. "Why didn't you ever tell me?"

"It never mattered. He went his way and I went mine. He remarried as well. Think he had five boys, last I heard." Which meant gossip-wise, or on a landline phone. My parents thought Facebook was when you fell asleep on the couch with a book on your face.

It happened more often in my house than you might imagine.

"Dante and I probably wouldn't suit either. Our worlds are very different. His normal is like something out of a movie or a book. I'm not sure I'd fit into that."

Another look of displeasure. "I didn't raise my only daughter to be a coward. You can go anywhere and do anything. It's not about your backgrounds being exactly the same. It's about how you feel and if you're willing to compromise and sacrifice. If he accepts you for who you are and how you are, and you do the same. If you're willing to commit through good times and bad, because I promise you, there will be both. Those are the things that matter."

She took a drink of her lemonade and continued. "He's from an excellent family, he's smart, charming, and handsome as sin. And most importantly, he loves you."

Those stupid tears were back, but I wouldn't let them out. "He's never said it."

"Some men aren't very good at saying it. Your daddy's one of them."

I couldn't picture Dante being the kind of man who would have a hard time saying he loved someone. What I could imagine is that he'd never said it to anybody because he'd never really loved anyone.

"Or maybe he hasn't said it because you won't let him."

This was what happened when people who knew you perfectly got to weigh in. Even though I hadn't told her, she somehow understood I wouldn't let him say anything inappropriate because of my relationship with Sterling.

But my mother didn't have all the facts, and maybe after I told her she'd feel differently. "I did a lot of research about him online, Momma. He's the worst kind of womanizer. He'd never be faithful."

"Haven't you ever heard that reformed playboys make the best kind of husbands?"

I slumped in my chair. She still wasn't on my side. "That's such a cliché."

"It's a cliché because it's true, darlin'. Look at your daddy. He was such a hound when I met him."

I looked at my graying father with his receding hairline and paunch that hung slightly over his belt. "Daddy? You're talking about my father?"

"Don't look so surprised. Every belle in a fifty-mile radius was after him. He fell in love with me because I made him chase me until I caught him."

"How did I not know any of this?"

"It's never been relevant before. There I was, a divorced woman, and I got renowned bad boy Montgomery Beauchamp to propose. Your Grandma Lemon was furious. But she got over it."

Sort of.

"And now here we are, happily married for three decades. And I've never doubted your father or his loyalty once."

She reached over and put her hand on the side of my face, like she used to when I was little. "You shouldn't hold people's pasts against them. You should decide what you want and then go after it. Don't make decisions based on fear. You're a Beauchamp. We're made of stronger stuff than that. Whatever you decide, your daddy and I will always support you."

We stood up and she hugged me, holding me close. There was nothing quite like a mother's hug. Even though I was super confused and didn't understand why she was giving me a pass to go after Dante when I knew she wanted me to marry Sterling more than anything. "I may be pulling for Dante just a little because of how jealous the women at the club would be if you married an actual prince."

"Momma," I laughed. That wasn't really an argument that would sway me.

"Can you imagine if my grandchildren were princes and princesses?"

"I'll probably still marry Sterling."

She closed her eyes for a second. "Just let me have this fantasy. I can just see their faces. So sweet."

I laughed again.

"What is that?" She looked at my eyes.

"What?" I asked, alarmed.

"Right there, on the side of your left eye. You have a little crow's toe," she said. "Welcome to true womanhood, darlin'."

I wanted to rush inside and check. A wrinkle? I was only twenty-four! But the camera crews came over to tell us that they were done for the night, and offered to drive Dante back to his hotel. He told them he would call a taxi after he had said good-night to my parents. It seemed like the crew didn't want him to stay, but didn't have anybody powerful enough to argue with him. We returned our mike packs, and they started packing up their equipment into their vans.

"Montgomery, Sue Ellen, it has been a distinct honor to visit you in your home. Thank you so much for having me."

"It was our pleasure, and you are welcome in our home anytime," my mother said with a big smile, as she picked up the tray. She looked at me. "Your daddy and I are calling it a night. Would you please let the dogs out? And maybe you can show Dante the game room before he leaves?"

She turned to him. "Her father has a whole wall filled with her accomplishments. You should definitely see them."

"I would love to."

And now I was caught, and they both knew it.

Maybe my mother wasn't quite as impartial as she claimed to be.

Chapter 21

HRH Dante:

All days are nights to see till I see thee, and nights bright days when dreams do show thee me.

I stopped by the hall mirror and saw that my mother was right. It was there, bare and faint, but definitely there.

Sad over my lost and squandered youth, I showed Dante to the basement, where we heard whines and scratches. My parents had put our dogs downstairs so they wouldn't interfere with the dinner and filming.

When I opened the door, our pudgy little basset hounds came scrambling up the top step, begging to be petted, tails wagging. I ruffled their long, floppy ears, and Dante crouched down to let them sniff his hand. He passed their test, and they pressed little doggie kisses all over his cheeks.

Good heavens, even my dogs loved him.

"This is Droopy and Snoopy." Dante raised one eyebrow at me. "What? I named them after the dogs we got when I was five. So more accurately, they're Droopy II and Snoopy II. Go find Momma and Daddy!"

They ran as fast as their little legs would carry them, and we could hear their nails clacking as they went upstairs to find their favorite people.

I started down the basement stairs. "Did you research my parents?"

"What makes you say that?"

"You mean other than you knowing practically everything about them?"

He grinned. "I have a staff. I got dossiers. I wanted to be prepared."

I nearly asked him why, but stopped because it might open a door I didn't want opened. I also wanted to ask him if he'd done it for the other girls, but knew I wouldn't like the answer either way.

Then he said, "I really wanted your parents to like me. I know that's important to you," and the sweetness and warmth that encircled me made my heart do a jig. I was so touched by the lengths he had gone to just to make me and my parents happy.

"The trophies are over here." My father had put in a built-in cabinet that he filled with all the sashes, crowns, and trophies I'd accumulated during my pageant days. But there was something new. Two big bulletin boards, filled up with newspaper articles. There were articles that quoted me about Nico and Kat's engagement. There was an announcement from a local paper from a press release I'd done about the launch of Lemon Zest Communications. Several pictures of my graduation days, both as an undergrad and when I got my master's degree.

My parents were proud of all my accomplishments, and not just the ones they preferred. Here I felt like I had to earn their respect because I'd disappointed them so often, and they loved me anyway. I blinked away the tears that formed and coughed to clear my throat.

I needed to stop constantly almost crying before I became that girl. Although, at this point, maybe I was her already

"You were busy."

"Busier than a one-legged cat in a sandbox," I replied, and he smiled at me as he read the inscriptions on some of my trophies. "Here I thought I could make you a princess, and you are one already."

"A princess of Monterra is probably a little bit different than the Georgia Peach Princess."

"I'm not sure our family's advisors would like it if you tried to put our children in pageants, just so you know. They have rules."

Our children? "And in this alternate universe, how many children do you think we're going to have?"

"However many you'll give me."

"I'm giving you zero."

"We'll see."

It was so infuriating how he would do that. I would say one thing, reminding him of reality, and he talked about a future with me like it was a foregone conclusion.

He stopped to study me. "You seem sad. What's wrong?"

How did he do that? I didn't want to share what my parents had done. It was still too new and too personal to tell anyone else. So instead I said, "You mean other than you wanting to turn me into a baby factory?"

"You would look adorable pregnant," he said, and it was getting too serious, too real, and much too hot in this room, so I decided to change the discussion.

"I have a crow's toe."

"A what?" He probably thought it was some Southern thing that got lost in translation.

"You've heard of crow's feet? Those lines around your eyes? I have a little one. A toe, not quite a foot yet."

He walked over to me and looked into my eyes. This turned out to not be a good conversation topic either, as he was standing too close and uncontrollable parts of me liked his proximity very, very much.

"You don't."

I wished he would move. Or that my legs would work so I could. "I do. I'm getting old and wrinkled and will have to start buying more expensive eye cream."

"The man who loves you will adore you even when you're old and gray." The unspoken message was very clear. Even I couldn't pretend he was talking about something else. "Every line around your eyes would be a time he made you laugh. Every wrinkle in your beautiful face would mark the journey you'd taken together."

So now he didn't care if I got old or fat? He must have seen the disbelief on my face.

"I don't fall into the camp of men who imagine their wives will stay young forever. And it doesn't matter. Don't misunderstand me, I like the way you look now, but I would still want to be with you, even when your outer beauty fades. Because we would still laugh, and I would still be excited every morning that I got to wake up next to you. I would always think that you were as beautiful as you were the day we met. If you were mine, I would never stop wanting you or thinking you were the most amazing woman I'd ever met."

My breath hitched and my heart put in its two-week notice, letting me know it intended to quit. You quite literally could have knocked me over with a feather. I was unable to respond.

First, he'd told my parents he wanted me to be the mother of his child(ren), and now he was saying the most incredible thing any man had ever said to me. It was like the gloves had come off and he was just going to go for it. It was probably the closest thing he'd made to a confession of possibly being in love with me.

But he still hadn't said it.

And did he mean any of it? Had he been saying the same exact things to Abigail, Genesis, and Michelle?

Was he kissing them? Holding them? Doing *stuff* with them? Was I special? Did I matter to him at all?

I didn't know one way or the other, which made it even harder to make a decision. Because if he meant what he said, if that was the way he felt about me . . .

Then I had a very serious problem on my hands.

Fortunately, he didn't push the issue or force me to answer. He took out his phone. It seemed like a strange thing to do. Who was he going to call?

He called a taxi company. I hated the way that I felt—wanting him to stay and wanting him to go at the same time.

Call finished, he walked over to the pool table. "I haven't played this in a long time. We probably have time for a game before my taxi arrives. Do you play?"

"Uh-huh." Wonderful. I had been reduced to single-syllable sounds.

"What if we made a wager?" He picked up a pool stick and chalked the end. "How about if I win, I get to kiss you, and if you win, you get to kiss me?"

Him trying to hoodwink me restored my speech. "I'm not one of your idiot bimbos. That's the same thing, smart guy." I also didn't know why he'd said it, because he'd already proven that even if I wanted to kiss him, he wouldn't cross that line until I was single and available.

"What do you propose then?"

I winced and wished he hadn't used that word. I was back to where I was on graduation day, thinking about kissing him but not being able to. Part of me fantasized about telling him to stay put, driving down to Sterling's law firm, and ending it. The other, smarter part of me urged me toward caution.

Sterling should have been there instead of Dante.

I hated this indecisiveness. It was so unlike me. I wanted something, made a decision, and went after it.

What I did know was that one man was with me here and now, and the other had been too busy. "Tell you what. If I win, you owe me. I can call on you at any time for any publicity reason, and you'll show up, no questions asked. If you win . . ." I took in a deep breath, hoping it wasn't a mistake. "I'll consider your offer."

His gorgeous eyes smoldered. "Let's play."

I grabbed my favorite cue and let him break. He called solids, and sank two balls. He missed the third shot. I surveyed the table, planning out what I would do first.

He came up behind me, and every nerve ending in my body stood at attention. "Let me show you."

Let him show me? I had just watched him play. I could have beat him blindfolded and with one hand behind my back. But before I could tell him as much, he had put his arms on top of mine, positioning them with the cue. He was so solid behind me, so strong. So tall. My blood pounded hard in my veins, making me go blurry-eyed for a second. I swallowed. "Shoot here." Then his hands traveled down to my hips, turning them slightly. "Stand like this."

"Okay, I've got it." My voice sounded ever so slightly panicked. He didn't move, and his breath caressed the back of my neck. My weak and apparently too-sensitive knees started to tremble. "I know you think you're helping, but you're not."

"I don't think I'm helping," he said in that soft, seductive voice of his. His lips were right next to my neck, and I actually felt his words on my bare skin. My mouth went dry. The group of rabid squirrels inside me liked this as much as I did, and they went crazy.

"You can move now," I tried. Ten more seconds of this and I would have to hit him with my cue or else embarrass us both. He finally moved, and I was finally able to breathe again. "Eleven ball, corner pocket."

The adrenaline rushing through me helped me to go quickly from one shot to the next, until there was only the eight ball left. I had an easy shot. I was going to win.

But did I want to?

I looked up at him and said, "Eight ball. Side pocket." Eyes still on him, I sank the shot.

"I know we can't kiss, but part of me was hoping you'd miss," he confessed, leaning on the side of the table.

Part of me had hoped for it too.

His phone buzzed. "My taxi is here. I'll see you back in California tomorrow."

He put the cue away. I thought he might kiss me good-bye on the cheek, but he walked over to the door instead. He halted and looked back at me. "I know you won, but will you consider it anyway?"

I already was.

I arrived back in California, tired and more confused than ever. I'd tried to call Sterling three times after Dante left, but there had been no answer. Which both worried and frustrated me. He was supposed to be working. If he was working, why didn't he answer?

The crew didn't give me much time to get unpacked and get ready for another elimination ceremony. As I'd predicted, Michelle was let go. She collapsed into a heap on the floor, hysterically sobbing. Everyone in the room who was not behind a camera tried to comfort her. She kept swinging her arms out and saying, "No! Leave me alone! I wanted to be a princess! A real princess!"

Finally she calmed down enough that she could be helped out to the waiting limo. The assistants packed her things during her meltdown. I felt so sad for her, and I said a little prayer that she would find the man she was meant to be with.

Abigail had stolen Dante to talk to him, and I figured it was better for me to not know where they were so that I didn't start hitting her over the head with those silicone chicken cutlets she kept stuffed in her bra.

I actually wanted to get some sleep, but a PA stopped me to let me know that I would be heading out first thing in the morning to visit Dante's family. He usually had me go last, and I wasn't sure what made him change the order, but there wasn't much I could do about it other than get a good night's rest.

Bright and early the next morning, after saying good-bye to a sleepy Genesis, I was on the show's private plane with my MSJ crew (Mike, Steve, and John). They still wouldn't talk to me, and they never said anything about what was happening. They only filmed it. So I looked out the window and wished for my phone, and I felt giddy and excited about being in Monterra again.

I missed Dante's family. And I really missed seeing Kat. It was weird to go from living with someone and seeing her every single day for years to just visiting.

I must have fallen asleep, because the flight attendant woke me up for landing. I rubbed my eyes and tightened my seatbelt. But when I looked out the window, I didn't see the Alps. I saw cars and buildings.

One building looked an awful lot like the Eiffel Tower.

"Excuse me," I said, turning in my chair. The attendant walked back over. "Yes?"

"Are we in Paris?"

"We are, and we will be landing shortly."

Paris? Why had Dante taken me to Paris?

It wasn't like anyone on this plane would tell me anything, so I'd just have to wait to find out what he had up his sleeve.

We got through customs quickly to find a black SUV waiting for us. Giacomo stepped out from the front seat in one of his tailored suits, and I almost hugged him. I didn't though, because he wasn't a hugger. He was one of the queen's personal secretaries, and the last time we'd been in Monterra he had helped Kat and me navigate around and dressed us in couture gowns.

Ooh, did this mean a shopping spree? I was so down for a shopping spree!

"Signorina Lemon, it is a pleasure to see you again." I half expected him to bow, because he was always so formal.

"I'm so happy to see you, Giacomo. What's going on?"

"I have instructions to deliver you to His Highness. He will explain."

A shopping spree with Giacomo and Dante? I hoped he didn't think this was going to be like some *Pretty Woman* montage where I modeled stuff for him. That wasn't going to happen.

The car arrived at our destination, a very old, very beautiful building with stone columns and pillars and gold statues along the roof. "Where are we?" I asked.

Giacomo got out to open the door for me. He handed me a dress bag and told me not to open it. "Leave your belongings here, and I will see that they are taken care of. His Highness waits for you inside."

Not caring if the crew was ready or not, I hurried in. If this was a mall, it was the most beautiful mall in the world. I entered through the one open door into a cavernous lobby, with multiple sets of stairs, and huge, gorgeous, twinkling chandeliers everywhere. My shoes echoed on the expensive floors, and I looked up to see that I was surrounded by murals on the walls and ceilings.

My heart leapt with excitement when I found him. Dante stood on the landing in the middle of the staircases, and I climbed up to meet him. He was wearing a tuxedo and looked criminally handsome.

"What is this? Where are we?" I asked.

"Come with me. I have a surprise for you."

Chapter 22

HRH Dante:

People may not always tell you how they feel about you, but they will always show you.

I followed him down a hallway, and then another, until he opened a set of double doors. We walked into a theater decorated in reds and golds. A luxurious red velvet curtain hung over the stage, and there were at least five levels of balconies on either side of the stage.

We walked down the center aisle and he stopped. "This is your surprise."

An empty theater? I heard a violin chord, then the sounds of other string and brass instruments being warmed up. So not totally empty, there was an orchestra in the pit.

"Thank you?"

He laughed. "You said you never got to do your solo as Clara. Your mother contacted your former ballet instructor, and she e-mailed me the sheet music for the part."

"I don't understand what you're saying. And you still haven't told me where we are."

"We're in the Opéra National de Paris, and some of the most famous ballet dancers in the world have performed here. Now it's your turn. You have your costume, a dressing room's been prepared for you, and there is a stage director backstage who will give you your cue to enter."

I gasped and put my fingers over my open mouth. And, predictably enough, the tears were back. "You can't be serious."

"I'm very serious.

"I can't do this. I can't just get out there and do a dance that I haven't rehearsed in almost ten years." My voice shook.

He put his hands on my shoulders, making certain that I was looking at him. "You told me that you still remembered every single step. There's hardly anyone else here, so you don't have to worry about being embarrassed. I just wanted you to have your chance to dance your solo."

Then I couldn't talk. I wanted to, to thank him, to tell him what this meant to me, to tell him . . . what? What else did I want to say but couldn't?

"Now get backstage and get ready. These people are charging me by the hour."

He gave me a little push toward the staircase on the side of the stage, where the woman I assumed was the stage manager waited for me. She spoke rapid French, and I had no idea what she said. I'd taken French in high school, but not enough to make heads or tails of what I could only guess were directions.

She opened a door for me into a little dressing room, where there was a bench covered in makeup with a large mirror and bright lights. Four vases of lemon lilies waited for me. She shut the door and I looked around, touching the table and smelling the lilies. I saw a small white card in one of the vases and opened it.

Break a leg. —D

That made me smile. I opened the dress bag and touched my Clara costume. I didn't have to try anything on to know that it would fit me perfectly. Giacomo had my measurements somewhere, and he'd probably used them for this costume, which had an empire waist and was pale pink with ribbons and lace at the sleeves and hem. It was supposed to have a nightgown feel to it, but still be suitable for dance.

A matching pair of pointe shoes waited, but they weren't broken in and I hadn't been *en pointe* in years. I would have to dance this on my tippy toes and balls of my feet, the same way that I had as a little girl. I put on some stage makeup and ran a brush through my hair. It was too short for a bun or ribbons, and I would just have to make do.

I finished lacing up my slippers and walked out of the door. The stage manager had been waiting for me, and she took me to the wings where I could hear the orchestra playing the opening bars of my piece. The stage lights prevented me from seeing out into the audience, and I couldn't tell where Dante sat.

The stage manager said something to me that I assumed was "go" or "start." I went downstage center and took my first pose. Nervous energy racked my whole body, making me shake just a tiny bit. I was already glistening like crazy.

The music began, and I felt like I was a teenager again. I couldn't extend the way I used to or hit every position correctly, but I didn't worry so much about the technical part of it. I just wanted to move to the music.

I had forgotten the joy, the exhilaration of this. Even if the theater was empty, it was enough just to be on stage again. I made mistakes and did jumps and turns that would have made my ballet teacher pull her hair out in frustration. It couldn't have looked all that great.

But that was okay. Because this was just for me, and I loved every second of finally dancing my last solo.

The music ended, and I bowed. Once the music was gone, I heard voices yelling, "Brava! Brava!"

I held my hand up to shade my eyes, and I saw Dante cheering for me, and his youngest sister, Serafina. She came rushing up to the stage carrying a bouquet of flowers for me. She jumped into my arms, and I hugged her tightly. "Serafina, darlin'! What are you doing here? I'm so happy to see you!"

"I wanted to surprise you. Are you surprised?"

"I'm very surprised," I told her. "What did you think?"

"You were so pretty! I'm going to ask Mamma and Papa if I can take ballet when we get home." I put her down as Dante walked onto the stage. The orchestra members had started to disassemble, putting away their instruments and sheet music. The stage manager said something to Dante, and he replied in French.

Serafina ran into the middle of the stage and started doing her own version of my dance.

"Do you think this would qualify as completing my final quest? Have I proven myself?" His light brown eyes sparkled in these lights, and he looked so happy.

"That's between you and your liege lord," I said, holding the giant bouquet of flowers between us like a shield so I wouldn't do something I shouldn't. "Did I do okay?"

It was sad how much his answer mattered to me. I told myself that it was because of all the expense and effort he had gone to, but his opinion mattered. Probably even more than I was willing to admit.

"You were . . ." He stopped, as if searching for the right word in English. "Poetic."

My heart stilled. "Poetic?"

He took a step toward me, making me cling tighter to my flowers. "Since I'm not allowed to tell you how beautiful, or amazing, or talented you are, it was poetic."

My hand went to his chest of its own volition, and he put one of his hands over it. Right above his heart. "This was the most thoughtful gift I have ever received. I'd forgotten just how much I love ballet. Thank you."

He looked at me for a moment, as if he wanted to say something but didn't dare. Finally he said, "I know that you thought it was better to settle and be real and to let go of your dreams. But sometimes it is better to still dream."

I looked at this man, really looked at him. This wonderful, beautiful, amazing man who had just let me erase one of my deepest regrets. Who wanted me to dream.

I loved him.

I truly, deeply, completely loved him.

And not just as a friend.

The realization stunned me, and I actually felt a bit dizzy. My skin flushed and I had to look away from him so he wouldn't see what I was feeling. I was in love with him, and probably always had been. Even if I had fought it with every fiber of my being. Heck, I'd even gotten engaged to someone else to keep from admitting it.

Because I was still scared to trust him.

"Did you do something like this for any of the other girls?"

He put a finger under my chin, lifting my face up to look at him. "That's why I had you come first. I'm not doing this for anyone else. No one else matters to me."

The words were beating against my chest, wanting to be let out. They flew their way up, to the tip of my tongue.

Tell him!

I opened my mouth, and Serafina came bounding over. "Let's go home! We're all having dinner tonight."

The moment passed. This wasn't the time or place to say anything, and I still needed to work some things out. I reluctantly pulled my hand away, and he just as reluctantly let me go.

"Sure thing." I smiled at her and then turned to Dante to ask him to have the stage manager get my things, because I was pretty sure I'd get lost backstage if I had to figure it out on my own.

"Darl—" I stopped. I'd nearly called him darlin'. I'd never called him that.

It seemed like my traitorous heart was trying to tell him what I felt against my wishes.

I hoped he hadn't heard.

He had. He wore the biggest grin I'd ever seen. "You almost called me darling." He didn't leave off the G the way I normally did. "You only say that to people you care about."

My eyes went wide. "No, I was trying to say Dante."

"I heard it. Or maybe you confuse words in English sometimes too."

Yeah. I confused them the exact same way he confused them. On purpose.

I felt pinned beneath his gaze. "I know what you said, and you know what you said, and that's good enough for me."

I opened and closed my mouth, like a live fish about to be fried. "I need to change and get my things."

"I'll find the manager for you." He left me alone on the stage with Serafina. She did a couple of leaps and twirls until she was standing next to me.

She put her hand in mine. "You did almost call him darling. I heard it."

I frowned at her. "Whose side are you on?"

"Dante's. I want you to be my sister too."

I didn't get to talk to him much on the plane ride to Monterra, as Serafina had an unlimited number of stories to tell me. Which was good, because she made an excellent chaperone. While I'd basically ignored Dante's texts after last Christmas, I had texted constantly with his two youngest sisters, Chiara and Serafina. They had a lot of messages for Kat, whom they adored, but she didn't want to talk to them or see them because anything that reminded her of Nico was too painful. So I was the one they chatted with, and we'd become even closer as a result.

She finally wore herself out when we got into the waiting car. She fell asleep within seconds, her poor little head falling to one side. I tried to move it to a more comfortable position, but she just kept flopping forward. I gave up.

"All of me is starting to hurt," I whispered to him. "I forgot I even had some of these muscles." I probably should have warmed up or stretched first.

"If you need any help massaging your sore muscles, I am at your service. I am excellent with my hands." He winked at me, and we both suppressed our laughter.

I nudged him with my shoulder. "I shouldn't humor you."

"I think you should. I thoroughly enjoy being humored."

As we drove through the cobblestone streets in the capital city of Imperia, I smiled at all the darling Swiss chalet shops with their gingerbread lattices that lined the main streets. Their red shutters were thrown open, and each window had its own box filled with colorful flowers. This time the only snow was at the very top of the Alps, and everything else was lush, clean, and welcoming. There was the medieval cathedral where I'd celebrated Christmas with the royal family. I saw the massive stone fountain where I'd made a wish and Dante had pretended to push Rafe in. I felt the same wave of homesickness that I'd felt in Atlanta.

Which I didn't understand, because how could two completely different places feel like home?

We sat in a comfortable silence, watching the scenery fly by. "Can I ask you a question?"

"Of course."

I kept my gaze trained on the window. "If you hadn't seen me for weeks and I came to Monterra for one day and I asked you to see me, but you were busy working and had a deadline, what would you do?"

"I would get in the car the moment you called and would spend every minute I had with you."

He would have. I knew it. And if he was playing me, if this was all a game to him, he was the best player who had ever lived. Because his answer was perfect.

I gently leaned my head on his shoulder. I just wanted to feel him next to me, to be touching him in some small way since I couldn't and wouldn't do anything more.

He sighed happily, but didn't move and didn't say anything. Right then, it was enough for both of us.

The car passed through the castle gate, and I was so excited to be back at the palace. As if she knew we were home, Serafina instantly woke up. I took my head away from Dante's arm.

I saw the whole family waiting near the steps, even the king in his wheelchair. The car came to a stop, and Kat jerked the door open. "You're here! You're here!" She crawled across Dante to hug me.

"Hey, darlin'!" I hugged her back. Dante winked at me when he heard that word, but I just hugged Kat tighter.

Nico told Kat to get off of his brother so that we could get out, and he directed some of the footmen to carry in our luggage. "You're going to stay in the room next to mine," Kat said as we climbed out of the car. "It'll be just like old times."

I hoped not just like old times. Not all of those times were good memories. Nico kissed me hello on my cheeks. "*Buonasera.* I'm so glad you've come back. It's all Kat's talked about for days."

Chiara and Violetta both tried to speak to me at once, while Serafina danced around singing. I saw Rafe, and I hugged him. "I haven't seen you in so long!"

"Good to see you," Rafe said.

"I have to tell you, I think I've found the perfect girl for you. I should totally set you up." I thought he and Genesis would get along like gangbusters. I wasn't one hundred percent sure, but I suspected that Dante did have deeper feelings for me and that he'd kept Genesis around for so long only because she was my friend.

"I'm actually seeing someone right now," he said with a weird look, before glancing at the cameras and pushing his glasses higher up his nose.

Really? I'd have to get that story from Kat later. King Dominic wheeled his chair over to me. I was pretty sure my mother would want me to curtsy to the king, but I just smiled at him instead. "It is nice to have you back again, Lemon. We've been very pleased with your work!"

I thanked him, and then Queen Aria kissed me hello. "We're so glad that you're here. We've missed you! We have dinner ready if everyone's hungry."

They didn't seem to mind the camera crew at all, for which I was grateful. In the past the king had preferred not to be photographed, but I had convinced one of the press secretaries that it would be better for him to come forward on his own terms before private pictures were taken of him that he would have no say over (because that had almost happened when a paparazzo had tried to bribe Kat). For the last few weeks the king had started making appearances near his home, and the people had responded with so much love and adoration that he had increased his activities.

We all went into the dining room, and I got my old spot back between Rafe and Dante, and across from Kat.

It was like nothing had changed.

But everything had.

After dinner, we went up to the family's lounge and played board games and talked until Serafina started nodding off. We said our goodnights, and I could feel Dante watching me as I returned my mike pack to the crew, and Kat and I walked off arm in arm.

I threw one last glance over my shoulder before we left the room, and he was still watching me with a smoldering look.

It made all the air evaporate out of my lungs.

Kat convinced me to change into my pajamas and come to her room to talk. The other girls would be flown out at the end of the evening, but because the family knew me and my job, the show had agreed to let me stay overnight.

We had so much to say to each other that the hours really did just fly by. There was a knock at her bedroom door.

"That's for me!" she said as she ran over to open it. She came back with a tray. "My moonflowers and gelato," she said. I smiled, loving that she had that daily romantic gift from Nico.

There were two bowls this time, and I took the second. "Do you ever think it's weird that the royal family just took us in and liked us?"

"Why wouldn't they?" she responded. "We're awesome."

"Seriously."

She paused, holding her spoon in her mouth. She removed it and said, "I think with me it was because Nico just seemed to like me a lot right away, and that had never happened to him before. And I bonded with the girls. And I think part of what royals do is be nice and make everyone feel comfortable. So basically I suck at that part of trying to be royal, but I'm working on it."

I took another bite. "That still doesn't explain why they've always been so kind to me. Because I'm your friend?"

"Duh, because Dante's in love with you."

I started choking.

She reached around to hit me on the back. "You're an important part of his life, which makes you an important part of their lives. You know how tight-knit they are."

I knew it was one of Kat's favorite things about being in Monterra. She had pretty much raised herself, and she absolutely loved being an almost-daughter and sister to Nico's family.

Although I think she loved being his fiancée the most.

"So tell me. Do you love Dante too?"

Chapter 23

HRH Dante:

If the truth is out there, I think it's playing hard to get.

"Dante told me this legend about his family," I responded, and filled her in on the gypsy magic and promise, hoping I might distract her. I didn't want to tell her the truth about Dante yet. Because if I told Kat, it would make everything real. It would limit all my choices. As it was now, I could still decide how things would go.

"So what you're saying is Nico fell in love with me because of magic. Huh. That actually explains a lot."

"Stop it," I said, pushing her shoulder. "That's not true."

"Cool story, but you didn't answer my question. Are you in love with Dante?"

"I'm not sure of anything right now," was my evasive reply.

"Let's put it this way. What would your relationship status on Facebook be?" She finished her gelato and put the bowl back on the tray.

"I don't think there's a 'romantically confused with disagreement over who I should end up with' as a possible status." I put my bowl next to hers.

"You said romantically! So there is romance!"

"I don't know," I sighed as I lay down on her bed. "What I do know is that I do not like being stuck in this Bermuda Love Triangle."

"The triangle is indeed a sucky shape. All those points and edges. People get hurt."

People would get hurt.

And I didn't want to hurt anyone. I also didn't want to get hurt.

But it seemed like it would be impossible to accomplish both of those things.

After Giacomo woke us early in the morning for my flight, Kat mumbled not-nice things about his mother. She hated getting up early. But she did it, because she and Nico had agreed to drive with me to the airport since Dante had to stay behind to welcome the next girl and Kat wanted extra time with me.

I hugged everyone good-bye and thanked them and said I'd miss them. Dante hugged me the longest, and I loved being in his arms. He whispered something Italian in my ear, which was both unfair and hot. How could I have ever said yes to Sterling?

We got into the limo and waved good-bye all the way out to the gate, until we couldn't see them any longer. Nico was on his phone talking in Italian and looking through his tablet. I heard him mention the word "London," and remembered that they had an interview there after the visits to their family home finished.

"While you're in London, you should egg Abigail's house," I teased.

"Do you have her address?"

"I'm kidding, darlin'." That was a PR scandal I needed like a hole in the head. "Future Princess Eggs Soap Star's Home!" "Should you be saying things like that in front of him? Does he know about your vengeful side?"

"Nico? When he's like this he doesn't hear anything. It's like he's not even here. We can talk freely."

The future king was always busy. He and Kat were scheduled to get married this December, and then there would be a coronation where his father would abdicate and Nico would become king. I anticipated a huge bump in our tourism numbers.

I hoped my best friend could handle becoming queen. It made some doubt creep back in when I considered their busy schedules. If I did end up with Dante, how could I keep my company?

"What is that look for?" Kat asked.

"If I was with him, I couldn't work."

"Not true. I investigated. Prince Alex has an aunt who married into his family, and she ran a PR firm while still being a princess." She looked far too smug.

Another reason shot down.

"Then there's the womanizing."

"Womanizing?" Nico asked.

"I thought you said he couldn't hear us," I hissed at her.

She looked surprised. "Usually he can't."

"Why would you say that about Dante?"

I started ticking things off on my fingers. "Um, the Internet. Living in the same house with him for the last few weeks. Watching him flirt with everything that breathes from the moment we met."

He studied me, and I could get why Kat waxed on and on about his ice-blue eyes so much. They just seemed to pierce you. "You don't know, do you?"

"Know what?" Color me thoroughly confused.

Nico put down his phone and his tablet, focusing his attention on me. "The Internet articles and tabloid reports were all a show for Rafe."

"Rafe?" I was turning into a parrot.

"Rafe was engaged."

Now Kat was the parrot. "Engaged? What? Nobody in this family ever tells me anything!"

"To his childhood sweetheart. She was murdered, and they initially suspected Rafe. There was a total paparazzi feeding frenzy. He had an alibi, and it was eventually discovered that she had been cheating on him, and the other man killed her. Rafe was completely devastated, and the tabloids refused to leave him alone."

I exchanged shocked glances with Kat. Neither one of us had known anything about this. It was like an episode of *Dateline*.

"They hounded him relentlessly, even after he'd been cleared. So Dante stepped in and started putting on a show for the media so they'd leave Rafe alone. He dates a lot, but only with women who understand that it's never serious and only for the publicity. My little brother is not a womanizer by any stretch of the imagination. It's all pretend to protect Rafe. Dante is one of the most loyal, faithful people you will ever meet. In fact," he said, giving me a pointed look, "he hasn't been out with another woman since you came to Monterra."

My mouth dropped open, and I put a hand to my chest, trying to prevent my heart from exploding.

As Kat would say, Oh. My. *Frak*.

He'd always wanted to be a knight, and he really was a knight in shining armor. I had totally misjudged him.

All this time I had been so worried he would cheat on me, that he couldn't be faithful or committed, and it wasn't true. It had all been an act. A way to take the focus off of his twin brother so that he could grieve in private.

And I'd accused him of being a cheater and a liar, and he'd let me believe it. He hadn't corrected me or told me how wrong I was.

No, even when it cost him something he wanted, he'd let me go to protect Rafe.

I owed him an apology. A thousand apologies. I felt sick. He was noble and kind and I was distrusting and awful. He deserved better.

"That was the one thing you were most worried about and it isn't even true!" Kat interrupted my self-flagellation.

I couldn't say anything. I couldn't collect my thoughts, and I didn't know how to make this right.

It changed everything.

I was tempted to have them turn the car around, but I decided that I wanted to be free when I went to tell him that I was in love with him. As soon as Dante eliminated me from the show, I would fly back to Atlanta and end things with Sterling. I supposed I could have called him, but ending an engagement a few days before the wedding seemed like a face-to-face sort of thing.

I hated the idea of hurting Sterling. I hated disappointing my parents and their friends.

But I hated the idea of being apart from Dante even more.

"Are you okay?" Kat finally asked, probably surprised by my inability to speak.

"I'm just in shock, I think," I managed. "He really hasn't dated anyone in the last six months?"

"No. And Dante's never been serious about anyone. We both know how hard it is to find a woman who will love you for yourself, and not because of your title or your money." Great, now I was getting it from Nico. That's all I needed. More guilt.

"Or someone who won't love you just because of that unbelievably gorgeous face of yours," Kat said to him.

"Gorgeous?" Nico raised one eyebrow and smiled. "The feeling's mutual." He moved in. They were seriously about to make out. I did not want to see that.

"Other people are still in the car!" I said.

I saw Nico mouth the word *later*, and Kat got all giggly and lovestruck.

That kind of relationship was what I had always wanted for her, and I was so happy that she had it, but I was also feeling a tad bit envious of it. It's what I thought I had with Sterling, but sitting here with the real thing, even I had to admit that I didn't.

Sterling and I would never be like Nico and Kat.

But Dante and I just might.

We arrived at the airport, and the driver went to get my bag from the trunk. I hugged both Nico and Kat at the curb outside of the departure terminal. "Promise me you'll be nice to Genesis. She's my friend, and she's so sweet and genuine. You'll like her."

"Why wouldn't we be nice to her?" Kat sounded confused. I couldn't say what I imagined she might do, because I could see her trying to sabotage Genesis in some misguided attempt to help me and Dante get together. But as far as I was concerned, Genesis wasn't even a part of this.

It was between me and Dante.

"No reason. You do have my total permission to make Abigail's life miserable, though."

Her eyes lit up. "Done."

Taylor passed along an e-mail from Kat a couple of days after I got back to California. She said she hadn't gotten to meet Genesis, as she and Nico had been called away to meet some famous visiting celebrity. I was glad they did, because it was what I would have told them to do. We couldn't miss out on any chance to bring more publicity to Monterra.

Then she went on to say that Abigail's visit was an unmitigated disaster.

> So, Serafina did her "let's be best friends and watch *Frozen*" routine, and asked if she could wear Abigail's shoes. Abigail told her that if she touched any of her stuff, she would smack her across the face!!! Can you even imagine??? Who would hit Serafina??? She came crying

into my room, and I decided that it was open season. I mean, I was just going to ignore her and be polite if I had to talk to her, which I thought was big of me considering that she tried to kill you. She brought it on herself, because nobody threatens my soon-to-be little sister.

And I won't bore you with all the details, but suffice it to say that Serafina organized a slight frog infestation in her room and "lost" all of Abigail's makeup. Chiara accidentally cut a huge hole in her dinner dress when she told her she'd try to tailor it. I did research on her online, and dropped little tidbits of gossip about her previous relationships into the dinner conversation. The king didn't feel well, and Rafe refused to come downstairs. Nico wouldn't even look at her. Poor Queen Aria tried to fix things, but there was nothing she could do. I figure Abigail will probably cry in her interviews about how awful we all are, but most of the bad stuff happened off camera and I have an excellent PR woman to release a statement to the contrary.

Why has Dante kept this luna-chick around???

Miss you!

Part of me wanted to gloat when Abigail and Dante returned to the mansion, but I thought Kat had done a pretty good job of handling her for me.

Genesis and I were in the kitchen making lunch and talking about Monterra, carefully leaving out any personal details, when Harris came in with Abigail. "I need to speak to you ladies for a moment if I could."

What now? Genesis and I sat on one side of the couch, and Abigail sat as far away as possible on the other end. She really was a good actress. I knew how badly things had gone for her in Monterra, but she sat there looking like she didn't have a care in the world.

"As you probably already know, at this point in the show we would send you out to some exotic locations for one-on-one time with Dante, and then we would give you the opportunity at the end of the night to share a Romance Room together. But we're not doing that this season."

He paused for dramatic effect.

"Each night we have arranged for one of you to travel to a nearby four-star luxury hotel, where you will be given the option to stay with Dante in his suite or to spend the night alone in your own room."

It sounded appealing mainly because I was tired of traveling. But something was definitely off. This was so unlike anything the show had ever done, that I didn't know what else to think. They always went somewhere for these overnights. Always.

"You will be delivered an invitation at the very last minute, so none of you will know when the others have left. And, you may or may not receive an invitation before the next elimination."

I could almost hear the gasping that would take place in living rooms across the country after that announcement. That had never happened before. Every girl who remained was always offered an invitation to the Romance Room.

"If you're given an invitation, I hope you make the most of your alone time with Dante, and that you will think seriously about the future you might have together. Good luck, and I hope you all enjoy yourselves and make the decision that is right for you."

He seemed to be looking right at me. After he finished his speech, the production assistants came to separate us, and asked us to stay in our rooms. They were keeping us apart so that none of us would know who got an invite and who didn't. As a reward for being stuck in solitary confinement, they gave us old gossip magazines to read. At least it was something.

I spent most of the time packing up my things. I would be leaving soon to go home and fix the situation with Sterling, hopefully with the least possible amount of collateral damage.

It surprised me when a PA walked in with my invitation. First again. My initial instinct was to assume that he wanted me out of the way first so he could devote his time to the other girls. I took a deep breath and decided to be an optimist. Maybe he was doing it to so that he could reassure me of his intentions. Maybe he wouldn't even give the other girls invitations, and I was receiving the only one.

I took my time getting ready, and put on a red dress that Taylor had bought me for the show. I knew he would like it. I finished putting together my overnight bag and sat down to wait.

A few minutes later they let me know that the limo had arrived, and a field producer was waiting for me in the car. He asked me if I was nervous, and what I intended to do about spending the night with Dante. I tried to give him generic answers, not letting him know how I was really feeling.

I knew from the beginning that if I reached this point, I would not stay overnight in his room. The whole "avoiding the appearance of evil" thing. That even if I didn't do stuff with him, everyone in the whole country would assume that I did by going into that room, and since I was engaged, it hadn't seemed like a good thing to do.

But now I wasn't going to go in there because I needed to break up with Sterling first. It was a shame. I would have liked the chance to spend time with Dante away from the cameras, to ask him about what he had done for Rafe, to give him the chance to explain to me why he didn't tell me about it himself.

Dante waited for me outside of the hotel in one of his custom-made suits. He flashed a megawatt grin at me and helped me out of the limo.

"You look so absolutely dreadful tonight," he said as he kissed me hello on each cheek, and then he put my hand on his arm to escort me inside.

We went into the lobby, and it had been cleared of guests and employees. Dante led me over to a couch in front of a roaring fireplace and sat down right next to me. He pulled two key cards out of his coat pocket. "They have two rooms for us. They gave me the penthouse suite, and you a room on a different floor. This key"—he put it on the coffee table in front of us—"unlocks the door to my suite. This key"—he put the other key down on the right of the first—"will let you into your room. Now all you have to do is decide."

This was hard. I didn't want to discourage him or make him think something that wasn't true. I wanted to let him know that my feelings had changed, but this wasn't how I wanted to start our relationship.

"I promise you, we can just stay up all night talking." He took my left hand and held it between both of his.

"You're the one who said that there's only one outcome when an attractive man and an attractive woman are alone together in a bedroom."

His eyes went wide, and he said fervently, "I take it back. Every word."

I laughed. I knew he would behave. I knew I probably would behave, too.

Probably.

But part of minimizing the fallout of the decision I'd made was not doing anything that would humiliate Sterling or me on camera. Dante could be patient a little longer.

On the other hand, I really, really wanted to be with him.

All that was left was to choose a key.

Chapter 24

HRH Dante:

Every saint has a past and every sinner has a future.

I picked up the key on the right to go to my own room.

"I had a feeling that might be what you chose." He sounded disappointed, and gave me those sad puppy dog eyes that melted my heart. Droopy and Snoopy had nothing on him. "What is it they say in baseball? A swing and a miss?"

"I just can't." He still looked sad. I wanted him to know that things had changed. I leaned in to whisper, "At least, not yet."

He raised his eyebrows in surprise. He started to say something, but the camera guys wanted to call it a night, so they arranged the final shot and asked us to head to the elevators.

There was something on the back of the key card. A piece of paper had been folded up and taped to it. He put his hand over mine and was trying to signal something with his eyes. Oh. He didn't want me to look at the paper yet. Not on camera.

The crew filmed us walking over to the elevators, and then arranged it so two separate elevators' doors would open at the same time, and we symbolically each got into our own. They reopened the doors and said it was a wrap. I unclipped my mike pack and handed it to them, desperate to get away and see what the note said.

A PA told me that my room was on the sixth floor. I nodded and thanked her, and then I stepped inside and pushed "Six." The doors finally closed after what felt like an eternity, and I pulled out the note.

I switched the keys. This is the key to my room. I'm in room 1201.

Please come, it's urgent. I need to talk to you.

My heart beat so fast. I couldn't say no. I didn't want to say no.

The doors slid open on the sixth floor. A man stood there with a suitcase. "Going down?"

"No," I told him. "I'm going up." I pushed the twelfth floor button.

The hallway from the elevator to his suite was the longest hallway in the history of ever. I finally made it to the door, nervous, excited, and worried all at once, and inserted the key.

The light turned green, and I pushed down the handle.

He was standing next to the windows, looking out at the city. I didn't even notice the room, because he was all I could see. He turned when he heard my heels on the travertine tile in the entryway, and pointed at an armchair. "Please, sit down."

"Dante, I—"

"Wait." He rubbed the back of his neck with one of his hands. "*Limone*, there's something I need to say to you, and I need you to just stay there and listen until I'm done."

I nodded and sat down in the chair. He had already taken off his suit jacket and his tie, and unbuttoned the first few buttons on his dress shirt.

He shoved his hands into his pockets. "I've been thinking a lot about that movie we watched on our date. *Gone with the Wind.* And I've been thinking about how much our situation is like that one. You're marrying Ashley Wilkes, and Rhett Butler is standing here telling you that it's a mistake."

I understood what he was trying to say, but some panicked part of me wondered whether he had forgotten that Rhett left Scarlett in the end.

"You're getting married in three days. The honorable thing to do would be to step aside and say nothing. But I can't be honorable right now."

He swallowed a couple of times, and I stayed quiet, not wanting to say anything to stop him from what he was building up to. My heart beat so loud in my chest that I wondered if he could hear it where he was standing. He crossed over to me, knelt on one knee, and took both of my hands. I went absolutely still, unable to move.

"I love you, *Limone.* I am so in love with you, and it is killing me that you're doing this. He will never know you or love you the way that I do. He will never make you happy the way that I will. He won't carry out quests or slay dragons for you."

Dante loved me. *Dante loved me.* I wanted so badly to throw my arms around him and tell him that I loved him too. But something held me back, and it wasn't just that he had asked me to listen. Some part of me was still afraid and still doubted.

"I know you don't want to be vulnerable and give up control. I know he feels safe. That you think you can keep your heart safe. But you can't control life. You can't control me or us. But I promise you this—your heart will always be safe with me. I promise to protect it with my life."

I tightened my hands on his, clinging to this one point of contact.

"I also promise you that despite what you think, I would never cheat on you. I saw what cheating did to Rafe, and it nearly destroyed him. I could never do that to someone I love."

"Nico told me . . ." My voice came out as a whisper.

"I know." He smiled, rubbing his thumbs on the back of my hands. "I'm glad he told you. I should have told you about Rafe sooner. I'm just so used to protecting him and pretending to be that man. I had hoped that you could see past it, which is why I asked you to stay on the show. I didn't want you to be a spy. I wanted you to get to know me, the real me. Not just my flaws, but the good parts too."

Carrying around my fearful, battle-scarred baggage was so exhausting. I wanted to believe in him.

"I'm tired of being hurt," I confessed. "I just want a man I know I can trust. Someone I can believe in. Someone I won't doubt."

"I am that man, *Limone*. I give you my word. You know that I would never break a promise to you."

I did know it. Even with my doubts, I knew it.

"Nico told me once that the thing he regretted most with Kat was not telling her how he felt before she left. He said he was worried that she would run away if he told her, a fear I now understand. I've been afraid that if I was serious with you, you would leave. And I'm not sure I'm strong enough to lose you. I need you. But you have to know that everything I've ever said to you, everything you interpreted as a joke or teasing, I meant every single word."

A big old lump formed in my throat, and my chest ached. There were so many emotions, so many things that I wanted to say but couldn't. Not yet.

"What about the others?" There was something going on with Genesis. At least on Genesis's end.

"I haven't noticed another woman since the moment I met you. Because you, *Limone* Isabel Beauchamp, are the kind of woman who would make a train take a dirt road." He smiled at my raised eyebrows. "I looked it up. I wanted to be able to say it in your language."

Then I couldn't stop the tears, and they got heavier and stronger when he whispered, "Don't cry. I can't stand it when you cry." He wiped the tears from my face with his fingers. My nose started to run, and he even had a solution for that. He handed me a white handkerchief embroidered with his initials. Who carried around handkerchiefs? There was no discreet way to blow my nose, but I did the best I could.

I tucked the handkerchief into my purse, and he reached for me. He put his hand on the back of my neck to pull me toward him. For a brief, shocking moment I thought he might kiss me, but he only rested my forehead against his. We stayed that way, so close but not close enough, his minty breath mingling with my own. There was so much warmth and love that I could have happily stayed an eternity with him just like this.

"I really want to kiss you right now and make things better."

"I really want you to kiss me," I whispered back.

He let out a groan and stood up. "That isn't fair, *Limone*. You can't say things like that. You're too tempting. Because I still stand by what I told you before. I won't make you a cheater. But if you end things with him, then . . . what did they say in your movie? 'You should be kissed and often and by somebody who knows how.'"

I agreed. My fears and doubts clawed at me, but I wanted to stand up and tell him how I felt. I couldn't. At least, not until I told Sterling the truth. I needed to do this the right way.

Besides, I was pretty sure my legs could not have supported me just then.

Dante gathered up his things. "I know it wasn't fair to spring this on you, and I wanted you to have time to think things over and make a decision. I am going back to the house and will wait for you in the gazebo. There is a car downstairs waiting for you. You can either take it to the airport or back to the mansion to find me. If you don't come back, then I'll know it's over and I will never bother you again."

He came over and kissed me on the forehead, much too briefly, and then headed for the door.

"How do you feel about dogs?" I called after him.

"Dogs?" That made him stop in his tracks and stare at me. "I just told you I'm in love with you and you want to know what I think about dogs?"

I nodded.

"All right. I am pro dogs. I like them. Violetta and Chiara are allergic, so we never had pets. Why?"

It was a crazy litmus test, and I knew it. But I always said that a man who didn't like dogs was the kind of man who would stand behind you in a bar fight. Cowardly, untrustworthy, and unreliable.

"It's hard to explain," I said. "I just wanted to know."

He looked at me for several heartbeats before he said, "There are no guarantees in this world. But without risk, there's no joy either. I love you and I will always love you, no matter what you decide."

And then he was gone, leaving me alone with my confusion and joy and terror and love and doubt and excitement.

I stayed in that chair for a while, running the scene over and over again in my mind. It was probably the most romantic, wonderful thing a man had ever said to me. How could I waste another minute apart from him?

I had wanted to tell Sterling in person, but I wasn't sure I could wait any longer.

Running into the bedroom, I sat down on the bed and picked up the phone to call him. It went straight to voice mail. I tried it again. "Pick up, pick up," I said.

Nothing. It didn't even ring. He must have had it turned off.

Which was strange, because Sterling *never* turned off his phone. I called his office, and there was no answer there either. I tried his landline at his condo, and that went to voice mail, too.

He wasn't at home, he wasn't at the office, and he didn't have his phone on. Where could he be? I wanted to call my parents or his parents, but it was too late. I didn't want to wake them up, because then everybody would know something was wrong.

It was so frustrating. Being stuck in this holding pattern. Wanting to end things with Sterling, wanting to trust and believe Dante, but not being a hundred percent sure if I should.

There was only one thing to do.

I called Kat.

She should still be in Monterra, and it would be super early in the morning. I'd risk it.

"Somebody better be dead," she muttered.

"I think my wedding might be."

"What?"

"You were right. I need to end it with Sterling and give Dante a chance. Because he is in love with me. He just told me."

She said nothing, but I knew what she was thinking. She proved it a second later when she said, "I hate to say I told you so, but . . ."

"You do not. You would toss Nico to the side and marry *I told you so* and have its babies if you could."

"Do you love him?"

His cologne still lingered in the air, and I could still feel the phantom pressure of his lips on my skin, his hands holding mine. "I do love him."

She was fully awake now. "Yes! I knew it! I told you s—never mind."

"But I'm so scared."

"I totally get it. I went to a different continent because I was scared of loving Nico. But you didn't let me keep being scared. So what would you say to you if you were me?"

There was a full-length mirror on the closet door, and I studied my reflection. I would tell me to trust myself. To trust Dante. I had once told Kat that if a man ever looked at me the way that Nico had looked at her, I would never let him go. Which had clearly turned out to be untrue. Because that was exactly the way Dante looked at me, every time he saw me.

With an incredible mixture of fire, adoration, and love in his eyes.

I didn't answer her question. "But what about the other people involved? Like Genesis and Sterling. I don't want to hurt either one of them."

"Genesis went on this show knowing she might not get chosen, and that she might be sent home at any time. It was a risk they all agreed to take."

The reality of the pain this would cause was finally starting to sink in. "That doesn't make it right."

"And Sterling deserves whatever's coming to him, the jerk."

"Why don't you like him? You've never really told me."

"Because he broke your heart and made you distrust all men." I had blamed my issues with men on Enrique, but Kat was right. Sterling was the first boy to break my heart, and I hadn't really recovered my ability to believe and trust. Even now, when I had someone like Dante who wanted to love me, it scared me just as much as it thrilled me. "I don't think he's good for you, and I don't think he'll make you happy. You and Dante belong together. My DVR even has documented evidence of how in love you two are, thanks to that dumb show."

She was right.

"I don't want to get hurt."

Kat stifled a yawn. "He won't hurt you. I won't let him. I will be the first one to kick him where it counts, even if he is going to be my brother-in-law."

"But what if he does hurt me?"

"What if he doesn't? This could be the greatest thing that has ever happened to you. Tell him. Now."

I could do this. I would tell him too, and then go home and break up with Sterling, and after the show ended I would be in Monterra to work for his family and we could real-life date. This would work.

"And just think about the publicity if we had a double wedding," she said.

Whoa. "Nobody's saying anything about getting married."

"Dante has been since he met you. What was it you said to me about marrying him? Oh yeah, that it was as likely as rain falling upward."

I glared, even though she couldn't see me. "You're not funny."

"I'm hilarious and owed some payback for the lack of sleep. Call me tomorrow after eleven o'clock my time and tell me how it went. You know I'm a mess if I don't get at least twelve hours of sleep."

I told her good-bye and looked at my reflection again. I was doing this.

I was going to tell Dante everything.

Chapter 25

HRH Dante:

I heard you should doubt your doubts. Does that mean you should lie to your lies?

I entered the mansion through the front door and grabbed the first passing PA. "Have you seen Dante?"

"I think he was out back," he said.

Right. The gazebo. I'd been so excited I'd forgotten he'd already told me where he'd be. I ran through the foyer and into the family room. Abigail lounged on the couch, reading one of the old magazines. Her eyes flicked up to me. "Have you seen . . . ?"

"He went upstairs." She didn't let me finish and sounded extremely bored. I was so happy I considered actually hugging her for a moment. Love really did make you crazy.

Turning, I headed for the staircase. I heard a loud commotion behind me, and it sounded like it was coming from the production room. People were yelling, but I didn't care about whatever technical issue they were having. I needed to see him. I didn't want to wait.

I got to the third floor, and I knocked on the door before throwing it open. "Dante, I wanted to tell you . . ."

The words died in my mouth.

Dante was shirtless, sitting on his bed with Genesis. And they were making out. They broke apart when they saw me.

A weight pressed down on my chest, suffocating me. My stomach felt like it had been hollowed out. I was raw. Empty.

I didn't know this kind of pain was possible. Like getting hit by a bus, having my limbs ripped off by wild dogs, or being cut a million times by tiny sharp knives kind of pain.

"This is not . . . you can't be . . . not happening," was all I could say, as I tried to drag air into my lungs. The edges of my vision blurred and my knees buckled. I had to lean against the door to stay upright.

"Lemon?" He had the nerve to sound surprised. Like he hadn't set this whole thing up just to humiliate me.

Now I was breathing hard, volcanic rage surging through me. Blood pounded in my ears, and the anger gave me strength. I grabbed a nearby vase and threw it at his head. He ducked and I missed, making the vase shatter against the wall.

"You filthy, no good, lying, cheating, miserable . . ." I probably could have gone all night, but now he yelled at me.

"What are you doing?"

"What am *I* doing? What are *you* doing? I guess I don't have to ask. You're doing Genesis. I can't believe you! 'Haven't noticed another woman since we met?' You may not have noticed her, but you're not having any problems sticking your tongue down her throat!"

He looked at Genesis, then back at me. "Wait, I think . . ."

"And you!" I pointed at her. "You were my friend. How could you?" If I'd been even a little bit rational, I would have realized that I'd never told her that I was in love with him. But in that moment, I didn't care. To think I'd been so worried about her feelings, and she betrayed me!

She looked stricken, and that was at least somewhat satisfying. But not enough.

He walked toward me, holding his hands out in a placating position, like I was a rabid animal. "Let me explain . . ."

"Explain?" I scoffed. "No, you can't. There is no explanation other than I am so stupid. So, *so* stupid. I can't believe I trusted you."

I couldn't stand there for another minute. I didn't want to hear his lies. I was going home. I never wanted to see stupid Dante and his stupid lying face ever again.

Running down the stairs, I went into my room and grabbed my half-full suitcase and threw it on the bed. I picked up my purse and strapped it across my chest. I started throwing my clothes and shoes into my case. Of all the stupid things I had ever done, this was by far the stupidest. I knew the right choice to make. To marry Sterling and live happily ever after. Dante had promised he wouldn't hurt me. Promised he'd keep my heart safe. Then he arranged that lovely little scene for me to find.

Why? Why would he work so hard to make me fall in love with him just to throw it back in my face? Was this some kind of revenge? Because I wouldn't sleep with him in Monterra? I was probably the only woman who had ever told him no. So what, this had just been some elaborate scheme this entire time to break my heart in the worst way imaginable and punish me for bruising his ego?

I flashed back to our first night on the show. He had told me then that he planned on paying me back. Had this been it?

My brain whirled with furious thoughts, not able to concentrate or make sense of anything.

"Lemon, I'm Rafe."

He stood in my doorway. Like I hadn't heard a million stories about all the times they'd switched places to fool people. Did he really think I was dumb enough to fall for it? It wasn't me, it was my evil twin? Not likely.

"Where are your glasses, *Rafe*?"

"I'm wearing contacts. Look! I can prove it to you." I kept packing while he fished around in his eye.

He let out a groan of frustration. "I dropped it."

Of course. I let out a laugh of disbelief. "I'm not going to stay here and listen to any more lies from a cheater."

Taylor came running into the room, shoving past Dante. "You can't leave," she said with big eyes. "The finale is in three days. You heard Matthew, you have to stay. You know what he'll do."

Not even that gave me pause. I would go into another line of work before I'd spend another minute in this house. I didn't care about the contract, the job opportunities, or the ruination of my career. None of it mattered. Nothing mattered.

Let him do his worst. "Tell him to stick it where the sun don't shine."

"Lemon, you don't know . . ."

Dante interrupted her. "Make her stay here. I'll be right back." He turned to me. "I will prove it to you." He ran off down the hallway. What was he going to do, go and get changed into his suit to keep up the façade? They had tricked so many people over the years, and I wasn't about to be added to that list.

I was so, so done. I started for the door, but Taylor grabbed my suitcase out of my hand. "You need to calm down and . . ."

"Shut up!" I told her through clenched teeth. My hand balled up into a fist, and I only just stopped myself from punching her. "I don't have to do anything but get out of this house."

Screw the clothes and shoes. She could keep them. I had my purse, and that was all I needed to get home.

I ran out into the hall and down the stairs. A cameraman got right up in my face, and I shoved the lens away. The car Dante had reserved for me was still sitting in the driveway, and the driver was texting on his phone.

I came around to his window and knocked. He rolled it down. "I will give you five hundred dollars if you drive me to the airport right now."

"Done!" he said. I got into the back, and just as he pulled out, I heard the muffled sound of Dante calling my name.

I didn't look back. I got played like a grand piano, and it would never happen again.

Ever.

I found the first flight out, which was headed to Salt Lake City. It was scheduled to depart about twenty minutes after I arrived, and from there I would get a flight back to Atlanta. I just had to leave Los Angeles. I couldn't be sitting in the airport waiting for a plane when he showed up with a camera crew to tell me more lies. Because the TSA would probably arrest me after I killed him.

The plane was somewhere over the Dakotas when my anger finally subsided. Then there was just an overwhelming sadness and a pain so acute that it hurt to breathe or to move. My heart physically ached. Like, really, seriously ached. I shivered and started to cry, curled up in a ball in my seat. I had the row to myself, and I turned sideways to pull my legs up to my chest, wrapping my arms around them.

I cried the whole way back to Georgia. When we landed, I had a taxi take me to a nearby hotel. I didn't want to wake my parents up. I would explain everything to them in the morning. I looked through my purse for my cell phone and realized it was another thing I had left in California, along with my dignity and my heart.

The crying didn't stop, no matter how often I told myself that it was dumb to be crying over a man who obviously cared so little for me. It was hours before I finally fell asleep.

My constant crying had apparently exhausted me, and when I finally woke up, the sun was setting. I had been asleep for hours, and the hotel charged me for an extra day since I'd missed checkout. They called a cab to take me home.

When I pulled up to the house, I had expected to see camera crews and Dante waiting for me. But it was quiet, normal.

I went inside and called out for my parents. No answer.

The day passed with me in a fugue state, numb with shock, crying all the time. A haze of misery covered everything. Poor Droopy and Snoopy kept whining at me, nudging me with their noses, and trying to cuddle. They wanted to make it better. They couldn't.

I didn't watch sad movies or listen to breakup songs. I couldn't do any of the things I normally did when this happened. Because this was different.

The suffocating despair made me wonder if I'd ever be happy again. I probably should have eaten, but I couldn't. I didn't want to. I stood in front of the liquor cabinet and wanted to get smashed. At least then I could forget for a few hours. Problem was, once I sobered up, I'd still be just as depressed, only then I'd have a hangover, too. I decided against adding to my suffering.

My parents hadn't returned by the time I fell asleep. I probably should have called them, but I couldn't bear telling them what had happened. It would be too humiliating. I wasn't ready to talk about it to anyone. Not even Kat.

The last thought I had before I drifted off was that every moment of the day, I expected Dante to show up. To try and fix things.

He didn't come. If that wasn't an admission of guilt, I didn't know what was.

I spent the next morning in my bed, well into the afternoon. I catnapped most of the day, and the image I saw whenever I would close my eyes was him with Genesis. Like it had been seared into my brain, and I would never be able to think about him again without remembering what I had seen.

My parents returned. I recalled my mother mentioning that they had a corporate function in downtown Atlanta, just before my wedding. They had probably chosen to stay in a hotel overnight instead of driving back home. It was something they did all the time, especially if they had both been drinking.

"Lemon?" My mother came up the stairs. "What on earth are you still doing in bed? Your rehearsal dinner is in two hours. The caterers will be here any minute. You need to start getting ready! Oh, and don't forget that Miss Lydia is bringing your dress by in the morning to do any last-minute alterations before the wedding. Get a move on, darlin'!"

She left before I could respond. I wanted to tell her what had happened and crawl into her lap like when I was a little girl so she could fix everything.

But there was no fixing this.

I got up and started to get ready, because if I stayed in bed, if I started crying, then I would have to explain everything. I had at least a week or so before the end of the show would air, and that would give me some time to pull myself together so that I could tell them what had happened.

And hopefully get through the evening without sobbing hysterically.

One of the thoughts that had occurred to me on my plane ride home was, "Thank heavens I still have Sterling. I can still get married."

Only that didn't seem fair. To him or to me. I couldn't treat Sterling like some kind of back-up husband. He deserved to be with a woman who loved him the way that I had loved Dante, before he had taken my heart and thrown it in a blender.

I didn't want to settle. Not for a lying, cheating prince, and not for a man I didn't really love.

Even if I wasn't going to be with Dante, I wasn't going to marry Sterling. It was over.

My timing sucked, and it made me feel sicker than a dog with tick fever. It was terrible of me to be doing this, but I would get through this dinner, and at some point tonight I would pull him aside and tell him that we wouldn't be getting married tomorrow.

I would have to pay my parents back for all the money they'd spent on this wedding. I'd have to return the gifts, write apologies—it was all going to be overwhelming. I was also going to have to shut down my business. Matthew Burdette would make sure of that. Everything I had worked so hard for was just gone. I sighed and squeezed my eyes shut, afraid I might start crying again. But I had so dehydrated myself over the last two days that there were no more tears.

All I had to do was get through tonight, and deal with everything else tomorrow.

I put my face on, and then the ivory sheath dress with a silver lace overlay that I had so excitedly picked out weeks ago for this night.

The doorbell rang, and I could hear voices downstairs. My family, Sterling's family, close friends, so many people were there to celebrate.

I came downstairs with a smile glued to my face. I said hello and hugged people and pretended like everything was fine.

And hoped that no one could see how devastated I truly was.

Sterling came in, and I had thought that there might have been something—a moment, a spark, anything. But there wasn't. I knew then that I had made the absolute right choice in letting him go.

He came to greet me, and I offered him my cheek. I didn't like the reminder of Dante, but I didn't want him to kiss me, either. He didn't seem to notice. "Lemon! I haven't seen you in so long!"

I thought, *And whose fault is that?*

He studied me for a moment. "You look tired." They should really give boys in high school a class entitled, "Things You Should Never Say to a Woman."

"You look like you've got some lines around your eyes. Although, I suppose that's what plastic surgery's for, right?" He actually laughed. Kat was right. He was a jerk. How did I not see that before?

"What if I get fat? Is that what plastic surgery's for, too?" He seemed a little bit surprised by the venom in my voice.

"Don't be silly. That's what diets and exercise are for. Excuse me a second, but I need to go thank your parents for hosting this evening." He walked away.

Dante had at least said he would love me despite those things. Dante. A sharp pain pierced my heart. How could I be thinking of him right then? He didn't deserve it.

Ellis Wetherly sauntered in the front door carrying a bottle of wine. I just got cheated on again, and the woman who helped the very first guy to ever cheat on me was in my house. That white-hot rage roared to life inside me, and my gaze flicked over to the antique candlesticks on my right. She was lucky I was more scared of getting blood on my mother's hardwood floor than I was angry.

It had been six years since she'd screwed me over, and I still disliked her just as much as I had back then. "Lemon, honey. How are you?"

She hugged me, but I didn't return her greeting. "What are you doing here?"

"Didn't you know?" She gave me a puzzled look, but I could tell she knew exactly what she was doing and how much she enjoyed doing it. "I work at Sterling's daddy's law firm as an associate."

He had told me he had to stay up all night with the other associates. I wondered if she was one of them, and what kind of work they'd been up to. "Are you working with Sterling?"

She gave me a catlike smile. "We do work together. Intimately."

I didn't know if she was just trying to mess with me, but in that moment I knew what was happening with them like I knew with Abigail and Burdette. No wonder he turned his phone off. They were sleeping together.

Strangely enough, the murderous anger faded. I just didn't care. "I hope the two of you will be very happy together," I said, and she looked both confused and shocked as I walked off.

I went out on to the back porch, needing to have a second to myself. It definitely said something that Dante's cheating had sent me into a downward spiral that made me wonder whether I should seek psychiatric care, and Sterling's wasn't even a blip on the radar.

Looking up at the stars, I had a moment where I wondered whether

I had misunderstood the situation at the mansion. What if that was Rafe? Something had felt off about him, but I had assumed it was the anger and the cheating. But what if it wasn't? What if he had really been there? But wouldn't I have known that?

Was it possible? Anything was possible. The South could rise again. Possible, but not probable.

What if I had been wrong?

I wasn't. If I had been wrong, Dante would have been here by now. He would have called his private plane and would have been in Atlanta before I got here. He would have called. He would have ridden up in his shining armor on his white horse to take me back to his castle, all his quests completed. Something.

Instead I had a big fat nothing.

No job, no fiancé, nothing.

I went into the kitchen, surrounded by the catering staff my mother had hired. Nobody tried to talk to me, and I liked being anonymous and ignored. Nobody to ask me if I was excited about tomorrow, nobody making innuendoes about the honeymoon, nobody telling me how lucky I was to be marrying Sterling.

I didn't want to be surrounded by my loved ones, standing alongside the man I was supposed to marry, because I realized that the only man I had ever truly loved was Dante.

Dante, who didn't come for me. Dante, who had cheated on me. Dante, who could never be the man I needed him to be.

The doorbell rang again, and I heard my mother calling my name. I didn't answer. I didn't want to stand around talking to people and pretending like my life wasn't in shambles.

"Lemon!" she said as she came into the kitchen, looking very bewildered. "There's someone at the front door to see you."

It was him. He had finally come.

Chapter 26

HRH Dante:

Sometimes I think it would be the best thing in the world to be someone's favorite hello and hardest good-bye.

Heart in my throat, I followed my mother. What would I do when I saw him? Should I tell him to leave? That I didn't want to hear any more of his lies?

Some part of my heart pleaded with me to listen.

But it wasn't Dante standing in the foyer.

It was Taylor. "Can we talk? Privately?"

I led her into my father's study and closed the pocket doors behind us.

"Is that your rehearsal dinner?" she asked, sitting down on the brown leather sofa. She started chewing the end of her fingernails. I sat in my father's favorite armchair, facing her.

"It is." What was she doing here? Did she think she was going to convince me to come back to film the finale?

That would not happen.

"So you're still getting married tomorrow?"

"Not that it is any of your business, but no, I'm not."

She leaned forward. "Because you're in love with Dante."

I could feel a massive headache coming on, and I pinched the bridge of my nose. "What do you want, Taylor?"

It was then that I noticed the clear case she had in her hands, small and thin. It was a DVD. "This is the whole show, with some unedited parts at the end of the finale. You need to watch it. It will explain everything. I wanted to e-mail it to you, but I still had your phone and I didn't know if you'd check your computer."

The finale wasn't scheduled to be filmed until tomorrow. They had filmed it early? Why?

She pulled my cell phone out of her pocket and handed both items to me. There were like a billion missed calls and texts, most of them from Kat and Dante. I turned my phone off and put the DVD down.

"You have to watch it. Because Rafe was telling the truth. That was not Dante. Dante was outside in the gazebo waiting for you, and you interrupted Rafe and Genesis."

Now he had Taylor doing his dirty work? I ignored the piece of my heart that leapt with hope. I knew better. "Did he send you here to lie to me?"

"I have no reason to lie to you. That's why I brought the DVD. So you could see that both men were on the show, and have been from the very beginning. It's another twist. Matthew felt that the show had become too predictable, and that blogger, Reality Joe, keeps spoiling who the winner will be every season, so we played everything very close to the vest to keep it from getting out. It's why we broadcast the show early, too."

I looked at the silver disc. She said it would prove that I had found Rafe, not Dante. "Why didn't Dante tell me?"

Now she looked uncomfortable and chewed on her nails again. "He might have been under the impression that you already knew."

"And who gave him that impression?"

"I did," she confessed. "When it became clear that you were the favorite of both the audience and Dante, they wanted you to be surprised too. They also liked the tension between you and Genesis, where you guys were trying to be friends, but you thought you were both falling in love with the same man. Only that wasn't how we wanted you to find out. You caused total chaos when you walked into that house and went upstairs. Not only because we wanted to film everything, but because you were about to ruin the surprise and we knew it would not be good."

"So sorry my pain messed up your TV show."

"It's okay." She shrugged, totally missing my sarcasm. "It worked. It's reality television. Everything's about the drama. It's what we do." She expelled a deep breath. "And I should probably let you know that the audience saw the whole story."

"What do you mean the whole story?"

"The whole one. Your engagement. Your previous relationship with Dante. We filmed everything. There are cameras in every room, including the bedrooms. We did censor out Sterling's name, because he didn't sign a release, but everything was filmed."

"Not everything," I corrected her, my heart thudding lowly. "There aren't cameras in the bathrooms. And there were times Dante and I were alone that there were no cameras around."

"The times you thought you were alone with Dante, we had cameras and long range microphones to pick up what you were saying. Even if we couldn't see you, we could still hear you. His bodyguard nearly took out a few cameramen a couple of times. And when you and I were in the bathroom together, I had a small camera on my shirt."

I felt so violated and betrayed. "The interviews when the camera was off?"

"Hidden cameras were filming."

I thought of everything I had told her, everything I had admitted to in those interviews, everything that was personal and private that was now no longer mine. Had everyone at this party seen everything? Did they watch the show? The only thing I had going for me was that my parents' crowd were not the television-watching type. Nobody here had said anything to me.

But that wasn't the point. The point was that Taylor had used me to advance her own career. My life had been used to entertain. My problems, my suffering, would be given to the masses to enjoy.

And I was not okay with that.

"You signed a release," she said defensively. She must have seen how angry I was getting.

"Are you filming me now?"

She paused. "Yes."

Unbelievable. She hadn't come here as a friend. She didn't care about my feelings or what had happened to me. She cared about ratings. She had come here to film my reaction, to see what I would do next.

"Get. Out." I marched over to the pocket doors, throwing them apart, and then to the front door, flinging it wide open.

"Lemon . . ." she tried.

"If I see you or any cameras on this property, I will sic the dogs on you. Now go!"

She looked sorry, but I knew it wasn't for the pain she had caused me. Only that she probably hadn't gotten on film what she had come here to get. I slammed the door shut behind her.

More than anyone else, I understood being devoted to your career, wanting to succeed more than anything. But I had also been willing to give it up, to put other things, like my own sanity, first. Taylor wasn't, and she was willing to sacrifice me and our relationship to get further ahead.

I never could have done that to someone I cared about.

Our friendship was over. One more thing for me to be sad about.

The DVD reflected the overhead lights in my daddy's study. My chest constricted tightly as I thought about what she said it contained. Weeks' worth of episodes showing that Rafe had always been a part of the show.

Which would mean that Dante hadn't cheated on me. He hadn't lied to me. I had been so quick to believe the worst of him, to automatically jump to the worst possible conclusion. After he had told me he loved me and promised to be honest and true to me.

I would have to spend the rest of my life apologizing to him.

First, I had to watch that DVD.

"Lemonade, it's time to go in and eat." My daddy had been sent to find me. He put his arm around me, and it was all I could do to not rest my head on his shoulder and sob my heart out.

"I spoke to your young man," he said. My pulse jumped and my whole soul lifted with anticipation. When had he talked to Dante?

"I'll tell you what. I set that Sterling straight." I felt deflated. "He said you were going to stay home after you got married, and I told him that my little Lemonade was just like me, and that you would figure out how to be a wife and a mother and have a career."

My heart caught. "Thank you, Daddy." I kissed my father on the cheek. He finally got it. He finally understood.

And I knew that had been thanks to Dante.

All I wanted to do right then was call him. Make this right. But I didn't even know where he was. If they had already filmed the finale, he could be on his way back to Monterra. I could call Kat to track him down.

But if he hadn't cheated on me and he wasn't guilty, why wasn't he here? Why hadn't he come after me?

With a sinking sensation, I wondered if maybe he had left me here because of what I had done. Because I hadn't trusted in him or in our love. That I hadn't waited to find a reasonable explanation for what was happening. He kept trying to prove that I could trust him, but I had shown him that he couldn't trust me. Maybe he didn't want to be with me anymore.

I couldn't blame him for that, even if it destroyed me.

Dinner was a blur. I smiled and nodded, unaware of what was happening around me. I was suddenly ravenous, though. After not eating for two days straight, I gobbled up everything they put in front of me. They brought dessert out, a gorgeous chocolate mousse, and as I went to take a bite, Sterling took the plate away from me.

"Don't you think you've had enough?"

I nearly stabbed his hand with my fork. That'd teach him not to get between a woman and her chocolate. I snatched my plate back and shot him a dirty look. I ate every single last bite, and then asked my mother if I could have the rest of hers. Sterling excused himself, as everyone sat around the table, still talking.

I had to get that DVD. I had to see with my own eyes what a moron I'd been. As guests started drifting away, I snuck over to the study.

Someone had closed the doors. I heard voices. I put my ear to the crack to listen.

It was Sterling and his father. "I don't know if I can do this, Dad. I don't love her."

"What's love got to do with it? This is a merger. After the wedding tomorrow, her father's going to sign the contract. Beauchamp Oil will be our newest and biggest client."

"It doesn't seem right."

"What she doesn't know won't hurt her."

I pushed open the doors, and both men just stared at me. "You're marrying me for my father's company? I think I would have preferred to catch you in here with Ellis." This seemed worse, somehow. That I hadn't ever mattered to him at all. I was just a means to an end. He hadn't loved me. I had at least thought I'd loved him, even though I had been wrong.

"Ellis?" His voice sounded strangled.

"You're together." I didn't need him to confirm it.

"We were." His eyes darted to his father. "Until . . ."

"Until your daddy promised you that you could make partner if you brought Beauchamp Oil in as a client." I crossed my arms and stared them both down. I guess the jerk apple didn't fall far from the jerk tree.

His father looked furious. "Now look, Lemon, don't go getting . . ."

"Quiet, please, Mr. Brown. Sterling and I are having a discussion about ending our engagement."

"I'm sorry, Lemon," Sterling said. "I never meant to hurt you."

"No, you just meant to use me and cheat on me. Because that's so much better." I let out a sigh. I didn't need to be taking my anger out on the idiot patsy. "It doesn't matter. You never had the power to hurt me. I never really loved you, either. I only did this because . . ."

The reasons were too many to explain to someone who mattered so little.

"I never should have said yes," I finished. "This will hurt my parents, so I hope you're at least enough of a man and a gentleman to apologize to them."

There was no ring to return. It was probably symbolic or a manifestation of both of our subconscious minds that we had never bothered to get it. Because we had both known this wouldn't work.

I left to find my mother and father first. I didn't want them to hear about the cancelled wedding from Sterling. I could imagine how disappointed they would be. I would just add the guilt to the emotional pyre burning inside me. They were saying good-night to their dear friends Eunice and Charles, so I waited until they were finished. With a trembling voice, I asked them to come with me into the parlor, and I closed the doors behind us.

They sat down, and I told them quickly what had happened, that I was calling the wedding off, apologized for taking so long to get to this point, and what Sterling and his father had planned.

Talking about Dante was still too painful, so I left that part out.

My parents sat in silence, both looking at me thoughtfully. I prepared myself for the lecture. To be told about the money and time I had wasted, and how I had let both of them down.

Then my mother said, “Well, thank heavens. Took you long enough to throw that boy over.” She turned to my father. “I never liked him. I told you they were all up to something.”

“You were right.”

There was nothing they could have said that would have stunned me more. “What? I thought you were so excited for me to marry him. Why didn’t you say something?”

“Because I didn’t want to influence your decision. I know we give you our opinions probably more than we should,” my mother said as she glanced at Daddy, “so I didn’t say anything.”

“I didn’t call it off earlier because I was afraid of disappointing you both. I know that I’m always letting you down.”

My daddy put his arm around me. “Why on earth would you say that, Lemonade? We are so proud of you! Don’t you know that your mother and I are thrilled by everything you accomplish? That we will support you in any decision that you make? That we think you’re the most wonderful girl in the whole world?”

Tears burned the back of my throat and my chest ached. All this time, I thought I was disappointing them. And it was all in my head. They loved me and were proud of me.

“Maybe we should all just start saying what we actually feel and not worry about what anyone else will think,” I said. My parents nodded in agreement. “And I will pay you back for whatever y’all have paid for already.”

My father shook his head. “Don’t you worry about that for one second. You and your happiness are what matters, not the money.”

Then he hugged me, and my mother joined him to hug us both, and the tears I thought I could no longer cry sprang up.

"You leave everything to us," my mother added, as she wiped the tears away from my eye makeup with a Kleenex. "We'll make all the calls and take care of everything."

I nodded, grateful and touched beyond words.

"First, the Browns and I are going to have a discussion," Daddy said as he walked out of the room quickly. I didn't envy Sterling or his father to be on the other end of that.

My mother kissed me on my cheek and then rubbed her lipstick away. "I'm going to send everyone home. So now all you have to do is go find the man that you're really in love with and tell him there's not going to be a wedding and that you are a free woman."

I couldn't tell her that I had ruined everything with Dante. That he didn't want to see me. The stabbing heart pain was back. "There's something I have to do first," I told her.

Chapter 27

HRH Dante:

Who ever loved, that loved not at first sight?

Wherever my father was confronting the Browns, it wasn't in the study. The room was empty when I went in for the DVD. I took it and my father's laptop and went up to my room. I changed out of my clothes into jeans and a T-shirt, preparing myself for what I was about to see.

I really hoped Taylor hadn't been lying to me again. I wasn't sure I could take much more of the hope-and-despair carousel. I heard the front door opening and closing and the sound of cars driving off as guests left.

Sitting on my bed, I put the DVD into the laptop and pressed "Play" when a screen popped up asking what I wanted to do.

It was the entire season of the show, and there was no way to skip to the end. So I had to fast-forward instead.

Maybe I would watch it later, when some of the pain had subsided and it didn't feel so fresh and terrible.

I slowed down during the horseback riding group date and watched as Dante and I had our race. I remembered that Genesis had gone to help one of the girls whose horse had wandered off, and she went down toward the stream. She got the girl back on track, and a rider emerged from the woods.

It had to be Rafe, because I knew for a fact that at that very moment Dante had been with me.

What about editing? What if they filmed it later? There were times we had to do things over again because the lighting was wrong or the sound guy had stepped into the shot. Maybe they'd had Genesis go to the stream again later on, only this time Dante showed up. I watched some of the Genesis and Rafe scenes, thinking it still might be a scam.

But now there was no question. As I listened to him talk, watched him move, saw his smile, I knew, without a doubt, that it was Rafe.

Rafe had been there from the beginning, romancing half of the women on the show while Dante had the other half.

Only there hadn't been any other half for Dante. There had been only me, and the show made very certain to show it. All of our dates, all of our conversations that I had thought had been private, out there for public consumption.

Kat had been right. I could see it on his face. Documented evidence that Dante had loved me. It made the breath catch in my throat to see what I'd had.

And what I had thrown away.

I fast-forwarded again, until a point when the footage was different. This hadn't been edited yet. There was no music, no slick scene changes, no voiceovers from Harris. It was me finding Rafe. I didn't watch that. I didn't want to relive it. But then there was Rafe in the backyard, getting Dante, who was waiting for me. I didn't want to hear what they said, because the look on Dante's face tore me apart. The cameras only barely kept up with him.

He came running out front, trying to stop me. And I just drove off.

Then it was the finale, and Rafe went first. Genesis waited for him in a beautiful jade-green gown that shimmered in the light. She didn't look happy as he approached, and he looked brokenhearted.

Before he could speak, she said, "I'm only here because I have to be. I'm not interested in hearing what you have to say."

"Genesis, please, let me explain why I did what I did."

"There's nothing you can say or do to fix this," she told him with a mixture of anger and sadness as she walked to the waiting limo.

I'd been so obsessed with my own feelings, that even after I'd realized that Rafe had been there, I hadn't given a single thought to what Genesis had been going through. I would force Taylor to give me her number, and I would call her first thing in the morning to apologize. I had been totally out of line and had no right to speak to her the way that I did. She was suffering from the deception, too.

Then there was Dante with Abigail. She wore a tight black sheath, leaving no room for her to even breathe. She must have had ten pairs of Spanx on under that thing. She held her left hand out in front her, as if she expected there to be a ring on it soon.

She looked far too smug and tossed her Disney princess hair as Dante approached. He stood in front of her.

"I'm sorry to do it like this, but I'm not in love with you. I'm in love with Lemon, and have been for a long time. I just found out that she saw my twin brother with Genesis and thought it was me. So now I'm going to find her and think of some way to make sure that she's mine forever."

My heart pounded so fast I thought it might rupture. He walked away from her, and she started screaming at him, and I couldn't understand what she was saying.

Because her real accent most definitely was not British. If I wasn't mistaken, that was one thick Cajun accent spewing out of her mouth. But what about her "family" in England? Knowing her, she had probably just hired some actors to keep up the lie.

A small part of me enjoyed that revelation as I imagined how that clip would play nonstop on the Internet indefinitely. Karma truly existed. But this was filmed last night. Why hadn't he come? I shut the laptop. It was late, but I needed to clear my head, and I felt like the walls were pressing in on me. I slipped on a pair of shoes and went downstairs.

My mother was in the kitchen, directing the cleanup. "Everyone's left."

"Thank you for handling everything. I'm going to go for a walk."

"Take the dogs with you. I'm sure they're dying to get out of the basement."

I would not think about the last time I freed them from the basement. When Dante had asked me to consider being with him, and I already wanted to. Even then my heart knew what my head refused to accept.

Droopy and Snoopy came tumbling up the steps, and they got even more excited when I asked them if they wanted to go outside. I grabbed one of my old jackets, still hanging by the back door, and went out to wander around the ranch.

Fireflies winked their little lights off and on, and for the first time, they didn't immediately remind me of Sterling and our first kiss. Which made me glad, because I had always loved fireflies and I didn't want him to taint everything in my life.

I ended up in the orchard, and I let the dogs off of their leashes. They started to frolic around, sniffing everything in sight.

It mended my heart just a little to see their joyful exploration. A full moon hung overhead, casting a mellow, soft light over everything. I found the family lemon tree. A soft wind rustled the leaves overhead, and the faint scent of lemon blossoms surrounded me. There were initials carved on it from the members of my family who had kissed their true loves here.

Something I might never have.

I sat down at the base of the tree, leaning my back against it. I had to find Dante. I had to explain. Kat would help me. She knew what this felt like. If I could just make him understand me, if I could find a way to make him see . . . but how could I? I'd ruined everything. Like in one of those romantic movies where you get so frustrated with the hero and heroine because if they would just talk and communicate, then everything would be fine. There wouldn't be an obstacle. I had been that idiotic. I had been totally irrational and unreasonable and let all my issues and baggage cloud everything, and it had cost me one of the best men I had ever known.

Snoopy perked up his ears, and Droopy followed. They started to bark, which could only mean someone was approaching.

I got the shock of my life when I saw Dante in his wrinkled Armani suit, looking exhausted. The dogs ran over to him, circling his legs. He patted them briefly and walked until he stopped a few feet in front of me.

"Dante! You're here." I stood up and leaned against the tree for support. "I didn't think you would come. I thought I had ruined everything and you'd never want . . ."

He held up his hand. "Are you still getting married?"

My tears made it hard to see. "No."

He came so close. "Do you love me?"

"Yes, I love you—" He didn't let me finish, and his mouth was on mine and everything exploded into flame. He grabbed me by the waist when my legs gave out. He literally took my breath away.

And whatever I'd thought about all the other kisses we'd ever shared, this one put them all to shame.

When he finally stopped, I felt like I had been drugged. He stroked the side of my face, my neck, my shoulders and arms. "My darling *Limone*, how could you ever think that I wouldn't come for you? I love you."

"Because I didn't trust you when you asked me to. I thought the worst of you."

He seemed to be considering this. "Maybe that should matter more to me. It doesn't. At some point, when I have loved you for many years and been one hundred percent faithful to you, there will come a time when you will be nothing but absolutely secure. I can wait for that."

I hugged him tight, and he rested his head on mine. Then I took him by the hand, tugging him to sit down next to me. I wasn't sure I was strong enough to keep standing if he kept kissing and holding me like that. He took off his suit jacket and laid it on the ground so we could sit on it. He pulled me to him, wrapping me up in his arms.

"About Rafe being on the show . . ."

"I thought you knew," he interrupted me. "I would have told you if I'd known. But to be honest, I don't know how you could have been confused. He's clearly nowhere near as handsome as I am."

I kissed him then, a soft sweet kiss, to show him how happy I was.

"I don't think I mentioned it earlier, but you look unbelievably awful right now," he said with such sweetness and love I wanted to melt.

"You look hideous, too," I said. More kissing. Then he looked up. "Wait. Is this the famous lemon tree?"

"It is. But we didn't get to share our first kiss here."

"We did," he said, kissing me on my temple. "It was our first kiss since you said that you loved me, and that's just as good." He played with the ends of my hair, and I leaned into his hand. "By the way, would you mind saying that again? I want to make sure I didn't imagine it."

"That again."

I giggled when he rolled his eyes. "*Limone*!"

This time I held his face in my hands, making sure that he could see it in my eyes, and then I told him with my voice. "I love you." Then I made sure to show him with my lips.

When that kiss ended, he again held me tightly, like he never wanted to let me go. "Why did it take you so long to get here?" I asked.

"There was a huge storm that grounded us, but first I had to deal with production issues. I wanted to come after you immediately, but Matthew Burdette started screaming about everything and threatening you and saying how he was going to ruin your company. I couldn't let that happen. I told him I would stay and finish filming, and that I had proof of his affair with Abigail and that if he was smart he'd do whatever he had to do to keep you happy."

"You blackmailed someone for me?"

He pulled my hand up to his lips and kissed it. "Technically it was a bluff, because I don't have evidence, but he doesn't know that. And I would blackmail the whole world for you. I think now I have finally completed my last quest by saving your company, and truly proven myself worthy, don't you?"

I did. He really was my knight in shining Armani.

He put my hand back down and looked at me intently, seriously. "I would give you the world if I could. I would do anything for you. Because you're going to be my wife."

"What?" I was both elated and terrified. "Let's not put the cart before the horse. I just put my parents through all this mess. I don't think I should be discussing marriage to anybody right now."

"But you will marry me." He sounded so confident and sure.

"That doesn't sound like asking."

"I'm not asking. Every time I ask you for anything you say no. So now I'm telling. You will marry me, you will be my princess, we will have babies, and I will have my nightclub and you will have your PR firm and we will live happily ever after in our palace."

I should have been mad. But he was right. We totally would.

"I know it's scary for you, but if you do me the honor of giving me all of your trust and all of your love, I promise you will never regret that choice."

Shaking my head, I stopped him. "You don't have to say anything else or promise me anything else. This time it's my turn to promise you. I promise to always believe in you. To always assume the best. To always trust you. To always, always love you."

He had that mischievous glint in his eye. "Those sound a lot like marriage vows."

"Hush," I told him. Then I made sure he couldn't talk.

Snoopy pounced on us, apparently tired of being left out of the affection. We petted him, but never took our eyes off each other. "I forgot to tell you that Rafe said he apologizes for anything that he might have done to upset you, and he promises to never do anything else that will make you angry ever again. He also said that if I cared at all about my own personal safety, I should be careful to never make you mad, either. So recognizing that I'm taking my life into my own hands here, I have something for you and I'm not sure how you will react."

He reached into his pants pocket and pulled out a black velvet ring box, making my breath hitch. Giddy excitement bubbled up inside me, my pulse skyrocketing out of control. My hands trembled in anticipation. He opened it up to reveal an enormous pale yellow diamond ring in an antique silver setting. "You don't have to say anything yet. But I got this from my mother's vault when we were in Monterra visiting my family. It was my great-grandmother's ring."

"The one from the gypsy legend?"

"The very same."

I had been right. Dante chose the absolute perfect ring for me. I had loved the magical story of how his great-grandparents found each other. I already adored this beautiful ring, but not nearly as much as I adored him.

"And guess what kind of diamond this is?" He took it out of the box. "A lemon diamond. It's fated, don't you think?"

I did.

I even let him put the ring on me. And, not surprisingly, it fit.

"How do you feel, Princess Lemon?"

I looked at my lemon diamond engagement ring in the moonlight, and then I looked at the handsome, wonderful, amazing man next to me who would be my husband. I put a hand on the side of his face.

"I feel happier than a tick on a fat dog."

"And that's a good thing?" he asked.

I laughed, and was so happy that I would spend the rest of my life loving and laughing with him.

"Yes, darlin'. That's a very good thing."

NOTE FROM THE AUTHOR

I know that there are so many ways that you could choose to spend what little free time you have, and I am beyond grateful that you chose to spend it with Dante and Lemon.

If you want to find out just how much groveling Rafe will have to do to win Genesis back in the next book, please sign up for my mailing list on my website: www.sariahwilson.com.

It's an e-book jungle out there, and authors need all the help they can get. Reviews will help other readers discover and experience that royal Monterran *amore*. I would love it if you could leave a review on sites like Amazon and Goodreads, should you feel so inclined.

Thank you!

ACKNOWLEDGMENTS

I have to begin by thanking Kindle Scout/Kindle Press, the Kindle Scout team, and most especially Caroline Carr, for going above and beyond for me. This book exists because of your actions behind the scenes.

Very special thanks to Anh Schluep, for calling me the day before my birthday and making a decades-long dream come true by offering me a publishing contract to write romance. I will always be grateful for that, and I'm still screaming on the inside. Thank you to Chris Werner for jumping onboard and taking care of everything.

Thank you to the Montlake team, to Susan, Marlene, and Jessica, for all your hard work in bringing Monterra to the rest of the world. Thanks to my developmental editor, Melody Guy, for helping me to explain what I meant to say but didn't, and for leaving LOLs in the margin, reassuring me that I'd made at least one person laugh. Thank you to Montreux Rotholtz and Jessica Fogleman for cleaning up all my grammatical messes and to Kerrie Robertson for the cover. My little sister, Charity Byrd, must be thanked for reading this book before anyone else in the world did, and for letting me know what she liked and what she didn't.

Thank you to the lights of my life, my four children, who are growing faster than I would like and who are becoming far too independent. Thank you for thinking that being a writer is no big deal and always keeping me grounded, and for filling my heart with so much joy.

And I always save the best for last—my love and thanks to my husband, Kevin, who supports me and loves me and makes this journey through life worthwhile. When people tell me that no fictional hero could actually be so nice, so charming, so smart, so handsome, or so loving in real life, I only have to look at you to know that they're wrong.

ABOUT THE AUTHOR

Sariah Wilson has never jumped out of an airplane, never climbed Mount Everest, and is not a former CIA operative. She has, however, been madly, passionately in love with her soul mate and is a fervent believer in happily-ever-afters—which is why she writes romance. *Royal Chase* is her sixth happily-ever-after novel. She grew up in Southern California, graduated from Brigham Young University (go Cougars!) with a semi-useless degree in history, and is the oldest of nine (yes, nine) children. She currently lives with the aforementioned soul mate and their four children in Utah, along with three tiger barb fish, a cat named Tiger, and a recently departed hamster that is buried in the backyard (and has nothing at all to do with tigers).

Her website is www.sariahwilson.com.

Made in the USA
Monee, IL
28 June 2023

37888806R00166